DUPED

STEPHEN MAITLAND-LEWIS

Black Rose Writing | Texas

ISBN: 978-1-944715-74-8
PUBLISHED BY BLACK ROSE WRITING
www.blackrosewriting.com

Printed in the United States of America
Suggested Retail Price (SRP) $22.95

Duped is printed in Garamond

*As a planet-friendly publisher, Black Rose Writing does its best to eliminate
unnecessary waste to reduce paper usage and energy costs, while never compromising
the reading experience. As a result, the final word count vs. page count may not meet
common expectations.

PRAISE FOR *DUPED* BY STEPHEN MAITLAND-LEWIS

"A realistic and engagingly descriptive novel."
—Kirkus Reviews

"Stephen Maitland-Lewis has secured his place as a supremely gifted writer of the cunning, courage and evil residing within the human spirit. With his special talent of developing characters capable of both heroic and treacherous acts, Maitland-Lewis relies on his wits to create another fabulous book. *DUPED* ranks as another masterpiece from this writer with a hugely impressive body of work."
—Jim Engster, President *Louisiana Radio Network*

"Maitland-Lewis delivers a sophisticated, high-stakes, international thriller that will make you grateful for the life you have, providing you aren't already caught in a web of corruption and deceit in the sweltering Nigerian streets. Be thankful you're a reader and not a character in this haunting tale of desperation, greed and power."
—Stephen Jay Schwartz, *LA Times* bestselling author

"With Stephen Maitland-Lewis' *DUPED*, the international thriller has been revitalized via expertly elicited, marvelous tension and a sympathetic yet flawed protagonist. *DUPED* excitingly hops the globe, as an Everyman must face his own ultimate moral code while forced into the world of espionage."
—Brad Schreiber, author, *REVOLUTION'S END, DEATH IN PARADISE*

"Exotic locales. intrigue, international monetary fraud and betrayal. Oh... and seamed stockings! Stephen Maitland-Lewis does it again with *DUPED*, a book that will keep surprising you up to the very last page."
—Pam Atherton, award winning talk show host

"I remember vividly, sitting with my husband Harold Robbins at our dining room table mesmerized by Stephen Maitland-Lewis' fascinating stories of international finance in third-world countries that he had experienced first-hand. The shenanigans, corruption and danger were shocking and stunning at the same time. Harold stopped Stephen as the stories unfolded... 'Stephen, you have got to write this story.' Stephen resisted at first thinking that if it was written as truth that there might be legal complications. 'No," Harold said, 'fiction always begins with truth. It'll be a best-seller. It's a story that needs to be told. Stephen Maitland-Lewis does not disappoint in this saga of greed."
—Jann Robbins, author of *HAROLD & ME* and co-author of *HONOR*

PRAISE FOR OTHER TITLES BY STEPHEN MAITLAND-LEWIS

HERO ON THREE CONTINENTS

"A moving, complex and well-crafted fictional biography… Maitland-Lewis renders the multitudinous cast of characters with marvelous detail … a touching read, with a fictional character to admire." –**KIRKUS REVIEWS**

EMERALDS NEVER FADE

"A poignant story of two men whose lives are forever altered by a period of history that should never be forgotten." –Robert Dugoni, **NY Times Bestselling Author**

"I couldn't put it down until the end. It is a page-turner – greatly enjoyable and informative. Perfecto." –Connie Martinson, TV Host of **Connie Martinson Talks Books**

"A story of intrigue that examines the human condition in all its layers." –Jim Engster, President of **Louisiana Radio Network**

AMBITION

"This financial thriller rocks and rolls with sex and skull-duggery and more money than Midas can count. It's un-put-downable. Chilling." –Kitty Kelley, seven times **NY Times Bestselling Biographer**

"Ambition creates the excitement of free-fall – it's difficult to put down. Who said financial institutions were dull? A wonderful book and a great reading experience." –Mickey Kantor, former **United States Secretary of Commerce**

BOTTICELLI'S BASTARD

'Botticelli's Bastard is beautifully written and to its further credit impossible to categorize. Part thriller, part intriguing mystery, this book is compulsive reading. Above all, it is a first-class novel." –Sir Ronald Harwood, **Oscar® winning writer**

'Botticelli's Bastard is a fascinating complex and completely compelling novel. It is everything I love, history, art, suspense, intelligence and creativity. I am captivated." –M.J. Rose, **International Bestselling Author**

"My interest in collecting important art came together with my love of thrillers. Stephen Maitland-Lewis' Botticelli's Bastard is a great read." –Arthur Kopelson, **Oscar® and Golden Globe® winning producer**

ALSO BY STEPHEN MAITLAND-LEWIS

Hero on Three Continents

Emeralds Never Fade

Ambition

Botticelli's Bastard

This novel is dedicated to the loving memory of Harold Robbins who inspired and encouraged me to write it, to Florence Henderson who inspired me with every smile, and to Lieutenant Douglas Dalzell MC whose heroism and sacrifice will be an inspiration forever.

DUPED

Is it possible to succeed without any act of betrayal?

~Jean Renoir

CHAPTER 1

Sam Marsh breathed in the brisk sea air as he looked out over the marina, boats bobbing on its waves like fat, content seagulls. The sky was clear blue, there was a good wind, and the sun's warmth enticed him to take off his shirt, savoring the afternoon's heat. He loved taking Birdland out to Newport Beach, Dana Point, even to Catalina Island. A few hours at sea in blissful solitude—no telephones, fax machines, e-mails, or meddlesome letters with collection agencies' letterheads—provided him his only happiness in recent months.

A day off the unpredictable Southern California coast prompted the constant checking of sails, winds, currents, mast, tiller, and compass along with vigilance for swimmers, other boats, water skiers, and buoys. These tasks for him weren't grunt work as they blotted out his other concerns; they culminated in a seafaring Zen he relied upon.

Sam now turned his gaze toward the empty bed. He recalled the past, of Karin, her naked body tangled in the sheets. He reminisced of the time they had gone sailing together and then spent the night together. How he'd stroked her face and nibbled her pouty lips until she had awoken.

"There are only two things I want to do in life," he whispered, as she rubbed her eyes. "Make love to you. And sail solo to Hawaii."

Her body shook with laughter. Even he smiled at the absurdity of it.

"Now why do you want to do a silly thing like that, Sam?" she purred.

It was a fair question—Sam was no hero. "I just need to do it. It was the same thing when I took flying lessons a few years ago. Had to try. Same with those martial art classes I'm taking."

He watched her brow stiffen as she contemplated the challenge. "But suppose you don't make it?"

"Well, I'll either be rescued at sea or drown."

She ran her fingers through his chest hair, arousing him. "Promise me you're not going anywhere too far away." She rolled on top of him and enveloped him with her lips and tongue. But her kisses stopped with a jolt. She stared down, wide-eyed. "Sam, you won't ever leave me, will you?"

"Of course not, Karin," he whispered.

Shaking his head in the present, annoyed at himself, Sam stepped into the shower.

A few minutes later, Sam was behind the wheel of his Maserati on the Santa Monica Freeway, en route to Palm Springs against a still-dark sky. It had more pep than the BMW 6-series Karin had received in the divorce settlement. The soft leather seats were like silk, something he appreciated when he came to the buildup of traffic headed east. Sam put on a CD of Fats Waller playing stride piano.

As Sam pulled up to the front of the Sunridge Hotel, he glanced at his watch. There was still plenty of time to slip into his new gray Armani suit and splash some expensive Caron cologne on his face. He may sweat over his hotel tanking and the way its restaurant now seemed able to dazzle would-be patrons only on the weekends, but nobody needed to smell his fear.

Karin had scheduled a nine o'clock meeting at the hotel's restaurant, La Sonrisa, but as usual, it was closer to ten when she flounced into his office. He'd often joked that his ex-wife was the only German born with no idea of time. Indifferent to the fact that she had kept anyone waiting, she breezed into the meeting beautiful and cheerful, bearing pastries.

Sam gave her a respectful peck on the cheek but hesitated to reach out for a Danish. His trim waistline, a perpetual source of pride, had swollen over the last year.

He had just determined to resist the sweet temptations when Karin announced, "I've decided to cut my hair. This length is not becoming at my age." Her blonde hair was long enough to tickle the belt on her tight designer jeans.

"You're stunning," he replied.

"I'm cutting it shoulder length," she said. "At my age, I can't dress like a teenager anymore."

"The issue isn't your hair. It's that T-shirt."

"What's the matter with my T-shirt, for God's sake?"

"Well, isn't it too tight? And those pink sequins—c'mon. Aren't they a little cheesy?" He said it with what he hoped would translate as a friendly wink.

"Go to hell," she snapped. "I didn't come here for insults. I came here to get some alimony you conveniently forgot to send me."

"I'm going through a cash crunch," he began.

"Is it any wonder the restaurant is losing money when you send over complimentary bottles of champagne to any table with a pretty girl?"

Sam grimaced and shifted in his chair. "I don't understand what you're talking about."

"Don't give me that. A friend of mine was dining at La Sonrisa the other night and noticed the Perrier-Jouet you sent over to two hookers."

"Karin, they weren't hookers, for goodness' sake. One of them is a well-known actress on a daytime soap."

"Have you been to bed with her yet" she raised her sharp but delicate brows "or are you still working on it?" If there were aspects of her physical appearance that substantiated these fresh worries about aging, Sam didn't see them.

"Karin, we have to rely on word of mouth to build the business."

"Your version of building business hasn't worked. We haven't been full here in ages. And now you're not paying me alimony. It's time you consider selling me your half of the company." Karin got up, not even wanting for his reply. "I need to talk to Maria about replacing that ancient washing machine."

Sam stood. "Karin," he began, but she was already out of his office, her back to him.

"Think about it," she tossed off, without looking back. "It would solve your problems—wouldn't it?"

Sam walked over to the bar to have a coffee with Rod, the young bartender he had recruited from New Orleans, his favorite on the staff.

"Bad meeting?" Rod asked. "How about adding brandy to that coffee?"

"Oh, it's nothing that winning the lottery won't solve." Sam smirked.

The phone rang and Rod handed it to Sam.

"Mr. Marsh?" The on-duty receptionist was on the other line. "A Mr. Tony Dobbs just called. He's phoned a few times. He needs to see you."

Sam grunted. "Sure. Tell him to come by."

He hung up, sighed, and felt a jagged edge in his thoughts; not that Karin's outbursts humiliated him, he realized, it was that he expected them. He gulped down his coffee before heading into the restaurant. His maître d' was hurrying across the courtyard, dinner reservation book in hand.

"Philippe, who do we have coming in tonight?"

"A good crowd tonight, Sam. Seventy-two reservations. Three parties of six. The mayor and his wife, a party of ten. It's their anniversary. The editor of The Desert Sun and his wife. It's her birthday. We've got the cake lined up."

"Good work, my friend." That La Sonrisa had received rave notices in the local and national press as one of the brightest jewels in California's buoyant restaurant world meant more to Sam than anything else. But it couldn't counteract a more ominous sign—one he hadn't shared with Karin—that he couldn't keep the Sunridge fully occupied, no matter what promotional gimmicks he tried.

Sam had done financial deals with Tony Dobbs back in his days of flying high as a banker and financier. Tony, a little younger than Sam, was an English accountant who had become active over the past decade in California real estate. It was Tony's condominium in Honolulu that had become Sam's temporary home when he'd taken his sailing lessons farther afield.

As the two lounged by the diving board at the far end of the hotel's pool, Sam thanked his friend for dropping by to lift his spirits after another godforsaken Monday meeting with Karin. Tony's silence made Sam wonder if that was the reason for his friend to drop by. The man always looked a little haggard since his daughters had entered junior high, but he had a diplomatic tidiness about him; this morning, even this seemed to have fallen apart, as if he'd just stepped off a ten-hour flight.

"Did one of your girls get hold of your wife's credit card again?" Sam ventured.

Tony shook his head and launched straight in. "Sam, I'm on to something. The deal is weird. I don't get it. I'm confused about it, very confused. It looks as if it could make millions and be a real life changer." A deal potentially worth millions explained his jumpiness, and the clipped rhythm of his sentences.

"What's cooking?"

Tony startled as Rod delivered a tray of coffee and water. He waited until he had receded far in the distance to start: "Hear me out. Over the last few months, I've been in touch with a firm of accountants in Lagos, Nigeria. In fact, the senior partner of the firm is a graduate of Birmingham University." Sam knew this to be Tony's alma mater. "We've become friendly. Well, as friendly as telephone, faxes and e-mail allow."

From his attaché case, Tony retrieved a manila file.

"Bill Kidogo is his name," he continued. "As you know, Nigeria is as corrupt as hell. The rich live like kings, and the poor starve. Typical third-world stuff. It's very difficult to get money out of the country legally. Bill contacted me because he has clients in Lagos who want to get their money out and have me help them buy homes here in the States, and then they'll emigrate. You'd be ideal for helping them get their capital out. You've been in this field for years."

Tony handed the file to Sam, who scanned the faxes and file notes. The first document was written on the letterhead of Knight & McPherson, the Lagos accounting firm that Tony had mentioned. The writer was Dr. Bill Kidogo, a PhD in international economics. He also mentioned, in the letter, that he was a former secretary general of the Institute of Chartered Accountants in Nigeria.

Dr. Kidogo explained that his firm represented the interests of three prominent Nigerian citizens, who'd granted him full power of attorney to act on their behalf with transferring the funds and authorization of investments. He emphasized that Knight & McPherson would totally comply with Nigerian regulations and that the Central Bank of Nigeria would consent to all transfers of funds overseas.

"Tony," Sam said, putting the file down. "It's Nigeria. Are you sure this is legal?"

Gone was the timidity of only moments before; Tony's smile was wide and enthusiastic. "It's like that transfer we did from Haiti to Panama. Remember that? Remember how much money we made?"

Sam nodded.

Tony went on. "It's three members of the Nigerian military. They're all rich but want to get the hell out of Nigeria and they can use connections at the Central Bank to wire-transfer money to a shell corporation. You still have your shell?"

"Yes," Sam agreed, annoyed, "but—"

"We could use your shell and have the money transferred to Panama, like before."

"Do you know how much they are planning to wire?" Sam asked.

Tony slid over to Sam and flipped over some pages in the notes. Pausing on one page, he pointed and smiled.

"Thirty-seven million." Sam knew how reverent his voice sounded. For moments afterwards, the only sound was the gentle motor of the Jacuzzi near them on the patio.

"What do you think, Sam? You want to get out from under these worries with the hotel? You want to tell Karin where she can stick her offer to buy you out?"

Sam shot Tony an intense look, and out of respect, Tony looked down for a beat.

"Sam, we both need this deal. It's a twenty percent commission. We'd be splitting seven-point-four million dollars, and you wouldn't even have to leave the country."

"It's a Nigerian scam," Sam said. "There will be a catch."

"No. Here's the best part." Tony's voice took on an energy of optimism. "We aren't investing any money. Use your shell and accept their money and wire it back to them when they get out of Nigeria. Pose as consultants. Kidogo tells his associates at the Central Bank we are consulting with the Lagos government on weapons procurement. Once the Central Bank wires it to your shell, you send it on to Panama and we are home free. Panama will never question a wire from a government bank. We take out our commission and we need not work again for a long time."

"Who are the supposed clients?"

Tony shrugged but smiled. "I don't know their names, but they're military guys who want to get out of Lagos and retire to live in big houses in Southern California. Can you blame them?"

"I still have a lot of questions."

Tony took a long sip of coffee and nodded. "Look before you leap, I get it. Let's set up a call to Kidogo and you can ask him yourself."

Sam let the morning sunshine, reflected off the pool, bathe his weary face. It sounded nice. Hell, it sounded more than nice; it sounded like salvation. But he wouldn't let his eyes fill with stars—not yet. He had too much experience in finance not to approach a situation that sounded this peachy with the utmost suspicion. "Set it up. But I warn you, Tony. I will grill him."

Tony sat back in his chair with an arm tucked behind his head. Someone who didn't know the inner workings of the men's lives, but was only seeing them from a distance, would believe them to be the very picture of affluent luxury. "Fine by me."

CHAPTER 2

It had happened during the intermission of a show at his favorite theater in London. He noticed her: elegant in a tight, low-cut black cocktail dress. She was chatting with a friend, yet she noticed him staring and offered him a coy smile. He took his first chance to buy her a drink, explaining he was alone in London on banking business. After the play, her friend took the hint and left them to their own devices.

At first all he knew about her was she was a wealthy divorcee, self-assured and overflowing with style and grace. At night, they had explored; in the afternoons, they had made love in her Chelsea apartment. If her sophistication encompassed certain inhibitions by day, in bed she had been unbridled.

For a long time, his career had been his exclusive focus. That he seemed able to turn investments into liquid gold was the only value he saw in himself—it was the only thing he did. Made money and then spent it immersing himself in cultural events that reinforced the image of himself as a man of means. Theater, art galleries, symphony performances. The stock leisure activities of the upper echelon.

At first, he'd been certain that's all he could be to Karin—a rainmaker in the world of investment banking. Not that he considered her shallow; but he considered money making his only standout quality, the only thing separating him from the scores of refined Englishmen who might have caught Karin's eye. As their relationship deepened, he couldn't help but let his insecurities slip out from time to time, and every time she would assure him it wasn't the money. Karin could make her own—she was no more just a pretty face than he was just a walking wallet—and besides, she emphasized, wealthy men were a dime a dozen in London high society.

Sam grew comfortable enough with this intelligent, ambitious woman that he asked her what it was about him. His curiosity was genuine. If it wasn't the money, then she saw something in him he didn't see in himself. The thought made him eager to view himself through her eyes. She told him that what she had liked, and now loved, about him was his unshakable core of confidence. It was with a sense of certainty in himself that he had approached her, and she had since witnessed this same self-assurance play out in many areas of his life. That solid inner core of his, Karin said, made him seem indomitable to her, and reliable. He had become one of the few people around whom she—a beacon of confidence herself—could allow herself to be vulnerable.

Sam considered it not ironic but interesting that she looked at him this way. For years, he had considered his confidence a product of his money, believing that if he lost one, the other would tumble soon after. After being with Karin for a while though, he felt the hub of his confidence shift. He even came to feel that he could withstand it if he lost his money, his money-making acuity that bordered on magic—so long as he didn't lose this woman who seemed to trust him.

Sam picked up the phone in his hotel office and called Karin, first to confirm she was not wandering the grounds of the hotel. When she answered, he breathed a sigh of relief and told her about the deal Tony had offered him.

The pause lasted long enough and Sam wondered if she was still on the line.

"Karin? Are you there?"

"Nigeria?" she hissed with equal parts disgust and astonishment. "Posing as arms dealers? Are you out of your mind?"

He tried to convey the minimal risk, the tremendous potential payoff, describing the Lagos scheme as the chance of a lifetime. The more she objected, the more adamant he became that there was nothing to object to.

He barked into the phone. "If I get paid three million on this deal, I won't ever have another discussion with you about late alimony payments."

"As nice as that would be," she said, "if you wind up in jail, that will not help me either with alimony or the hotel. I have to go."

The indecision Sam felt afterward—this terrible fresh weight in his gut—made him question his own motives, about calling her, about getting involved in this. What kind of reaction had he hoped for? Was there some part of him hoping that she, like him, would view this as a saving grace for at least the hotel, if not more? He knew he had to be crazy to think that way; there was far too much resentment between them now.

Sam left his office and walked to room 305, where he'd put up Karin when she first visited him from London. Knowing no one was staying there, Sam used a master key to open the door.

The room offered one of the best sweeping views of the property; its scenic window had rendered the perfect backdrop that first night for Karin in her diaphanous gown. He remembered the satin folds of it lapping at his legs upon their greeting—him trying to kick the door shut, her reaching for his zipper.

How different she'd been then. Animated. Daring. Almost wild. After Sam had driven her to gasps and spasms with his tongue, she'd said, "Now it's your turn." Eyes aglow, she suggested, "Let's go for a swim."

No one was at the pool. Though the speed with which Karin stripped down to her gold jewelry made Sam wonder if even a crowd would have deterred her. She struck him, from the beginning, as the woman who always saw a mission through. From the three-and-a-half-feet marker, she beckoned Sam—who was shyer to disrobe, more mindful of the security measures in the place—to join her.

He aimed for nonchalance as he pulled her hips against his in the shallow waters; the gleam in Karin's eyes and her bright, teasing laugh said she wasn't buying it. She knew it made him nervous, even as it thrilled him. If anyone was mellow about this, it was her.

As they toweled off in the room, Sam invited her to stay permanently; she could have 305 as long as she liked. Karin, who had built her own small empire in the computer programming world, claimed she needed to consider it. However, their week of bold bliss was all the persuasion she needed. She could work from anywhere in the world, returning to London only to pack. Back in Palm Springs, she bought a three-bedroom condo.

Six months later, on a hiking path atop the San Jacinto Mountains overlooking the valley below, Sam had proposed. The thrill of her yes and her kiss had made him feel like the most powerful man on earth.

From ornate carved frames, past presidents stared down at the current president in the Oval Office. The silence in the historic room was thick as his director of Central Intelligence and his secretary of Energy awaited his reply.

"Is there any sense whether the troop movements inside Iran are an exercise versus a potential attack?" the president asked.

Zeke Reilly, the DCI, like many previous heads of the CIA, spoke only with great caution. He took off his glasses and rubbed the earpiece against a temple. He had paid little attention to George Laney during the meeting. In his opinion, the Energy Department had no business being involved. His legendary air of superiority vanished before the president but extended to a ruthless temper with agency subordinates.

"Well, Mister President," Reilly began, "our attitude at the agency will be this: hope for the former but be ready to find out it's the latter."

"In other words" the president filled in, "we cannot say, yet."

"Not at this point. No, sir."

Though Laney cleared his throat, it was enough to snag the president's and Reilly's attention.

"I wonder," Laney offered, "if we might consider if even border skirmishes between Iraq and Iran could affect the flow of oil. It's wise to look to Venezuela and Nigeria to increase our imports in case the worst happens."

Reilly rolled his eyes. "George, they're not at war."

"Not yet," said Laney.

"Does the Energy Department have intel from one of your agents in the Middle East we're not aware of?" Reilly's snide tone was unmistakable.

The president jumped in. "You both have valid points." He looked at Reilly. "We don't want to create a panic, since there has been no major military engagement." Now the president turned to Laney. "We should be ready to look to other oil nations to help us out if Iraqi oil stops flowing."

"Yes, sir," Laney agreed. "No need to stir up trouble. But it will hurt our numbers if there is an Iran–Iraq situation that leaves us unprepared to pick up the slack with, say, Nigeria."

"I'd prefer going to Venezuela first," said the president. "They're a lot more stable."

"Of course," Laney replied.

"Zeke, I appreciate the report," the president said in his slow southern drawl as he wiped his brow. He loosened his red tie. He was a handsome man: a mop of thick gray hair, a body kept in shape and tanned through years of golf and tennis.

"Reason I had both of you in here is that if we need to up oil imports, I want you working together. Harmoniously."

"Of course," Laney repeated. The director of Central Intelligence managed only a silent nod.

"We need to think how we will deal with this eventuality. Zeke should let the Israelis know we want intel from anywhere we can get it, long as it's reliable."

"I will make sure our Mossad associates in the area know of our concern," Reilly said. "We can't allow any interruption in our oil supplies."

"Two of you get back to me the second there are new developments." When the president thanked them, Reilly and Laney rose and gathered their papers in unison.

"Don't worry, Mister President. Zeke and I will get on top of this." George Laney cast a quick look at Reilly and nodded. Reilly ignored him.

"I'll check in with you tomorrow, Mister President," Reilly said.

With the president's parting nod, Reilly was out the door. George Laney loitered, fumbling and then reorganized the few papers he held.

"Was there anything else, George?"

"No, sir. Just a comment, sir."

"Yes?"

"Our department has relationships with several government officials in Nigeria. I know there is a lot of corruption in Lagos, but one thing I can say, sir, is that if there were a crisis and we needed oil, we could buy additional supplies at a discounted rate from Lagos rather than Caracas."

The president frowned. "Let's hope it doesn't come to that. But good to know. Thanks, George."

"Thank you, sir."

Laney rushed to catch up with Reilly, who waited at the elevator bank.

"Quite the alarming report, Zeke. What do you think the timeframe is? When do you imagine the Iranians might strike?"

Reilly pushed hard on the button again.

"You think they might move within the next couple of weeks—based on their positions?"

"I've said all I'm at liberty to say," Reilly answered. "As soon as I have any news, I'll alert the president."

The elevator doors opened. Unfortunately for Reilly there were no other passengers.

"I hope you'll let me know too, Zeke. We're supposed to be working together on this."

"Of course, George."

Laney paid no attention to the slight. He didn't give a damn what the spy chief thought. He was too excited about the news. No sooner than he'd waved goodbye to Reilly, who returned a brusque nod, Laney pulled out his cell phone.

"Annie, it's George."

"How are you?"

"I'd like to stop by to make a couple calls, send a few e-mails. It's urgent. I can be at your place in half an hour?"

"See you then."

He hurried down the corridor and out the door and to his car. Normally, Laney would have a driver but he did not want anyone, not even his own employees, to know about Annie.

CHAPTER 3

Sam closed the door to his office behind them. At eight thirty in the morning, he was already on his third cup of coffee. He glanced at his watch. Lagos was eight hours ahead of California.

Sam checked his watch again and then leaned in toward Tony, who had set up the call. "Remember. I'm not committing to anything."

"Fine," agreed Tony. "I'm telling you, all the risk is on their side."

"What risk is that?"

Tony sighed. "Look, there's so much corruption in Lagos, a bribe will make anyone look the other way. But if Kidogo's clients are caught, they will go to jail."

"And us?"

Tony wore the impatient mask of someone consoling a child frightened by imaginary creatures. "We are military consultants who did not get the money they owed us. They will not pursue us. And this deal will change our lives."

Sam dialed. Tony, on an extension, greeted Kidogo. In no time, their conversation hit that effortless stride of long-time acquaintances. After Tony had introduced Sam, Dr. Kidogo spelled out the confidentiality of the transaction. His heavy accent and the unfamiliar pattern of emphasis made it difficult for Sam to understand him, so Sam listened.

"Mr. Marsh, the three gentlemen I represent are heroes, men who have served the Nigerian military for years, and now that they are retired, they want to live a better life than all their money can buy. I am helping them with transferring thirty-seven million dollars. I have relationships with employees in the Central Bank, and when they are paid their share, they will enable the transfer of the funds to a shell corporation. Can you handle that, gentlemen?"

Tony looked over at Sam and nodded.

"Doctor Kidogo—"

"Please, call me Bill. And I would like to refer to you as Sam."

"All right, Bill. I have a Panamanian offshore account I've used in the past.

Bedford and Clifford." He detailed for Kidogo information about the shell corporation and its officers.

"Very good, Sam. I will check into this and call you back."

"Thanks," Tony offered.

"Just a second," Sam jumped in. "I have some questions of my own. And I want to make clear I need some answers before agreeing to work with you."

If it is possible for a pause to be confrontational, this one was.

"What do you wish to know?" Kidogo asked.

"Go easy," Tony whispered. But Sam was retrieving a pen, ready to take notes.

"Tony tells me that Bedford and Clifford would receive the funds from the Central Bank of Nigeria, not from an independent bank. Is that correct?"

Kidogo confirmed this.

"Good. Now, Doctor Kidogo"—it was hard for Sam to call a man like Kidogo by his first name, even on request. "I assume you would want Bedford and Clifford to wire the money to a Panamanian bank." This was one aspect of the transaction that didn't tie his stomach in knots. "And there is one I've worked with before."

"No." There was force in Kidogo's reply. "We will use the Union Bank of Switzerland, the main Geneva branch, or there can be no deal."

Sam gave Kidogo the benefit of the doubt; a man in his position had a reason for being this insistent. "Have you previously dealt with someone at UBS?"

"We use that bank because they have the most liberal rules regarding acceptance of wire transfers. And because they will safeguard the identities of those involved."

"So you have dealt with them before."

"Yes, Sam. I have."

Sam tapped his pen as a new concern occurred to him. "And why are you not dealing with the last person to help you wire money to UBS?"

The blood drained from Tony's already gray face. The desperate way he shook his head felt incongruous with the brief silence on the other end, and with Kidogo's even response: "I cannot discuss the details of previous business dealings. I am sure you have clients whose names you do not discuss."

"I don't need the name, Bill," Sam continued, undaunted. "I just need to know why you're not going back to the same person."

Tony had switched from shaking his head to letting it hang.

"If you must know," Kidogo said, "he was a banker from here in Lagos and he made so much money, he has retired from the field. And he left the country."

Tony and Sam covered their mouthpieces, the former appearing hopeful now. At least Kidogo had answered; at least he hadn't hung up to move to the next candidate on his list.

"What do you think?" Tony asked in a loud whisper.

"I know someone in Geneva who might help." Sam dashed a note to himself. "Tony and I will discuss that," he said into the phone. "I also need to know how they will pay us after the wire transfer goes through."

"Once my clients know the funds have reached UBS in Geneva, they will keep Tony to secure homes for them in the Southern California area."

Sam looked at Tony and smirked. Tony shrugged and smiled.

"Then," Kidogo continued, "my clients will get permission from the government to visit the Ivory Coast, using the excuse of meeting with military contractors there. Once safe in the Ivory Coast, they can fly directly to the United States. Upon their arrival in Southern California, they will wire $7.4 million dollars to the account of your choosing."

Sam could see the explanation reassured Tony and he tried to take his own reassurance from that fact. But he couldn't help wondering if Tony was experiencing a personal financial crisis of his own. Just how high could his daughters be running up the credit card bill? Or was it something different altogether? Did Tony's resume have a blank spot just itching to be filled with white-collar crime? Sam himself had done financial work in the past that, while technically legal in America, would have put him in jail if he was a long-term resident of another country. But he'd come to his senses. He'd gone into work that seemed, by comparison, smart and safe. The hotel business.

"I want the option of using someone in Swiss banking," Sam said.

"Please, consult with anyone you like, but their fees will come out of your end, not ours."

"Let us call you back tomorrow, at the same time."

Tony nodded again.

"That is agreeable," said Kidogo. "In the meantime, I wish to check on your Bedford and Clifford. Until tomorrow."

When they'd hung up, Tony moved to the chair alongside Sam's desk. "Well, that's Doctor Kidogo," he said, studying his friend's face for some telltale sign. "What say you?"

"I need to talk to my friend Pierre in Geneva. I know more about Panama than Switzerland."

"I don't like the idea of another partner. What about this Pierre's fee? Who will pay him?"

"We will if we move ahead."

"I am not doing this, Sam, if I have to split it three ways."

"We'll worry about his cut if he believes we're not dealing with swindlers. And don't worry. His cut would be a fraction of ours," he said, growing annoyed with Tony's lack of concern for the finer details. Whether he wanted to do this to save his own neck, for the thrill, or out of simple greed, he should recognize the importance of knowing all he could about the voice on the other end of the phone.

"What is it, Phillipe?" Sam snapped. He'd hoped for some solitude that night—unlike Tony, he was a planner, and he wanted to prepare for his call the next day—but his maître d' had scurried up to him, anxious, as soon as he'd walked into La Sonrisa.

"Sam, we have a lively group in for dinner. A party of six. They've just ordered their third bottle of Dom Perignon. Five men and one woman. She's stunning. Go over. She looks your type."

"Thanks, I'll be there in a few minutes." What the hell does Philippe know about my type? He asked himself. Since Karin, he'd dipped his toe in the dating pool once or twice, but he wouldn't say he'd dived in. His attention focused on making sure his business—the one he owned with his ex-wife, who'd represented a pillar of his own identity—was a success. Sam hadn't dabbled enough to have a type. Still, he reasoned, there was nothing wrong with saying hello to a beautiful woman and her associates.

Sam downed a glass of white wine and went to the mirror to check on his appearance. He didn't look as haggard and dog-tired as he felt. Then he inhaled, smiled, and scurried across the courtyard to enter his restaurant.

"They're in the back at the round table," Philippe pointed out. Sam had only to follow the loud voices and laughter.

His approach stopped their conversation.

"Good evening. I'm Sam Marsh, the owner. I hope you're all having a good time."

Jesus, Philippe was right. She wore an immaculate white dress, a large emerald pendant caressing her neck. Her eyes sparkled when she smiled at Sam as she put down her fork, granting him her full attention. Her black hair swished across her bare shoulders.

"Shimon Zahavi," one man announced, stretching out his hand. "Your restaurant has been the perfect place for our celebration."

"If you don't mind—a birthday, an anniversary? If there's anything that our chef or maître d' can do, please let me know. We'll take care of it."

"No, no birthdays. We've stopped counting those." They all laughed. "Except Dina. She remains as young and as beautiful as she was when crowned Miss Israel a few years ago."

"Shimon. Stop it. It was more than a few years ago," she said with a smile.

Sam was no exception to the norm in that he appreciated looking upon a beauty queen, but countless attractive women had wined, dined, and brunched their way through La Sonrisa over the years. There was something else about this woman, an indelible self-assurance behind her steady gaze. The word solid flickered through Sam's thoughts, and for a moment, he remembered how Karin had used this very word when justifying her initial attraction to him. She bewitched him. He had to know what this magnetic woman did when she wasn't winning pageants.

"We're here to celebrate a business deal," Shimon explained. "These three gentlemen—Shlomo, Arik, and David—are my partners in Tel Aviv. We have a business there. This is Dina, David's cousin." Sam smiled at each of them as they were pointed out, but his eyes could not wait to rest upon Dina again.

"Well, please let me know if there is anything you want. Enjoy yourselves. It was very nice meeting you all." Sam knew how long to remain at the table playing the role. He turned and walked toward the far side of the restaurant. At the vacated bar, Rod the bartender had been surreptitiously reading a copy of Playboy.

"I'm looking for new drink ideas," Rod lied. "The usual, Coach?"

"Thanks, Rod."

While waiting for his white wine, Sam looked out onto the courtyard. It was a beautiful, clear night. It was surprising more people weren't in the restaurant. Then he remembered—big charity ball in town that night. The thing many of his regulars would attend. It was a one-night event; he told himself, this dip in patronage.

"Hello again, Mr. Marsh."

Sam pivoted and saw it was Dina. She was almost as tall as he was, and her emerald eyes held him in thrall.

"Dina. May I get you a drink?"

"Just a glass of mineral water. They're drinking champagne like crazy and I don't like it with a meal." Her voice had a distinct Israeli accent, friendly and warm but firm.

"It must be quite a big deal that you're all celebrating."

"Shlomo is the chief executive of a high-tech company in Israel. Don't ask me what they do, but it is related to the manufacture of specialized equipment used in operating rooms. Hospitals around the world are clamoring for it." Her eyebrow peaked with the last statement. She made the description of hospital equipment sexy.

"And how are you involved in it?"

"They needed to raise additional working capital for expansion, and I introduced them to a computer company in Silicon Valley that agreed to invest twenty-five million."

Sam whistled. "Those are the deals I loved when I was in the financial sector. I hope you get the customary finder's fee."

Sam's pulse pounded. He looked for, but did not find a wedding ring.

"So, you live near Silicon Valley?"

"No. I'm here in Palm Springs."

"How wonderful!" His smile was enthusiastic, hers enigmatic.

Sam transferred the bottle of mineral water from Rod to Dina. "Well, a toast to this wonderful business deal, and to our meeting." Sam raised his glass to his lips.

Dina sipped her water without taking her eyes off him.

"I'm very flattered," Sam said, "that you left five successful, powerful men to come talk to me."

There went her eyebrows again. "Well, don't be too flattered. Your maitre d' gave them permission to light up in our section. I cannot abide smoke, especially cigars."

"Philippe couldn't say no, with all the Dom Perignon that Shlomo has been ordering."

She chuckled.

Sam pressed his opportunity. "You said you have a place here in Palm Springs. I hope you become a regular here. It's such a pleasure to meet a neighbor in the desert." He handed her a card. "Perhaps you have a card as well?"

Dina took the card and Sam felt her fingertips linger longer than necessary when she withdrew her hand.

"Mr. Marsh—"

"Sam," he corrected.

"Your attention is flattering but you're very obvious."

"I see," Sam said, smiling. "I hope you will forgive a man who was expecting just another night and finds his heart beating out of his chest."

"You seem very relaxed," she teased him.

"You never get what you desire if you never go for it." While Sam didn't pretend to live his life by a single motto, if there was one consistent quality he could pinpoint about himself, it was that he did just that: he went for it. He could be mistaken, but it already seemed that Dina was someone who went for it too.

"Again, I'm flattered, Sam. But I'm only recently divorced."

" As your new friend, I hope we can have lunch together soon." He took another sip to divert the *please* that was also on the tip of his tongue.

"You're an interesting man, Sam. There's something captivating in your eyes."

"Lust?"

Dina laughed. "Well, perhaps that."

He watched, spellbound, as she moved away and disappeared back into the restaurant. He did not know what to do about his alimony payments to Karin or Tony's dubious Nigerian deal. Amid such confusion, it was a relief to feeling anything with clarity, and he felt this: he needed to see Dina again.

CHAPTER 4

"What's the rush, George?" Annie Curtis asked in her soft Louisiana accent as she greeted him at the door of her Bethesda home. George had known Annie since his wild oil-drilling days thirty years before, when the two of them would spend up to sixteen hours a day together in a makeshift office in a dusty mobile home.

He remembered those times at Grainger Oil in Texas with mixed emotions. The office hadn't had the air conditioning it needed. Their round trip commute had exceeded a hundred miles a day, on rugged and often unpaved roads. Yet she'd been a bright spot—loyal and hard-working. Their brief affair had ended when she'd met her future ex-husband and he'd become an oil lobbyist.

"Where's your car?" she asked. She stood in her doorway and looked up and down the street.

"Don't worry," Laney assured her as he stepped past. "Parked around the block."

In her living room, he asked, "How are the kids?" without a glimmer of interest, his eyes already moving deeper into the guts of the house.

"Mike has a tryout for the tennis team and Janet's landed a part in a college play." She straightened a cushion on the sofa. "Coffee?"

"I must have drunk a gallon at the White House." To Laney, time spent on pleasantries was time wasted. In the office he had paid her to set up and maintain, he logged on to the computer. "Annie, I just need to make a few calls and send a couple of e-mails."

She grew animated. "Anything interesting?"

"Oh, not much." Laney smiled. "Just a potential crisis in the Middle East that could mean a huge payday for you and me and a few others."

He checked the phone equipment, making sure the secure phone line was operational.

"Off the books, I'm guessing," Annie mused.

"Hey, don't knock the oil business. The president and I have both done well with it. Not to mention your family." He had a point: they lived in a nice house and vacationed in Europe every six months.

"I'm not complaining," Annie replied.

Laney took out a notebook from his pocket to check a number. After a few minutes he heard his cousin's groggy voice on the line.

"Mark?"

"George? Jesus Christ, it's the middle of the goddamn night here." Here being the Middle East.

George didn't care if he'd woken his cousin from a coma or death. "I've just come from a cabinet meeting and I have some news that will make us both a lot of money. If we act fast. Call me back at Annie's."

Laney put down the phone. "Mark sends his best," he lied. "He's calling me straight back."

"And how is your dear cousin?" Annie asked with an edge of sarcasm. She had never forgiven Mark Woods for stuffing a twenty-dollar bill down her cleavage at a Washington function years before. When the phone rang, she left the boys to it.

"Here's the situation, Mark. Reilly at CIA says there are Iran troop movements near the Iraqi border, and I've planted a seed in the president's head that we need to stockpile oil in case of a military conflict."

"And what country did you have in mind?" Woods asked.

"I'm calling Lagos next to speak with Tambo. Remember him? I will tell him to put together a group to stockpile oil as fast as they can. You should contact him in a few hours. You stand to make big commissions on this. But," Laney said, making his voice harder, "handle it with discretion, you understand." It was George's polite way of saying keep your damned mouth shut. "There must be no mention to anyone of Iran or Iraq. If anyone gets wind of it, they will know there's been a cabinet leak. And fingers will point at me."

"Yeah, yeah, I get it. What if Iran and Iraq don't go to war?"

"Well, that would be a terrible shame," Laney said, eyes twinkling. "But it doesn't matter. Because after we buy up huge quantities of Nigerian oil, whether there are border skirmishes or not, I will convince the president we have to buy Nigerian oil at slightly inflated prices."

"How slight?" Woods inquired.

"Not enough to send anybody to Venezuela and those leftist Commie bastards. Just enough to make us a hefty profit with no one knowing. You and Tambo can handle the transportation details. I will call Miguel in Lisbon to discuss storage in those new undersea facilities they've built off Madeira. After you've spoken with Tambo, be ready to get your ass over to Lagos. The price per barrel has been holding steady at a hundred and twenty, but if anything happens on the Iraqi border, God knows how high it will go."

"Sounds juicy. When I wake up later—at a normal time—I'll call Tambo."

"And Mark," Laney said, "watch the drinking."

In Annie's kitchen, Laney poured himself a cup of her coffee he hadn't wanted just minutes before.

"Something to go with it? I made some oatmeal raisin cookies yesterday."

"Why not? It's a celebration." He popped a cookie in his mouth. "You know it's easier talking to Mark when you've woken him from a dead sleep than when he's drunk."

"Which is usually, right?" She fiddled with the cookie tin, printed with a Japanese motif. "The guy still seems like a loose cannon. You believe he can handle it?"

"As long as he keeps his mouth shut."

She appeared unconvinced. "But can he?"

"He owes me everything. And he knows if he screws this up, I won't bail him out next time."

Back in the office, he punched in another long, international number. The phone rang and rang. It was an ungodly hour in Nigeria. He hung up, waited, and dialed again.

He heard a gruff deep voice answer the phone. "Who is calling me in the middle of the night?"

"Glanville, it's George Laney. I have news that can't wait." In the long pause that followed, Laney hoped that Glanville Tambo's infamous temper wouldn't persuade him to slam down the phone.

"All right." His voice was terse but, at least, not enraged. He understood that Laney knew better than to call if it wasn't vital. Following Laney's summary, Glanville stated—rather than asked—"So, this gives us a good opportunity to make money again. Yes?"

This was the response Laney had wanted. He beamed.

"You should put together a syndicate in Nigeria to stockpile oil. As much as possible. Ship it out of Nigeria. Secure as many Suezmax and Aframax tankers as you can. Miguel will call you from Lisbon to arrange storage in the Canaries. My cousin Mark Woods will call you. Don't go back to bed, Glanville."

"And if there is no fighting between Iran and Iraq?"

"I will convince the president to buy surplus oil. At an increased price."

"Hmm." Now Tambo sounded alert and pensive.

"What is it?"

"I wonder, "Tambo's words had a slow, sibilant quality to them—"if perhaps there's someone we can hire to blow up part of the pipeline and make it look like the Iranians."

Laney squeezed his eyes and rubbed his forehead. "Sounds mighty tricky." There was no reply. "But we can consider it. You make inquiries and I'll do the same."

Tambo promised he would.

"Use Mark to buy the oil. We'll give him the usual commission and I assume they will pay the normal percentage to me."

"Agreed."

With their conversation winding to a close, Laney promised to e-mail Miguel. Securing tankers, he acknowledged, would be the hard part. He could almost hear Tambo nodding on the other end of the line. "But I'll do whatever it takes," Tambo assured. "Good work, George."

"Do you want to do this deal or not?" Tony hissed at Sam on the patio beside the Sunridge's pool. Sam had hoped Tony would be less likely to raise his voice with hotel guests swimming and sunning themselves nearby. Tony did not share Sam's caution.

"I'm waiting for a call from Pierre," Sam explained. "If Kidogo will make us use UBS in Geneva, I want to be damn sure of their laws, including how we get paid.

"But Kidogo has used that bank before!" It wasn't only Tony's volume drawing attention—it was also the increasingly red shade of his face. Noticing the sunbathers who looked his way, Tony said, "I'm sorry, Sam. Kidogo is asking me what is going on and I don't want him to go to someone else.

"Kidogo needs us," Sam assured him. "If he could have used someone at UBS or anywhere else, he would have already done so. And listen." Sam did his best to moderate his own voice; the sunbathers had just returned to minding their own business. "I'm leaning toward saying yes. So far it doesn't seem like a scam—mostly because Kidogo hasn't asked us for any money. If he does, though, this is over. Understand?"

Minutes later, Sam took Tony to the Sonrisa's bar and asked Rod to prepare them Sam's favorite libation: Between the Sheets. It was a mix of brandy, rum, Cointreau, and lemon juice. Russ, the cocktail pianist, had introduced Sam to it when both of them had tired of their nightly martinis and had searched for an agreeable substitute. The drink had become Sam's standing companion after he and Karin had split up.

"When we had that money from the Mexican guys go through your shell to Panama," Tony said, "there was no problem."

"Because it came from a central bank. If the same holds true for UBS, we should be all right. But if Swiss law or UBS policy demands they investigate the source of the thirty-seven million, then we have a major problem. Or if they don't monitor wire transfers but still Nigeria raises their suspicions, we're screwed."

They drank their drinks, celebrating only a possibility, not a fact.

"How much did we make on that Mexico City deal, anyway?"

"I remember," Tony took a slug of his drink. "It was 750k a piece." Tony shifted the liquid around in his glass. "I need the money, Sam. The real estate market is awful right now. We're not even going away for a vacation this year. You should have seen the look on the girls' faces."

"Sorry about that," Sam mumbled. "Listen, just between us, I'm unsure how long I can continue to lose money here. And if I lost the hotel..." It was a sentence Sam couldn't find an ending because he didn't want to imagine it. What would happen to him if he lost the business that had been his sole focus, refuge, and a source of pride following the end of his marriage? "I want this as much as you."

"Report back to me," Tony said, finishing his drink in a gulp, getting up from his stool, "and tell me what Lucky Pierre says."

CHAPTER 5

Mark Woods rolled out of bed with a groan. Standing up—for a man six feet four and 270 pounds, from a platform bed, after an evening of sweaty intercourse and heavy drinking—was no easy task. He glanced over at his Philippine maid, who was still asleep. Lusting after his maid was a matter of both convenience and increasing his odds. He walked naked into the kitchen and poured himself some orange juice, which he decided against spicing up with vodka.

As Woods sat at his desk, perspiration formed on his forehead. The air conditioning was so damned noisy that he didn't run it at night. He got up now to turn it on, muttering resentfully about the Kuwait heat. He grabbed a cigarette from an open pack on his desk and lit up.

His smoker's cough combined with the noise of the air conditioner awakened Lourdes. With a white towel wrapped around her thin body, she rushed into the living room. She could have used more sleep; she still had circles under her eyes.

"I'll make you some coffee, Mark," she offered, not a trace of affection in her voice.

"Yeah," he croaked, sounding half alive. It wasn't only the heat he detested; it was the sandstorms and frequent power outages. He wasn't too fond of the Kuwaitis either, and the distaste seemed to be mutual. When the emir had banned all public celebrations of Christmas and the big yuletide party at the Sheraton was canceled on twenty-four hours' notice, Mark had raised his voice to the Crown Prince at a social function. He'd just escaped a humiliating public arrest. On another occasion they had escorted him from a party after slipping ten crumped hundred-dollar bills into the hand of a mistress of one of the emir's nephews promising her a good time.

It was George Laney who'd banished him to Kuwait, though it was also Laney who had saved him from serving time back in Oklahoma for driving drunk and possessing an illegal handgun. And from fraud indictment. And from bankruptcy. Laney saved him many times, but it didn't mean he appreciated all this help.

Here was what Woods appreciated in Kuwait: the Filipino maid and a bottle of vodka close at hand. These were the implements of his comfort whenever he experienced a slack time in his business—which comprised himself, a part-time bookkeeper, a phone, a Rolodex, and a legal pad. He ran it from his apartment overlooking the Gulf; he'd launched the firm after he had quit his job working for an oil broker, furious that they had cheated him out of a year-end bonus.

Lighting another cigarette, he dialed Glanville Tambo. He'd met Tambo a few times at conventions around the world and at George's home in suburban Maryland.

The man's voice was as deep and pompous voice as ever. "I've been speaking with George. I understand we will do more business together."

"That's right," Woods said. "George thinks I should fly to Lagos immediately."

"You should. I have already spoken with my friend, our ambassador to Germany. We don't want any of the usual visa problems at the airport. As you will have to fly via Frankfurt anyway for your connecting flight, our ambassador will meet you at the Lufthansa executive lounge. You will fly to Lagos together. A government car will bring you straight to my home. You will work from there."

Cigarette ash dropped into the hair on Woods's chest, but he did not flick it off. "Does the ambassador know why I'm coming?"

"He is a member of our syndicate," Tambo said with undisguised pride. "Since I spoke with George, I have already put together a powerful group of investors, and I have many more people still to contact."

Mark Woods liked the sound of that, though he worried about the shipments—and told Tambo as much. "The tanker market is tight at the moment." Out of habit, he reached for the bottle of vodka to top up his orange juice.

"We will try to charter as many tankers as we can. Those we need and can't arrange. Well, we have other ways. I can handle that. I have a brother with a high military ranking. He'll assist us."

"So I gotta meet this guy—the Ambassador—tomorrow?"

"At noon. His name is Leonard Mobete. My assistant, William Kidogo, will make your flight reservation from Frankfurt to Lagos."

Mark scribbled down the ambassador's name on the corner of a magazine cover. He remembered William Kidogo well.

"Meanwhile," Tambo said, "I have another nine or ten people to contact. I already have seventy million committed."

By the time he put down the phone, Woods was happier. "Jesus Christ," he said, both to Lourdes and to himself. "George was right. I could stand to make a ton in commissions over the next couple of weeks. Maybe enough to get out of this goddamn place forever."

He grabbed an airline schedule from his desk. There was a flight for Frankfurt departing at eleven. It was still too early to call the travel agent to book his ticket, but it wasn't too early to pack.

Sam had known Pierre Bloch—paragon of sophistication and European culture—for fifteen years. Sam assumed he learned his impeccable manners from attending boarding schools in his native Switzerland and in England. After qualifying as an attorney, he had taken the banking route. Pierre had spent a few years on Wall Street before returning to Geneva, where he established a worldwide reputation as an investment advisor. His expertise in international banking equaled his linguistic skills; fluent in four languages, he'd proven invaluable to Sam on many European deals.

"Pierre, it's Sam. How are you, mon vieux?" He awaited his friend's voice on the line; a conversation with Pierre was like setting down a heavyweight.

"Just ordered my opera season tickets. You should join me in Geneva."

Normally, Sam would have lingered on the pleasantries, but time was of the essence. "Pierre, I have a business deal for you. I'll warn you it sounds too good to be true. But if it's genuine, we stand to cash in."

"Tell me."

Sam launched into a monologue explaining the deal, including how the unemotional Tony had become overbearing about their going into partnership on the Lagos deal. He then welcomed advice from Pierre. He wanted some finality from their conversation, either reassurance that it was worth the risk or irrefutable proof that it was a bad idea so he could give Tony a reason to give up.

"Well, it sounds interesting," Pierre said, with hesitatation. "Without having to go there, Sam, and with the shell corporation you have, it minimizes your risk."

There was a very long pause on the phone.

"And what about the downside, Pierre?" When he did not get an immediate reply, Sam lowered his voice and sighed in exasperation.

"Pierre, just tell me. Is this something that can work? And do you want to help us with UBS?"

"Sam," Pierre began. "I am most honored you asked me to help you. I have to wonder, as you do, if it is for real. And even if it is, do we have any way of knowing if they will catch your people on the inside? Are they thorough? Are their bribes sufficient? And are they being watched, right from the start?"

Sam had to admit these were good questions, for which he had no answers.

"But, then again, where would Swiss banking be today but for the billions of dollars that left Latin America, the Congo, Iran, the Philippines, and so on? I have my doubts, but we can work on it a little and see how it unfolds as we go along." Pierre's voice was the picture of equanimity, revealing neither worry nor enthusiasm.

Typical Swiss, Sam thought.

"I can speak to people at UBS in Genève," Pierre offered. "I will find out if there is a threshold for investigating wire transfers. Especially those from Nigeria. And if the origin of the funds is the Central Bank, it will help us."

Sam expressed his gratitude. "If you will work with us," he explained, "we'll prepare an agreement between Dr. Kidogo's accounting firm, his clients, my shell corporation, Bedford and Clifford, and yourself, which will cover all of us. It will specify your fee and ours."

Pierre agreed to this, specifying only that he wanted to see a draft of the agreement. Given the uptick in publicity about money laundering, he said, he wanted to make sure the contract would stand up to the scrutiny of the Union Bank of Switzerland. Sam didn't finish expressing his profound gratitude when Pierre cleared his throat.

"There is one other matter we have to discuss."

"Your fee," Sam said. "Yes, for all your efforts on our behalf, Tony and I want to give you a considerable finder's fee. Did you want to suggest something or should I?"

For a moment Sam's only answer was the long-distance crackle on the line.

"Yes," Pierre replied. "A fee. I am sure you would agree that if we work together, my using a known and trusted officer and finding out about UBS current policies, which are not available to the public, would be worth a considerable amount."

"I want you happy with whatever fee we agree upon."

"Then you agree that my services are essential in making this Lagos deal happen?"

This was unlike Pierre, who had a number in mind that usually spilled off the tip of his tongue. Anyone with whom he worked understood his value.

"Yes, Pierre, we need you. So tell us what number you have in mind."

"It sounds to me," Pierre said carefully, now starting to frustrate Sam, "that all three of us are essential parts of this potential deal. Tony brings you the deal with the contacts in Nigeria. You have the shell corporation and legal knowledge about wire transfers. And I have the contacts in the bank in Switzerland. So, why don't we split it three ways?"

Sam recovered quickly.

"I won't argue that we need you. But Tony may well object to his share shrinking. I'd have to ask him."

"I hope you can convince him," Pierre said, " how important my contact at UBS is—and the risk it is for me to go to him about this. If he is not willing to help, I will have compromised my relationship with that bank."

"I understand your position, Pierre." What else could Sam say? He needed to buy some time. "Let me talk to Tony and then get back to you as soon as possible."

"Thank you," Pierre said evenly. "I hope we can all get our fair share and celebrate together in Europe soon."

At the hotel bar, Sam and Tony sat blank-faced and exhausted, neither cheered by the bottle and glasses placed in front of them, nor the bartender's jab at humor: "Let me know if you two need straws or anything."

Tony did not look up and Rod took his leave. When he was far enough away, Tony asked his friend, "So, is this a celebration or a wake?"

This was the most convivial rendezvous Sam remembered because he knew that Tony tired of meeting poolside and Sam wanted a place somewhat less cloistered than his office.

"So, good news or bad?" Tony began.

"Bit of both." Sam poured for Tony and then himself.

"What do you mean?"

"He's in."

"I'll call that good news."

Agreeing, Sam saw his opportunity to extol the virtues of using Pierre. Then he launched into how difficult the process might be, even with money coming from the Central Bank, without inside information about UBS.

"How much does he want?" Lines of concern formed on Tony's face as he watched his friend pour him a second glass of wine no sooner than he'd drained the first.

"He wants to be a partner. He wants a third."

Tony's mouth flopped open. "A third? Almost two and a half million dollars for an introduction to some guy at a bank?"

"The only bank Kidogo will deal with. Tony, we need him."

"The hell we do. We'll find someone else."

"Who else do we know connected to UBS." The way Sam said it, it wasn't a question. "This is the only way."

"Let him take a flat fee or forget it."

"Tony, Pierre wouldn't do this for anything less. He will be in some jeopardy when he asks about the wire transfer."

"Let's negotiate with him."

Sam just shook his head.

"You're telling me you're willing to kill this deal. I brought it to you. I did not make your friend a full partner."

"No, Tony, you're saying you will kill the deal by not giving a third to the guy who can get the 37 million into UBS."

Tony looked around the bar, scantily populated at this hour—as it was so much of the time now—and wondered how his friend could be so cavalier about money, especially now.

"Tony." Sam tried to soothe his friend's anger and disappointment. "Come on. It's better than nothing. And it will not happen without him."

Tony drained glass number two.

"You said you wanted to talk to Kidogo before agreeing," Tony reminded Sam. "I want to talk to Pierre before we decide anything."

"We should draft a document to send Kidogo. The transfer of funds from Nigeria must be in strict conformity with Nigerian regulations. We must see that they obtain all the necessary consents and any taxes that might be due are paid.

The funds cannot be connected with any drug trafficking or money laundering and all that stuff."

"And your friend, lucky Pierre?" Tony asked bitterly.

"We'll draft an agreement making sure he has to reveal information about UBS wire transfer policies to us and give us the identity of his contact at UBS in order to receive his share of the monies."

Tony eyed Sam. "I don't like it. I don't like him getting a third and I don't like our not negotiating with him."

"I understand. Are we moving ahead?"

" I have to talk to Pierre."

CHAPTER 6

In Lagos, the air inside Mark Woods's destination terminal was muggy. Perspiration trickled from his neck down his back. The ambassador, whom Wood's had met-per Tambo's plan- in Franfurt, did not look half as sweaty. Wood's stained, cream-colored jacket clung to his red shirt, which stretched to its maximum. If he was sober and less tired, he'd have noticed, too, that the terminal needed a coat of paint. The other passengers had sour and apprehensive expressions as they approached the immigration officers. One of them stamped Woods's passport without a second glance, he and the ambassador were waved through.

When Woods's bags careened onto the baggage carousel, another official approached them with their cases and took them outside to a limousine parked nearby.

"Shall we go?" offered Mobete.

"Not until I get a couple drinks under my belt," Woods replied. "Man, you do not understand how hard it is to travel that long in the air. And those damn Kuwaitis. Can't find any alcohol anywhere in the stupid country."

The ambassador held up a hand to the driver, showing he should wait. Mobete accompanied Woods to an airport bar.

Woods took his seat with a thump. "I don't have any local currency."

"Please, allow me to buy you a drink," Mobete offered.

"I need more than one."

As Woods gulped down a second and then a third vodka, Mobete considered his burly American companion. The ambassador, immaculately dressed in a dark-blue double-breasted suit, pressed white shirt, and silk tie. His polished black shoes contrasted the faded, scuffed, and neglected brown footwear of Mark Woods. Wood's belly hung over his belt and the top of his too-tight and stained trousers, his face was splotchy and stubbled. His breath, normally unpleasant because of indigestion, seemed all the worse now for being coupled with his pungent body odor.

Given the opportunity, Ambassador Mobete would have preferred to sit well away from Mark Woods on the drive in the limousine, but he had his orders: to facilitate Woods's entry into Lagos, and to extend to him hospitality fit for a king.

Exhausted from his trip and drunk, the opulence of Glanville Tambo's residence stunned Mark Woods. The gold leaf gate, the guards in dress uniform, the long, circular drive leading to the white, marble, three-story home all belied the poverty Woods had done his best to ignore on the drive from the airport.

Inside, the house was so glutted with antiques Woods became claustrophobic—and as though he'd fallen backward into an earlier era.

"Looks like there's no place a guy can put his feet up," he said to Mobete. Smiling, the ambassador led Woods up a long, gracefully curving marble staircase to the second floor, down a plush Berber runner, toward the office of Glanville Tambo.

In the office, a tall slender man in his early sixties arose to greet them. Tambo projected the unmistakable aura of wealth and power.

"Sit down, Mark. William Kidogo will be here in a minute to help you settle in. We have had more telephone lines, and a fax installed for you. If you need a secretary, William can arrange that too."

He turned toward the ambassador. "Leonard, thank you for your help and for coming so."

After shaking hands with Tambo and Woods, Mobete made his grateful escape from the ugly American.

Woods stretched his legs until he was reclining more than sitting. "So, Glanville. I guess we will make a big oil score at the expense of my government."

"I'm happy to tell you, "Tambo's smile revealed oversize, bright-white teeth "that I have received commitments from investors totaling one hundred and ten million. I still have more people to approach."

Woods whistled. Tambo regarded this reaction as he might have a full outburst. Woods leapt out of his chair and shouted. "That is mighty impressive, Glanville. You have wasted no time."

"Yes, my contact has assured me of his cooperation regarding tankers, so we have no reason to worry anymore about transportation issues. My friend will do as I say. Also, I've been speaking with Miguel in Lisbon. I have completed storage arrangements."

Woods laced his hands behind his head with a yawn. Oblivious to how Tambo assessed him with stifled distaste, he ploughed ahead.

"So, Glanville, I will buy oil and oil options for you. I need the name of a company. Do you have a name in mind?"

"Why not Madin Oil? I can have that registered as a Panamanian corporation."

"Madden?"

"M-a-d-i-n." Tambo spelled it slowly.

"That some Nigerian name or something?"

"There's a pill I take every day called Coumadin. When I was looking at the bottle this morning, Madin struck me as a good name."

"Look here. The world's got itself a second Shakespeare."

Tambo furrowed his brow and leaned in. His penetrating stare made Woods sit up straight. "What do you mean?"

"Just you got a way with words, that's all. What's the pill for?"

Tambo continued to stare at Woods. The American was no stranger to the art of annoying those around him—whether he'd just met them or had known them for years—but now he was wearing on the nerves of someone who could have him killed.

"I have a blood clot that is very dangerous. I did not want the doctors to operate on the base of my skull. So I take a blood thinner to stay healthy. They tell me I must stay calm." If Tambo's eyes had seemed penetrating before, now they were bullets. "So I hope there will be no problems with our project with George."

Woods attempted to swallow his fear. "Should be a breeze, Glanville."

"You look as if you need a rest and a bath." It wasn't a question. "My butler will take you to your quarters."

Tambo picked up his phone, whispered into it, and then hung up. "Now, Mark, buy oil as soon as you're ready. Tell me at the end of each day how much you have bought, what the total costs are, and where we will wire the funds. I'll send my assistant, Doctor Kidogo, up as soon as he arrives."

A butler, dressed in a white suit complete with a bowtie, appeared at the door.

"Thank you, Glanville," said Woods. "I'm looking forward to getting started."

Woods stood and shook hands with Glanville.

"Contact me each day," Tambo reminded him. The small portion of Woods's dignity not pulverized by the civil beating it had just received allowed him to nod his head.

Woods followed the butler out of the office and downstairs toward the back of the rambling residence.

"Glanville Tambo lives high off the hog," he muttered.

"I am sorry?" the butler said.

"I'm living in Kuwait," Woods explained. "Even some of the richest sheikhs in Kuwait don't have a place like this."

"Oh, yes." The butler spoke with cautious decorum. "Minister Tambo has done much for our nation. The oil has helped us become a more prosperous country. Without him, we would have much less. We owe him a great deal of gratitude."

Woods followed the butler down a marbled foyer, past rooms the size of tennis courts, and filled with expensive Italian furniture. The whole way, their feet padded on thick Persian rugs.

When the butler led Woods outside, they entered a courtyard with an enormous fountain. Flamingoes wandered idly about, dipping their beaks in the water. In front of them stood another house, not as large as Tambo's residence but still grand enough to wow even those accustomed to the real estate of Beverly Hills. It was two stories, also white, with many balconies overlooking the courtyard and surrounded on both sides by thick foliage.

Inside the butler guided him up another winding stairway.

"No elevators around here, huh?" said Woods, his bluster coming back to life now that there was a courtyard and marble walls between him and Tambo.

"I am sorry, sir," the butler replied. "Minister Tambo designed the homes this way. He says he likes the exercise."

"Good for him." As the two ascended the marble steps, the butler slowed down to match the American's pace. In his room, Woods's sweat dried thanks to the noiseless air conditioning, yet another factor that set this place apart from his apartment in Kuwait.

After the butler took his leave, Woods walked to the casement windows and opened them to step out onto a balcony that overlooked not only the fountain and flamingoes but, in the distance, a gold-tiled swimming pool. The perks of robbing a country of its oil.

A knock at the door interrupted his reverie.

Woods shouted, "Come in!"

A short gentleman with very dark skin and horn-rimmed glasses entered carrying an ornate box.

"Hello, Mister Woods. I am Doctor William Kidogo. I have a welcome gift for you, from Minister Tambo."

Woods shook the man's hand and then pulled from the box two bottles of Chivas Regal scotch. For the first time in a long time, Woods smiled. "Well, this is just about the best present I could ask for. Unless you brought me a woman."

"Minister Tambo remembered you like this brand," Kidogo said, bowing his head.

"I will open a bottle and celebrate all the money we'll make, Bill."

"Well, I will drink to that, but later," the Nigerian said. "I have to get back to my office."

"I could be here for a couple of weeks, Bill. Maybe more. So please keep the Chivas coming." Mark opened the first one. Not bothering with the glasses that accompanied his gift, he gulped straight from the bottle and smacked his lips.

Kidogo watched with a lack of expression. "I've set you up in an office in the next room. Tell me if you need anything."

"What about a calculator? I'll need that to monitor how much money we're making."

"There's one on your desk, Mark," Kidogo chuckled. His eyes wandered over Mark's suit. "Also, if you need any laundry, just press this bell over here for the houseboy. If you press zero on the phone and ask for the kitchen, you can order your meals and they will bring them to your room or office. And please use the pool and the rest of the house whenever you wish."

Woods flopped down in a chair and unbuckled his belt, acting no less relieved that a man free to scratch an inflamed patch of skin that had itched for hours. His trousers dropped a few inches to reveal the top of his red tartan shorts.

"Any women staying down the hall?" Woods smiled.

Kidogo shook his head. "His Excellency would like a daily update from you regarding what you've bought and all the settlement details. You can let me have them too. I'm here for an hour every morning. The rest of the time, I'm at my office downtown. I'm an accountant."

"Don't worry, Bill." Woods raised the bottle of Chivas to his greedy lips again. "You'll be seeing big numbers. Huge."

CHAPTER 7

The halibut from Sam's kitchen lay half-eaten on Tony's plate.

"What's the matter, Tony? Was it too dry?"

"Not at all. It tasted fine."

"You're still annoyed about Pierre."

Tony shook his head. "No, I told you, he sounded reliable and I agree we have to have him. There's another wrinkle."

"The wrinkle that calls for coffee or something stronger?"

"Let's start with coffee."

On his way through the dining room, Sam checked on their few lunchtime guests. In the kitchen, he poured coffee—he would need it, and likely more, to re-energize him about this deal. Was it logical to expect something that started with this many wrinkles to work out? When he got back to the table, Tony, at least, appeared calmer.

"So what's cooking?" Sam asked.

"Bill called around one in the morning. He's okay on the draft agreement. No problems. We agree on everything."

"But . . . ?"

Tony looked down at the remains of his halibut as if he expected it to bite him. "He wants us to go to Lagos to meet with him. He wants to introduce us to his clients. After which we must go to the Central Bank and sign—in person—something called the payment release order. This allows the Central Bank to release the funds to the shell company, and then the money will be transferred to Union Bank of Switzerland."

Sam thought it over as he sipped his coffee. Thirty-seven million was a lot of money; it was reasonable that they wanted to meet Tony and himself.

"What if we suggested meeting in Europe? Pierre is in Geneva. Or Paris is not so terrible." Sam chuckled, trying to cheer Tony.

"Already suggested it," Tony answered wearily. "He wants us in Lagos."

"Let's try to call him now."

In Sam's office, they dialed and redialed Nigeria. Between attempts, Tony informed Sam that Kidogo had filled him in on the requirements: they had to contact the Nigerian Embassy to discuss visas. The embassy needed, from Dr. Kidogo, a copy of a formal invitation to Sam and Tony, citing their business. The embassy also needed to see photocopies of their round-trip tickets.

At last a tired-sounding Dr. William Kidogo picked up the phone.

"Bill," Tony began. "How are you?" To Sam, his friend's enthusiasm sounded forced.

"We're ready to discuss the next step," Sam offered when Tony passed him the phone.

Kidogo wasted no time. "The next step is that you come to Nigeria, right away." He then reiterated the same points Tony had already relayed to Sam: they would meet the three clients, they would sign the requisite form at the Central Bank. "Can you be here within the next few days?"

"Bill, slow down. Why can't we meet in Europe? That would be much more convenient."

"It is impossible. The three clients are all important men in Nigeria. They are watched all the time." Kidogo let this sink in. "We have a military dictatorship here, don't forget. If they were all out of the country at the same time, it would look very suspicious."

However sound Kidogo's logic, Sam was still loath to travel to Lagos. "Well, suppose one of them came to Europe, with you. That would be enough."

"Impossible. You must come here to sign in person the payment release order at the Central Bank."

Sam didn't like people making demands of him. Nor did he like the prospect of globetrotting for work that was, in his opinion, on a par with dotting the i's and crossing the t's. "Isn't that something you could do under a power of attorney from us?"

"I have spoken to Tony about all this already." Kidogo's tone ruled out a compromise. "If you are serious about this business, you must come to Lagos."

Tony shook his head, saying nothing and looking defeated. He did not have the fight in him to convince Kidogo. But Sam was not used to people dictating conditions to him.

"Our expenses of flying to Nigeria from California will be enormous. We will come, but will you wire the funds to us as a sign of good faith?"

This time, the answer was longer in coming.

"There are Central Bank restrictions. I would like to do that, but I cannot. I am doing this at great risk and I assure you, any money I receive will be much less than yours. But I assure you I will take care of all your expenses in Nigeria."

Sam and Tony eyed each other. Tony looked helpless. Sam covered the mouthpiece of his phone.

"Let's talk," he mouthed.

Tony nodded.

"Bill," Tony said into the extension, "we will plan and call you back with a progress report. All right?"

"Call me back later today," said Kidogo. "It is important, if we are to do this business with you both, that you come immediately or else I will have to find someone else. Please send the visa applications and photocopies of the plane tickets to our embassy in Washington."

They all hung up.

"If this jerk keeps threatening me," Sam grumbled, "I will walk away." That Tony insisted it was just a tactic provided him no comfort.

"Where else is this low-rent white-collar criminal from the Third World going to find guys who know finances, have a shell corporation, can help buy real estate in Southern California, have a Swiss guy with inside contacts and our willingness to pay out-of-pocket expenses to fly to his godforsaken country? Tell me that!"

Tony put his arm around Sam's shoulder. Outside of shaking hands, they were not the type of friends who indulged in physical contact—not even a casual slap on the back, not a brotherly punch or tap or smack. Perhaps it was the rarity of this expression of warmth that caused Sam's mood to veer. "We will make this happen," he said.

Tony shrugged. "Hell, we got this far. Might as well go all the way."

While Tony used Sam's fax machine to ask Bill for an official invitation on his firm's letterhead, Sam phoned the Nigerian Embassy in Washington to request visa application forms. On the second phone line, Tony checked round-trip flights to Lagos.

"The cheapest tickets are about six grand, and that's via Paris," Tony reported.

"If we have a stopover in Paris, I might not go the rest of the way."

The resurgence in Sam's momentum had carried him this far, but now, with Tony making reservations, it was all becoming real. It was coming down to numbers—sizeable ones. He'd asked Kidogo for good-faith money, but he's the one who needed faith now. He was about to open his wallet to make this deal happen. It had better be worth it.

"Bill needs to tell us where we'll be staying in Nigeria," he said to Tony. "God knows what the hotels are like."

"So we will insist on a five-star hotel in the middle of hell."

Both men laughed, but Sam found it hard to shake the image. In the hospitality business himself, he understood a hotel was only as good as its immediate surroundings; he couldn't help but expect the grim circumstances that awaited him. But there was something else he also couldn't help thinking about— something more pleasant.

Sam was not in the habit of getting butterflies when he called a woman, the schoolboy nerves rattled him. He was so preoccupied with Dina he rarely worried about or was preoccupied with the Nigerian deal.

"I knew you'd phone, Mr. Marsh." Her tone was as soft and friendly as he remembered. "I half expected you to call me the next morning."

"Please call me Sam. And you must forgive my delay. There's a business matter I've been dealing with that's a bit . . . outside my wheelhouse. But calling you has been on my mind every day."

"And here we are." He could practically see her smile. "What can I do for you?"

"You can have dinner with me."

"Under no circumstances. I've told you already. I am not ready to go out on dinner dates with men, let alone strangers."

He had expected he may need to plead his case, not that he minded. There was something thrilling about working hard to impress a woman as successful and self-assured as Dina. She was equally deserving of his respect and worthy of pursuit. "I can understand that," he said, "but I'd like to see you again. You made a big impression on me."

"Thank you, Sam. I enjoyed your company, but I don't see a dinner date in our near future."

Sam acknowledged her boundaries, but his ears also perked at the words near and future.

"How about lunch, then? Something casual."

She hesitated. "Okay. The Hilton at one o'clock tomorrow?"

"Terrific."

The next day, at precisely one o'clock, he watched her climb out of her white Mercedes 560SL convertible, take a ticket from the valet, and hurried into the hotel. Her skin glowed in contrast to her white jeans and a pale blue shirt.

As they headed for a table overlooking the pool, he heard a woman whisper to her companion. "She looks just like Audrey Hepburn." Sam smiled. There was a resemblance between their faces, and both women always appeared poised and elegant, with a star quality that bordered on royalty.

Perusing his menu, Sam commented on how open and light the restaurant was.

Dina smiled. "That's why I chose this place. If I had let you select the restaurant, I'm sure you would have chosen some dark romantic place."

"Smart move," Sam said. "I would have done that."

Dina snapped her menu closed. "I will have the quiche. What about you?"

"You always know what you want? You don't strike me as a woman who waffles in her decisions."

"That's true," Dina agreed. "I had to learn to make quick decisions in my previous career."

"And what was that?"

"Oh, let's just say I worked in security."

"Securities?" asked Sam, knowing that was not what she said. "The financial sector?"

"No security, Sam. As in safety." When Dina shifted, their legs bumped under the table. She apologized while he savored the brief contact.

When their waitress, whose long blonde hair was in a severe ponytail, came to take their orders, Sam noted how Dina smiled genuinely at the young woman. Exceeding the perfunctory thank you, she left the server feeling valued. She had a way of doing that with everyone—including him. Her gossamer touch when she brushed crumbs from his chin during lunch seemed to erase everyone else from the room.

When their espressos arrived, Dina told him, "Sam, I confess, I'd intended to spend only forty-five minutes with you and then leave with an excuse that I have a meeting to attend. But I'm having a very nice time. Tell me, why did you leave Wall Street for Palm Springs?"

"I'd been in banking on Wall Street for many years, but I was worried night and day about its fluctuations. Eventually, I realized that my confidence fluctuated every time the market did. It was something I had no real control over. I decided

I needed something more . . . solid. Something where I could put in a good day's work and control the consistency of my results."

"And the hotel business gives you that?"

Sam looked away, torn between guarding his pride and vulnerability with this woman whom he hoped would reciprocate. "It gave me that." thickness coated his voice. "For a while."

"The hotel isn't doing well?"

This time Sam didn't have the same internal struggle; vulnerability had won out. In the steady beam of Dina's eyes, he felt helpless to do anything except tell the truth, the whole truth. "My ex-wife, Karin, and I run it together. For years, it was doing well, and we were happy. Somewhere around the time our relationship crumbled, the business stopped doing so well. I'm just hoping the two aren't inextricably linked. I'm hoping even though we couldn't make our marriage work, we can save the hotel."

Without dimming in intensity, Dina's eyes took on a new softness. "Were you married a long time?"

"Long enough that it's hard to see any aspect of the hotel without being reminded of our history." Clearing his throat, Sam attempted to change gears. The conversation had gotten far heavier than he'd expected. "But I'll admit a different association comes to mind when I think of the restaurant. Particularly, a certain table toward the back."

He may have been ready for a little levity, a return to his attempts to romance her, but Dina was of a mind to share as Sam had. "I was married to John for over twenty years," she said. "It takes time to figure out who you are again after a relationship like that."

While he had trouble picturing the dauntless woman in front of him ever questioning her identity, he was grateful for her words. She had managed, so succinctly, to say something he'd struggled both to describe and to understand. He said, "I agree." And from that point, Dina, it seemed, became an open book.

She told him that her family had fled Spain at the time of the Inquisition. After a few generations in Turkey, they had made their way to the Holy Land and settled in Jerusalem. If Israel had an aristocracy, her family would have been part of it. Over the years they had produced many eminent businesspeople, rabbis, university professors, diplomats, and archeologists. "I was in the Israeli army before emigrating to the United States."

Sam raised his eyebrows. "No wonder you are in such fantastic shape." Seeing her face deadpan, underscoring that idle flattery did not move her, he jumped back in. "I mean everything I say. How would you like to come with me on my upcoming business trip?"

He saw her gearing up to object.

"As security only, of course. I'm going to Nigeria."

She sat up straight and pushed back her shoulders. "You must be mad. Anyone who goes to that godforsaken country is an idiot. It's dangerous—plus it stinks."

"Well, I have a deal that's too good not to explore."

As he outlined the plan, she fidgeted with her napkin and endlessly stirred her coffee.

"Well?"

"I'd advise you not to go," she blurted. Then she paused and sighed. "But I also believe you won't be satisfied unless you do."

"I'm going next week."

"Why are you taking such a chance?" she asked. He noticed, with some pleasure, how concerned she sounded.

"It's hard for me to say this," Sam began, "but I trust you. I need this deal or I will probably lose my half of the hotel."

He could sense her weighing various unknown factors as she stared at him—or, more accurately, through him. "I will give you the name of a cousin of mine in Lagos. He's a civil engineer working with Soleh Boneh, an Israeli company, and they are partners with a local company in Nigeria. They're involved in highway construction projects. I'll phone you later with his telephone number. You should contact him when you get to Lagos and stay in touch with him. He knows many people over there, in case you get into trouble."

Sam laughed. "Dina, for crying out loud! How come you have a cousin in Lagos?"

She appeared taken aback by the question. "My mother was one of eight children and so was my father. I have thirty-six first cousins. They're everywhere, Hong Kong, Manila, Sao Paulo, Tokyo, all over the place."

Sam would have pressed for stories of this far-flung family, but Dina drained her espresso and then said, "This has been very nice. But I must go. Today is my shooting day."

"Your what?"

"I have a pistol. I go to a shooting club in LA."

"How often do you do that?"

"Whenever I'm not doing judo or kickboxing." With a wink, she arose. "It's damn good fun."

Sam rose with her, moving to kiss her cheek, but she turned away. He watched longingly, first as she left the restaurant for her car, then as she vanished into the thick afternoon traffic.

CHAPTER 8

Roni Kahan had been waiting for Philip in the hotel's lobby for a few minutes, but he wasn't worried. Considering the traffic and general chaos of everyday life in downtown Lagos, being ten minutes late was the equivalent of being on time. It always amused Roni at the sight of arriving guests quarrelling about the room rates and those checking out who couldn't reconcile their bills. When the arguments intensified, hulking security guards made their presence known.

Roni smiled at the two attractive, uniformed young women who worked the front desk. Hotel employees by day, hookers once their shifts ended. They smiled back. Occasionally he used their services, both as escorts and sources of information.

He stood out not only for being an Israeli among Africans but also for his tanned, rugged physique. The suit he wore without a tie looked good on his tall frame.

Philip Carlisle looked like any other Nigerian businessman coming to the hotel for lunch or to check into his room. He walked past the attractive women Roni had passed, but he didn't lend them flirtatious glances; he stared ahead. It was typical of the pair not to say much until they sat across from each other at a corner table, where they snacked from a bowl of peanuts while awaiting their order.

"Roni," Philip began, "I've always appreciated your knowledge about Nigerian politics and local business, and I'm hoping you can share some insight regarding the sudden jump in oil prices."

Roni tossed a few peanuts in his mouth and chomped on them before replying. "I've been watching closely too. And I wish I could tell you what was going on."

"The word from my associates in the oil industry is that some group is stockpiling. But why would they? I haven't been told about any threat to oil supplies."

"I know as much as you," Roni said. "One thing I've learned from working on construction projects here is that the government is volatile. People in government can lose their jobs or their lives suddenly. Plenty of speculation with that kind of instability. That's why they hire us to oversee their projects. Make sure it keeps the bribery to a minimum."

No sooner had drinks arrived than Philip placed his credit card on the server's tray. "You hungry?"

"I could eat," Roni shrugged. "But later."

Philip waited until the server was well out of earshot to say, "I was at the embassy, and even they weren't sure if there is any truth to the rumor that a Nigerian oil tanker has been hijacked."

"But I've heard it too."

They drank silently, sizing each other up. "Look," Philip began again. "We mix in the same circle and I'm sure we both have good sources to tell us what's going on."

Roni flashed a brief grin. "Just two consultants trading information?"

"Our bosses need information. We need not tell them where it's coming from."

Roni leaned in toward Philip. "Then inform your bosses that Israel ordered oil from Lagos, and it hasn't arrived, and the Nigerian government has provided no explanation. According to an unnamed source."

"Maybe it was being shipped in the hijacked tanker," Philip suggested.

"Or maybe there is no hijack and the Ministry of Oil is lying and saying there has been nonpayment, even though they've already received the money from Tel Aviv."

"All right," Philip said. "We'll help each other."

Roni raised his glass. "And each other's countries."

Sam was comparing notes with Tony and determining what they squared away for the upcoming trip and what they still needed to do—when Rod interrupted. "Coach, a call for you. "

"Anyone I want to talk to?"

Rod beamed.

"It's Dina?"

Rod's playful expression was answer enough. After the bartender left, Tony cast a jealous eye toward his friend. "Don't you have your hands full already?"

"Don't mind if I take this call in private, do you, Tony? Partner?"

"Well, make time with her fast. We leave in three days."

Tony's heel wasn't out the door before Sam pressed the blinking button with gusto. "Hello, my dear."

"Sam, forgive me. I'm in a rush. But I don't want to forget this before you go—I'm giving you Roni's contact information in Nigeria." She read the number off to him. Distracted by her voice, Sam wrote the digits down. "Try to commit the number to memory. In case you lose it."

"I will commit my lunch with you to memory."

"Promise me, Sam. I'm worried about you in Lagos. Please promise me you will memorize his number."

The mental image of her consumed him. He tried to reconcile her pristine beauty with both the toughness and maternal concern she exuded.

"How about I promise you, and I seal that promise with a kiss?"

He dreamt that she didn't move away when he leaned in. When his lips met hers, she kissed him with a passion that made him sure he wanted nothing more in life than her. For a moment, Lagos and the rest of Nigeria and everything about this deal faded from his thoughts.

CHAPTER 9

In front of a mirror in the privacy of his own home, George Laney had rehearsed everything he wanted to say when he got his few precious moments alone with the president. Now that the time was here, he wasn't confident. Agnes, the president's aged but astute executive assistant, showed he should walk straight in.

The president always appeared on the cusp of unraveling: his glasses so far down his nose they were almost falling off; so much ash burning at the end of his cigarette, it looked almost ready to fall; the top button of his shirt tugging at its hole, almost ready to pop through.

"Pour yourself a drink, George."

"Mister President, I'll come right to the point."

The president looked up, surprised at anyone's refusal of a stiff bourbon on an afternoon like this.

"Why is it this couldn't wait until our next meeting with Zeke?"

Laney let out a breath he'd been holding. Maybe all his practice would pay off. He hoped so.

"Mister President, I've been thinking about the Iran-Iraq situation."

His old friend nodded, inviting him to go on.

"The Iranian troop movements may result in nothing. But the real problem is if there is military engagement, it will be too late to do anything about the jump in Iraq oil prices."

"I know that, George. But we don't want to alert the world right now to our vulnerability and dependence on the Iraqis. That could ensure a disaster in oil prices."

This response was what Laney had so diligently prepared for. Sounding casual, he said, "Why don't we increase our imports from Nigeria? I have excellent contacts there, and we can get good prices per barrel and stockpile, in case things in Iraq get bad. The Nigerians will cut us a deal. We did enough business with them in the old days, remember?"

"Yes, I remember. We could do more with them." The president's expression turned grim. "But not now. We still need more information from Reilly. It's not time to panic just yet."

"It's not a question of panic, sir." All those hours in front of the mirror had taught him how to position his eyebrows, how to hold his chin, what sort of look to maintain in his eyes so that none of his trepidation showed. "It's a safety measure with no downside. If things get ugly, we won't get taken on Iraqi oil. If things normalize, we'll still have bought the oil at a lower price than our other sources."

Laney waited out the president's pause. "When did you last talk with Reilly?"

"Not since the cabinet meeting, sir."

The president shifted nervously in his chair and his voice rose. "You two have to work together on this, George. You've got to bury the hatchet and get rid of whatever tension there is between you and cooperate. Okay?"

Laney grimaced. "I don't have any problem with Zeke Reilly. Did he say something?"

With a perceptible flinch of his mouth, the president shifted gears.

"George, we're not going to create havoc in the oil market by increasing our imports from Nigeria or anywhere else. Maybe next week or in two weeks, if things continue to get tense on the border. And we'll need a pretext that makes it look like we need extra barrels, if we do. But not now. Got it?"

"Of course."

"I appreciate your Nigerian contacts, if we need them. I'll see you and Reilly next week."

"Thank you, Mister President."

Laney walked out of the Oval Office with a certain energy in his step. "Have a great day, Agnes."

"I'll try," said the dour-looking assistant, surprised by his mood, "but I can't make any promises."

Laney took out his cell phone and called Reilly's office. He waited, unsure if the director of the CIA could not take the call or if he had decided to make Laney wait.

"Reilly."

"It's Laney. How are you?"

"What can I do for you?" The director's voice was flat.

Eagerly, Laney explained that he was calling because of the president's command that the two communicate. He'd just left him, Laney reported. Important issues to discuss—couldn't be put off. When Reilly asked, some acid in his tone about the subject, Laney told him everything. His concerns. His proposed solution of upping the imports from Nigeria.

"And the president agrees with that?" Reilly asked.

"The president agrees we need to cover our asses in case any military involvement between Iraq and Iran affects the flow of Iraqi oil. He told me to communicate with the Nigerians about stockpiling and stand by. So I'd appreciate being in the loop, if you find out anything from your agents in the field."

"The second I'm told anything. And I'll see you next week in the Oval Office."

Laney snapped his phone closed without saying goodbye. The rigid line of his mouth gave way to a smile.

At 7:30 Tony pulled up in front of the Sunridge Hotel in a bright red Infiniti, his wife, Shauna, at his side. Sam, who had met her only once or twice, cringed as he watched them kiss and hug. He couldn't help overhearing the *I'll miss you's* and *Promise to calls* of a couple still in love. She drove off, leaving Tony standing at the curb with his bags, clad in khaki shorts and sandals like a summer tourist.

Sam was overdressed in his blazer and slacks. He helped Tony carry the bags to the car Sam had rented for the drive to the airport.

"You will not believe this. Bill called me yesterday! He told me to buy watches and some sunglasses as presents for the people at the Central Bank. How the hell can I buy sunglasses and watches when I do not understand if I'm buying for a man or woman? It's crazy."

Tony growled as he unzipped a pocket of one of his bags. Sam looked in, seeing a variety of watches and sunglasses. "I had to go to Target and pick up all this crap at the last minute."

Sam's jaw dropped. "Well, if that's all it takes to bribe employees of the Central Bank, we're in good shape. Split the cost with you?"

"Forget it." Tony waved away Sam's offer as he loaded his bags inside the rental. "I wouldn't mind your pal Pierre paying for something. He's getting two million of our money for making some local phone calls in his own hometown."

They headed out on Interstate 10 toward Los Angeles International Airport. Sam hummed to a Louis Armstrong CD.

"Sam, it doesn't stop there. Kidogo said he'd try to meet us at the airport in Lagos. If not, he'll send his driver, Joseph. Joseph will be wearing a white shirt, gray slacks, and a black and white polka-dot tie. We're not to get into any car unless the driver repeats the agreed code, 'Geneva 94.'"

"Sounds like a spy novel," Sam smiled.

"Oh, and we should have about five hundred in cash to cover bribes at the airport."

And just like that, the smile left Sam's face.

The next night, in France, Sam and Tony had dinner at Charles de Gaulle before taking off on their next overnight flight to Nigeria. They stood with the other passengers waiting for their flight to be called. There were a few white faces, expatriates, probably oil company employees willing to exchange a civilized way of life for big, tax-free salaries and the perks that went with the assignment to a hardship post. By contrast, the Nigerians returning home looked morose and apprehensive.

Sam picked up a copy of Time from the newsstand and flicked through the pages. Just before boarding, he noticed a commotion. Airline employees pushed passengers waiting to board back. Several gendarmes escorted three handcuffed Nigerians onto the plane; they were being deported for criminal activities on French soil.

"That's who you're sitting next to on the plane," Tony said, half in jest.

When the pilot announced they were about to land in Lagos, Sam checked his watch: four a.m. Two consecutive overnighters had taken their toll. He ran his fingers across his face and felt forty-eight hours of stubble, he was too exhausted to care.

As the passengers disembarked, Tony waited for Sam to catch up. They dragged their feet through the muggy airport to the immigration control area, where they stood, tired and bewildered, in a long line of weary travelers. A group of uniformed officials examined each arriving passenger's passport several times, passing it from the one to the other, always with an accompanying lift of an eyebrow. The old hands, the oil company workers, slipped fifty-dollar bills, neatly folded, inside their passports. Sam and Tony noted the skill with which the officials located and remove them, with the dexterity of the magician's sleight of hand, before finally stamping passports and allowing the passenger to pass into the baggage hall.

Sam and Tony's turn came. They watched as their passports were inspected and passed down the line to the militant, aggressive-looking officer at the end who, after examining them, put them at the bottom of the pile. He then abandoned his post behind the glass booth and left for a cigarette. There was nothing they could do but watch as the pile of passports grew taller.

Throughout this ordeal a lanky distinguished military officer, the corners of his uniform appearing well-pressed, stood watching. The swagger stick under his arm was a relic of imperial days. The original officer lumbered back from his smoke break to stamp their passports.

Sam's and Tony's baggage had already arrived on the carousel when they reached it. They took it over to a table where, yet again, they stood in line waiting, this time for not just one but for three coarse female customs officers to attend to them.

"Open," one ordered.

Shirts, socks, pants, underwear flew from the cases, the entire contents strewn across the table, some items falling onto the dirty concrete floor.

When she had finished, she asked in a soft voice accompanied by a menacing grin, "Do you have any dollars for me?"

"I'll give her ten bucks, Tony," Sam said in his friend's ear.

"Think that's enough?" Tony asked.

"Let's pace ourselves with the bribes."

It was the right call. Preoccupied with the crisp ten-dollar bill, the woman waved for them to repack their bags.

As they were about to pass through the glass doors to look for Joseph, in his white shirt and polka-dot tie, a plump middle-aged woman in a navy uniform barred their way.

"Christ, now what?" Tony muttered, gritting his teeth.

The plump woman shrieked questions and orders in a language that bore nothing more than a third-cousin sort of resemblance to English. She demanded he tell her their business in Nigeria, see their passports and reinspect their cases. Ten more minutes of nonstop incomprehensible verbal abuse, and they were allowed to pass into the arrivals hall.

They found a porter to assist them with the baggage, a youth with tired brown eyes, wearing a filthy white shirt and tattered jeans.

They looked in vain for someone in a polka-dot tie and gray slacks. After several minutes of scanning the area, they saw a man approach. Early thirties, nondescript build. Navy-blue shirt and slacks; sunglasses that veiled his eyes.

He said, "Come with me."

Tony and Sam looked at him, then at each other. "Who are you?" Sam asked.

"Come," he snapped again.

The young porter gave them an insistent shake of his head; the man's dangerous, his eyes pleaded.

"Come with me."

The porter's tongue loosened. "Don't do it."

Tony and Sam stopped in their tracks. In their fatigue and confusion, they recognized their vulnerability.

The man in blue berated the young porter for questioning his purpose. Amid this frenzied scene, a military policeman, with three junior soldiers standing behind him, approached. Once again, Sam and Tony had to produce their passports. Again, they faced interrogation regarding their visit to Nigeria. Satisfied with their answers, the military policeman allowed them to continue, indicating it was safe to follow the man in blue. By this time, the young porter had vanished.

The man in blue did not help them with their baggage. Sam and Tony followed him out of the terminal building, knowing neither who he was nor where they were being taken.

"There's no way I'm getting in a car with this guy without the password," Sam murmured. Tony, fearful and depleted, nodded.

After a hundred yards, they came to the end of the building. The sidewalk and the street lighting had also ended. By six-thirty in the morning, they had spent two and half hours just to get to this point. They stood in total darkness in what appeared to be an empty parking lot.

"What the hell is going on here?" Tony anxiously asked.

"Where is Kidogo, or Joseph?" Sam added.

"Hurry," ordered the man in blue, who had walked on ahead at a faster pace.

Exhausted, they did their best to keep up. Crossing the deserted parking lot, their shoes slipped into either a pile of trash or potholes. Reaching a low wire fence, and having to suffer the indignity of climbing over it, with their suitcases getting heavier by the minute, they arrived at a second deserted, unlit lot. The man in blue led them to a parked Volvo, a late sixties model, and tapped on the window. The driver jumped out.

"Good morning, Mr. Sam. Good morning, Mr. Tony. I am Joseph." It was difficult to estimate the age of this stocky Nigerian.

"What is the code?" Tony asked him.

"What code? What do you mean by code?" Joseph looked as puzzled as he sounded.

"Jesus Christ," Tony snapped.

The man in blue left them. Joseph told them to sit in the car while he loaded their cases into the trunk, and then they would set off to "Doctor Beel."

After a sigh of relief, they took their seats in the back of the Volvo. In their state of exhaustion, bordering on full collapse, they wanted nothing more than to believe this ordeal was over. By this point, however, they realized that any such thoughts could be premature.

"Sam, look out of the window," Tony whispered.

Sam leaned forward and looked out of the car's rear windows. A group of Nigerians, each one intimidating in stature, had encircled the Volvo.

"Stay in the car. Lock the doors and keep the windows closed!" ordered Joseph, opening the driver's door. He quickly closed his window and locked the car from the outside.

Sam and Tony were all too conscious that they were now sitting alone, in the back seat of an antiquated car, in the middle of a dim, unpopulated airport parking lot, surrounded by twelve hulking shouting men. Seconds later the car lifted a few inches from the ground, where it was suspended due to unfathomable manpower, before being dropped back to the ground. Their jaws rattled on impact.

Joseph tapped on the window. "They want two hundred dollars."

Sam and Tony both grabbed bills from their wallets.

"Christ, Tony. This is only the beginning. Offer them a hundred."

"Don't be stupid, Sam. Our lives are at stake."

With the doors again locked, they counted out two hundred dollars in twenties. Tony lowered the window a quarter of an inch and handed the money to Joseph. Against another barrage of shouting, Joseph jumped back in, and gunned the engine. The sound of screeching tires and screams faded.

"What was all that about?" Sam asked.

"Nothing to worry about," Joseph answered. "They wanted more money. They are bad men. Now we can go to Doctor Beel."

For over an hour, they drove through dark and poorly paved streets, unable to talk. They thought they had prepared themselves well for Lagos, the intensity of it, the desperation. Now both men realized the possibility that there was no such thing as preparing for this place.

By the time they arrived at Bill Kidogo's house, it was daybreak. While the early morning light boosted their spirits, it did nothing to improve the landscape of suburban Lagos. Doctor Kidogo's house stood at the end of a road full of deep potholes around which Joseph maneuvered the Volvo. A tall brick wall surrounded the house, and large steel gates hid any view of the building from the street. Joseph sounded the horn. Seconds later, the gates opened from the inside by a shirtless gatekeeper who, after letting the car pass, closed them again before he disappeared back into his corrugated tin hut. More potholes needed to be dodged.

The house and grounds were extraordinary. The ramshackle building, four stories high, was reminiscent of a crayon-drawing by a young child. It was one of the ugliest private homes imaginable. The stucco was gray with age and dirt. There had been no attempt at landscaping.

When Tony and Sam got out of the car, it was impossible to avoid stepping into stagnant puddles that emanated a smothering stench. Dank moisture and scattered trash stained their polished leather shoes.

"Christ, the stench is obnoxious," Sam whispered.

"All I care about," Tony whispered back, "is getting some sleep."

They followed Joseph into the lopsided house.

CHAPTER 10

From inside, the windows overlooked the quagmire from which Sam, Tony, and Joseph had extracted themselves. Two yellow sofas and an armchair popped against the wall-to-wall navy carpet. In a corner was a television on a card table, and a servant, introduced as Patrick, switched it on. They were graced with an ancient rerun of Tom & Jerry. Sam caught a glimpse of Tony's look of horror.

"Sam," he whispered. Sam followed Tony's eyes to spot a large brown rat in the corner.

Patrick remained seated in an armchair, watching Tom & Jerry, his presence preventing them from speaking freely. Another servant brought them tea.

After an annoying wait of close to thirty minutes, the door opened and in swept the senior partner of Knight & McPherson, and former secretary-general of the Nigerian Institute of Chartered Accountants, still in his pajamas. It was enough of an insult that Kidogo had not been at the airport to meet them on their arrival—but to greet them in scarlet pajamas was too much for Sam.

"We've been waiting for you for half an hour. We've had a lousy journey, and our reception at the airport was horrific. If we will work together on this deal, let me tell you, Kidogo, you need to show us greater respect or I'm taking the next flight back."

"Sam, for Christ's sake, have you lost your mind?" Tony snapped.

"I'm sorry I kept you waiting, gentlemen," Kidogo responded evenly. "It's good to see you. I had a late night working on our deal. Forgive me." Five feet eight and in his late thirties, early forties perhaps, Kidogo spoke clear English, unlike many of the Nigerians they had met since landing; still he had that staccato inflection of the locals. "Was your journey that unpleasant?" He sat in the armchair, crossing his legs and flexing his ankles.

"The flights were okay, but the problems at the airport here were horrendous." In his anger, Sam stuttered. "I mean, we had threats and paid bribes and, and we can't begin to tell you of the ordeal we have been through between landing and arriving here at your house. We assumed we would stay at a hotel. Why aren't we?"

Tony didn't chime in on the diatribe, but he nodded along.

Kidogo swiped his hand dismissively. "Oh that's just Lagos." His mannerisms added, Nothing to worry about.

Tony shot a glance at Sam, who looked astounded.

"Tony, Sam. You both look tired. I suggest you use a bedroom and bathroom to freshen up."

"Such consideration," Sam said in a stage whisper.

Suitcases in hand, they followed Kidogo down the uninviting corridor to a bedroom. It was a relief to contemplate getting out of the clothes they had been wearing for over sixty hours and to shave and shower.

Tony staggered into the bathroom and let out a loud groan. Sam looked in to see what was wrong.

"There's no bloody water!" Tony moaned. "Nothing is coming out of the faucets. I suppose this bucket of cold water is for our use."

"So much for the hot shower and shave." The development was minor, but now the absence of running warm water added fifty pounds to Sam's shoulders. If he was tired before, now he was bone-weary. Weakened. He could imagine nothing except crawling into a bed—on which he did not allow himself to expect any comfort.

They rejoined Dr. Kidogo in his living room.

"Is there a problem with the water?" Tony asked in strained graciousness. "We weren't able to shave or shower."

"The electricity went off and the pump isn't working. It will come on again in a few hours. Nothing to worry about. It happens every day. Remember, this isn't California. The problem is that we never know when it will happen so we cannot plan."

"Jesus Christ!" Sam muttered.

"Anyway, gentlemen," Dr. Kidogo continued, again dodging Sam's anger, "did you bring the presents for our friends at the Central Bank?"

Tony handed the gifts to Dr. Kidogo, who placed them beside his chair without a second glance.

"Let me explain what will happen," Kidogo began. "Tomorrow afternoon there will be a meeting at the Central Bank. You will sign the payment release order."

Sam and Tony did their best to fight off exhaustion and to concentrate.

"Our clients, let's call them our good friends, have seen many of their friends and colleagues grow rich. Sadly, they themselves remained poor. Our friends have the responsibility for procurement of equipment for certain departments of the military. So, we have constructed a large file showing that your supposed consulting corporation, Bedford and Clifford, has for two years been providing the Nigerian Ministry of Defense with consulting services. The Nigerian Ministry of Defense now owes Bedford and Clifford thirty-seven million dollars."

A tall slender man with a pencil-thin moustache, around Kidogo's age, entered the room. His navy-blue attire appeared silken to the touch.

"Gentlemen, welcome to Lagos. I'm Dr. Bill's assistant. My name is Ford Obete."

Obete shook hands around the room. "I have arranged your meeting at the Central Bank for tomorrow afternoon at four o'clock. I have just come from there. They are very much looking forward to seeing you both."

"Very good. Here are the presents for our friends at the Central Bank." Kidogo showed what sat on the floor beside his chair. "Take them there today before tomorrow's meeting."

Obete stooped to pick up the gifts.

Kidogo stood and opened his arms in a wide-open, welcoming way. "Gentlemen, now we must separate. Ford and I have an appointment this morning at my office. We will meet you for lunch at a restaurant in town. Joseph will take you there. Afterward, we will meet in my office, nearby, with our lawyer, to sign the agreements. And tomorrow morning we will meet with our friends at eleven, here. Then in the afternoon, there is the very important meeting at the Central Bank. Understand?"

"What we would like to do now is go to the hotel, shower, change, and rest," Tony said. "Can we do that? We could do with some rest."

"After this afternoon's meeting." As they had grown to expect, Kidogo's dominating tone and demeanor left no room for argument. Sam, his fury spent, shrugged at Tony.

"Bill," Sam said, "do we have anything to worry about as far as tomorrow's meeting at the Central Bank is concerned? I mean, do you have people you can trust there?"

Kidogo laughed. "Our country is much poorer than yours. So, when money is offered to anyone to help in a matter, there is never a problem."

Kidogo instructed Joseph to drive them into downtown Lagos and to show them the city before taking them to their lunchtime rendezvous.

They followed Joseph back through the house and into the quagmire outside, toward the parked car.

"Is it only eleven o'clock?" Tony whispered. "It seems we've been here for days."

"Same," Sam murmured as they climbed into the backseat. "But we're here and I will be damned if we are leaving without getting our two mil a piece."

"Well," Tony said, "you've gone from leaving immediately to leaving only after you're paid."

Once out of the fortress, the scenic tour began. For almost two hours, they skirted endless traffic jams, broken-down vehicles, poverty all along the roadside, deformed beggars at traffic signals, decayed buildings, open sewers and the heavy fumes of leaded gas. Sam said little to Tony, he figured it was already more complicated than he expected. He thought of Dina's cousin and the slip of paper on which he'd written Roni's number, torn down to a smaller size and inserted in his wallet. It was time to call Roni, with or without Tony's support.

In the car, they tried to catch up on lost sleep. This had the added benefit of sparing themselves the sights they were being shown.

At a Chinese restaurant in downtown Lagos, they found Ford Obete already seated next to Dr. Kidogo, immaculately dressed. His double-breasted suit was dark gray, his shirt crisp and white, his tie a conservative forest green. Sam was aware of the stark difference between Kidogo and Obete, on one hand, and Tony and himself on the other. Unshaven and unwashed, he and his friend looked too disheveled to break bread with their lunch companions.

Sam speculated that keeping them exhausted, and failing to tell them where they would stay the night, was a psychological ploy of Kidogo's, meant to quash any objections to whatever he might suggest. Lunch turned out to be purely social, a protracted exchange of pleasantries that forbid discussion of the deal.

If we had gone to our rooms first, Sam thought, we might have talked to each other. We might have decided there's no way this is worth it; we may have taken turns showering off the Lagos grime and preparing to travel back home. Kidogo has his eye on us all the time.

After lunch, Kidogo tapped on the back window of the Volvo, where Joseph was napping. Kidogo instructed him to drive Sam and Tony to his offices, just a few blocks away.

"I once spent two weeks in Bombay." Tony kept his voice low in the back seat of the Volvo. "Bombay is like Monte Carlo compared to this."

"I've never seen Bombay, but I've seen some of the less savory parts of Cairo and Mexico City. I agree with you." Sam took a long look at Tony. "Is your lip okay? Looks like you've broken out in sores."

"Jesus Christ. It's weird." He ran his fingers across his mouth, encountering blisters.

There were no signs to show the office of Knight & McPherson was an actual office. Joseph led them up some iron stairs into a formal conference room, where seated around the table was a group of Nigerians. Besides Dr. Kidogo and Obete, there were, among others, a Mister Williams, introduced as Kidogo's attorney and his brother-in-law. Joseph guarded the door.

Kidogo sat at the head of the table. In front of him was a stack of six copies of the agreement, the same document Sam and Tony had drafted in Palm Springs.

Each copy had to be signed, every page initialed and witnessed. No air conditioning made an already long and monotonous process unbearable.

"Joseph. Take them in the Volvo. We will follow in Ford's car."

While it was a relief that they could soon wash and shower and finally sleep, their hearts sank each time they had to travel the streets of Lagos. Their apprehension increased when, forty-five minutes later, Joseph brought the car to a standstill in a residential suburb, outside a small boarding house that rose behind high brick walls with two armed guards at the gates.

"Well, this isn't the Sheraton," Sam said. He was already out of the car when Kidogo's car pulled up behind them.

"Bill, you said we'd be at the Sheraton. That's where we told our friends and family and business contacts we would be. What the hell is this?"

"This is much better, much more convenient. You will be safer here."

Sam could read the concern on Tony's face, but he also understood his friend would leave the talking up to him. "No," Sam said. "This is not what we agreed on. You promised us…"

"Patrick will stay with you," Kidogo interrupted. His voice developed an edge they hadn't heard before.

"How is this place safer than staying…"

"This is how it has to be." It came across as a threat, as Kidogo intended.

Their suite's jungle-green walls and plastic drapes served as a fitting backdrop to the scuffed, faded living room furnishings. Considering everything, they should have thanked their lucky stars they had separate bedrooms, even if the double beds were fitted with musty linens. In the bathroom there was no mirror—only a yellowed hint at where one had once been mounted—but they had a toilet and a narrow shower.

Sam had no desire to see what he looked like in a mirror, anyway.

The view from the bedrooms and living room was of an open-air, all-night auto repair business.

Patrick would sleep on the living room sofa, Kidogo decided. "See that they do not leave the room. The door must be double-locked at all times." He then addressed his guests: "Only Patrick will open the door. Only Patrick will answer the telephone or make calls. Is all that clear?"

Though he was too drained for a fight, Sam said, "Why are we not being allowed to stay at the hotel you promised? Why are we not being allowed to communicate? Our cell phones don't work here."

"I am trying to protect you," Kidogo said, sounding exasperated. "I do not want officials to find out where you are staying. If you had checked into a major hotel, you would be most easy to find. There is no reason for the government to suspect you, but we should do this for the first day, as a precaution. Then you will have your standard hotel room."

Patrick, a stocky man in his mid-twenties, showed none of his prior gentility now—the soft tone, gentle smile, and kind eyes were all gone. It was as if Kidogo had flipped a switch in him. He no longer had to charm these men; he could now assume his proper role as the enforcer of Kidogo's will and whim.

Tony and Sam disappeared into their rooms. If there was no other good news, at least now they could sleep.

Philip Carlisle and Roni both recognized the value of switching their meeting spots; this time they sat in the corner of a dimly lit bar, each holding a glass of scotch. "So, what's the bad news?" Carlisle asked.

Roni took another sip. "I cannot tell you my source, but I've been informed by someone reliable there's military buildup by the Iranians on the Iraqi border. We don't know if it is an exercise, a provocation, or an invasion. But there is troop movement."

"Any news on the oil tanker disappearance?"

"Not a word."

"Seems to be a lot of oil being bought on the Nigerian exchange," Carlisle observed. "I sure would like to learn more about that."

"Well, when I tell you the next bit of business, you'll owe me a case of scotch."

"I'll order you another right now." With a smile, Carlisle raised his hand to call over the waitress, but Roni blocked his motion.

"Later, Philip. For now—listen. There's an American here who is attempting to scam the Nigerian military out of thirty-seven million, with the help of some guys on the inside in the Central Bank. I'm not sure if this has anything to do with the oil prices or the hijacking, but I must find out."

Carlisle's mouth opened slightly, then closed. He would need another scotch straightaway. "I'd like to get to the bottom of this."

"Which is why," Roni said, "in the spirit of cooperation, I would like to give you his name and his American cell phone number."

Somewhere in a decrepit but supposedly safe Lagos boarding house, Sam had a slip of paper in his wallet. Given that he'd obtained it through Dina, he trusted it almost as much as he trusted her. Sensing its presence among the meager belongings he's brought to this place gave Sam as much comfort as an American could hope to glean here in Lagos. Roni retrieved a slip of paper, from his own wallet and slid the folded square across to Carlisle, who studied it.

"Since I am being helpful," Roni continued, "I would appreciate your being honest with me. Is this guy working for your government in any capacity?"

"Never heard of him," Carlisle insisted, putting the paper in his wallet.

"Well, I thought you should monitor him," Roni suggested.

"I am. I have no idea where he is staying but my boss wants him watched. Whether this guy is working for someone in your government or just out for a big score, he could screw things up here."

"In addition to embarrassing my country."

"Almost as bad," Roni said with a smile, "as a war in the Middle East."

CHAPTER 11

Here was the plan: Tony, in one bedroom, would start moaning and groaning as though besieged with stomach issues (they could always blame the Nigerian cuisine). With Patrick, as their guard, drawn to the racket, Sam would sneak out of his own room, out of the paltry suite, and out of the hotel to call Roni. It was a plan Tony had readily agreed to, not even protesting that, so far, he hadn't known of Roni's existence. When he asked about it, Sam said, "I didn't expect to need to call him. But I don't like how things are going."

Tony played his part admirably, wailing until Patrick's heavy feet could be heard padding down the hall. Sam listened as Tony's door opened, just as Tony gasped, "My stomach! What in God's name did you feed us?"

Nice touch, thought Sam. After slipping away from his lodgings, he hurried down the street. After Patrick dealt with Tony, he'd likely pop in to check on Sam. His absence there would stand out as sorely as his presence did here: a white man by himself, rushing down the quiet unlit streets of Lagos.

Speeding up to a clip close to jogging, Sam wondered if he would soon hear Patrick shouting behind him. An icy feeling settled in his gut, he began to wonder if Kidogo had instructed Patrick to handle any escapes with force, if necessary.

His fears were interrupted only by the assault on his nostrils. There was no escape from the stench. Discarded cans, old tires, and other trash had been abandoned. When Sam got to the end of the block, he looked in both directions. To the left, a few small apartment buildings. To the right, nothing but a waist-high wall that separated a parking lot from the street.

Sam looked back. Far down the street, he saw someone. He could not tell if it was Patrick, and he did not wait to find out. Sam climbed over the wall and trotted through the parking lot. He saw the alleyway that ran between the buildings from the street side and ran towards. Beyond, in the next street he saw shops to the left and right.

The first shop was a repair business, broken radios and sound systems scattered all around. An elderly man stood behind the counter, working on a television set with a screwdriver. His attention was on a soccer match airing on a black and white set at the back of the shop.

Sam burst in through the open door. Besides the light metallic clinking of the old man's ministering to the TV, there was a horrible cranking sound. Sam looked up and saw the decrepit fan making slow aching rotations. From the sound of things, it would crash down on the old man any moment now.

"I want to use your phone. Here's ten dollars. I must use your phone," Sam said, out of breath.

The old man pushed back his spectacles and grunted. He sized Sam up for only a moment and then took the bill and pointed at the phone at the edge of the counter. Even the phone smelled bad. Sam dialed.

"Mr. Kahan, please," Sam said, catching his breath.

"This is Roni Kahan. Who's that?" The voice was gruff and unfriendly.

"It's Sam Marsh. Dina's friend. I'm here in Lagos. I don't know what I've got myself into." His face was slick with perspiration. Maybe this is why the phone retained such an unpleasant odor—maybe it was always being used by men who'd just jogged through a network of dangerous streets; maybe all phones in shops here in Lagos were used by people desperate to escape Nigeria, phoning their contacts in secret.

"Shalom. Welcome to Nigeria. Where are you?" His voice, although still gruff, sounded friendlier.

Sam realized the absurdity of not knowing where he was.

"Where am I?" he shouted at the old man, who had gone back to tinkering with the television set.

"This is Walter's Repair Shop on Santa Theresa Street," the man answered.

Sam repeated the information to Roni. "My partner and I are being kept in a building near here, under guard. We can't even use our cell phones."

"What is the address where you are staying today?" Roni asked.

"I—I don't know," Sam mumbled sounding defeated. "It's on, uh." Sam paused and dug the fingers of his right hand into his temple as though it might help him think.

"Somolu!" he shouted. "Somolu Street, about three blocks from Walter's place."

"Stay at Walter's," Roni replied urgently. "I am sending a man who works for me, Tawfiq. We'll talk as soon as he gets there, okay?"

"How long?" asked Sam, unable to hide the panic in his voice.

"About twenty minutes."

"They've got my partner in the house. I can't see the number on Somolu Street but it's the only four-story place. I can point it out to you or Tawfiq."

When Sam hung up, the shop owner Walter, presumably, looked at him. Maybe sweat-soaked men calling for help was a commonplace occurrence here.

"That may have been the best ten dollars I've ever spent," Sam said.

"Do you want to buy a radio?" Walter asked. There was no response from Sam. Walter returned to his repairs, Sam took in all the radios and televisions that sat on old tables and chairs and even cinderblocks.

"You repaired these?" Sam offered.

A smile revealed teeth missing from Walter's lower jaw. "I try to fix everything."

"I wish you could fix the mess I'm in," Sam whispered to himself. He meandered closer to the counter when he heard the voice from the open doorway. "Stop!"

It was Patrick, although at first, Sam thought he looked different due to the fierce expression on his young face as well as the gun he pointed directly at him.

"Come here, slowly," Patrick said.

Out of the corner of his mouth, Sam murmured toward Walter, "After I leave, call the police." He did not look at Walter but instead, walked toward Patrick, who had not moved from the doorway.

"Shall we go back to Somolu Street?" Sam said, in a falsely friendly tone, hoping Walter would remember it.

"Shut up!" ordered Patrick. "Come outside!"

Sam did what Patrick told him to, but he looked back at Walter, hoping for a last moment of eye contact. When Sam glanced into the shop, he saw Walter had his head down, working away, paying no attention. Patrick grabbed Sam by the arm, thrust the gun into his back, and marched him down the street.

"You're lucky my boss ordered me to bring you back alive. But if you try to run, I have instructions to shoot you."

In other parts of the world, one man being steered down the sidewalk at gunpoint by another man, clearly not a cop, would have sparked an uproar. Here, they received curious glances, perhaps, but not concerned ones.

The walls of Roni's office were lined with maps, while rolled-up blueprints and architectural drawings formed a carpet. Next to his filing cabinet sat his weights. Several times a day he would pump iron. Now he began a set of curls with his barbells, ruminating while he exercised. Ready, he put the weights down and sat down at his desk.

Roni dialed and waited, listening.

From Dina's hello, he could hear her exhaustion and worry.

"Roni, tell me. Is he all right?"

"Well, my man visited the TV repair shop but Sam was gone. We're not sure where he and his partner are staying but have the street name. Tawfiq is still in that neighborhood, looking for them."

"Was he hurt?"

"I don't think so." Roni paused and then asked, "This guy, Sam. He means a lot to you?"

"I care about him, yes, and you and I both are aware he's in over his head."

"From what you told me, the real problem" Roni sighed, "is they're trying to get money out of Lagos with guys who may scam them. And even if they're not, Sam and his partner cannot register with the American Embassy and tell them what they are doing. So, they've got no one to turn to."

"I tried to talk him out of going."

Roni hesitated. "These foreign businessmen who come over here on their own, with no protection from a major corporation or a government agency…"

"Roni, can you please just keep an eye on him? As a favor to me?"

"Probably, their deal sounded so good, they jumped in too fast. What was it your father used to say? 'Too much is the brother of too little.'"

Dina chuckled. "I haven't heard that phrase in a long time." After a few moments of silence, she asked, "Is there anything I can do? Should I come over?"

"There's nothing you can do that I'm not already doing. I will tell you what we find out. When we find him, we'll tail them. Tell me, Dina, are you in love with this guy? Or shouldn't I ask?"

She paused, considering, and then avoided a direct answer. "Thank you, Roni. Thank you. Please call me as soon as you have news." And she hung up before he could ask her again.

After a fretful sleepless night, notwithstanding their exhaustion, Tony awoke with lips more sore than they'd been the previous night and Sam with an upset stomach. Kidogo telephoned Patrick to advise that the two meetings scheduled for that day were confirmed.

Sam and Tony spent the morning watching a Lassie movie and early episodes of *Dynasty*. After the endless locking and unlocking of doors, a greasy and unrecognizable breakfast was delivered. Sam and Tony were not hungry, and Patrick chowed down on the leftovers. At least Sam and Tony could shave, wash, and change into clean clothes, tasks that Patrick chose not to perform. The resultant body odor did nothing to enhance the experience of sharing their quarters with him.

Patrick and Sam, both uncomfortable about the drama of the night before, avoided eye contact when they spoke to each other.

At noon, Joseph arrived to take them to Kidogo's office. Upon arrival at the office building, Patrick ushered them inside, his coat open, his gun visible. Sam and Tony sat with Kidogo and Obete awaiting their three new friends.

"Where did you think you were going to run?" asked Kidogo.

"We are not your prisoners," Sam said. "You have not given us a proper place to sleep, we are ill, and you won't let us communicate with others. We're supposed to be partners with you."

"You are our partners," countered Kidogo, "but we do not want our government to realize your intentions. Our hiding you, however unpleasant for you, is the best action."

The first of Kidogo's friends to arrive turned out to be his brother-in-law, Mister Williams, the attorney. He announced that he needed to pay notary and court fees for filing the agreement that, to be binding, had to bear an official court stamp. He based the fee on the underlying value of the transaction. As the beneficiary of the funds was a foreign corporation, namely Bedford & Clifford, and as the transaction was in United States dollars, those fees had also to be paid in dollars. Mister Williams demanded nine hundred dollars.

"Oh, God," Tony moaned, "here we go."

"Oh, come on, Kidogo," Sam groused. "You make us pay to come here, hold us under armed guard, and now you will hold us up for nine hundred dollars? Tell you what. Since you didn't pay for a hotel room last night, how about you guys pay the nine hundred? You owe us."

"Let's just get this done," Tony said.

Sam scowled at his friend. "You may be okay getting screwed, but I'm not."

"There is no need to be vulgar," said Kidogo.

Tony looked at his partner, now seething. "Sam," he said.

"The fee," Kidogo said, in the tone of providing a simple reminder, "is nine hundred dollars."

Sam didn't bother injecting any such false equanimity in his own tone. "We're not paying it. You guys are. And we're staying in a hotel tonight."

No one dared speak. Patrick, leaning against a wall with his hand on his gun, looked to Kidogo and then started moving toward Sam.

Sam sensed the movement in the room but he did not relent. Kidogo, never breaking eye contact with Sam, held up his hand. Patrick stopped.

"In order to waste no more time," Kidogo announced, "you and Tony will pay half of these fees and Knight & McPherson will pay the other half."

Sam did not answer, but Tony blurted out, "Fine. We agree."

Tony opened his wallet and counted out the money. "I'll cover this, partner," he said to Sam, trying to lighten the mood.

Mister Williams took the money from Tony's hand.

"So you see," said Kidogo, "we are very reasonable here."

"I don't like the way we've been treated," Sam said bluntly. "And I don't trust you."

"Well, you are in my country now," replied Kidogo. He said nothing else, but everything from his incisive tone to his squared shoulders delivered an addendum message: It doesn't matter if you trust me. You're stuck here.

CHAPTER 12

Prince Adedeji was tall, slender, and handsome in flowing white robes. He wore an embroidered gold kepi on his head, a hat with a flat, circular top and small visor. The prince entered the room with the self-possessed gait and aloof gaze of a man always mindful that people were watching. He acted as if he were in a fine palace, not a rundown office in the middle of Lagos.

He was the first of the three clients Sam and Tony were to meet, led by the example of Kidogo, Obete, and Mr. Williams, they had stood and bowed when the prince entered the room.

After official introductions and shaking of hands, Kidogo announced in a loud and official tone, "The prince is a longtime friend of mine. He is the one who brought this transaction to our two other friends, who will join us shortly. He and I have spent many hours discussing this operation, and you may be sure we have planned it carefully."

Upon sitting down, Prince Adedeji was brought a cup of coffee, a simple courtesy that Kidogo had denied Sam and Tony.

"Gentlemen, let me explain my position," the prince began in flawless English, his accent less pronounced than Kidogo's. He was educated overseas, Sam guessed. "I am a civil servant. I have the specific responsibility for the airport authority and civil aviation. In fact, I am in charge of our airport here in Lagos, one of the busiest in Africa."

So, you're responsible for that corruption, Sam thought bitterly. He glanced over at Tony, who nodded back at Sam.

"My share in the transaction, like that of my colleagues, will create a new life. I wish to live in America, after this is all over." He paused as though he expected Sam and Tony to applaud his decision, compliment him on his choice of a new residence. But no words came from them. Prince Adedeji continued. "It is my plan to invest in a modest home in California, say up to one million."

Despite his exhaustion, Sam managed a weak smile. "Prince, I want to advise you that you can get a very nice home for that much money. It will not be modest at all."

"Then I will need you both to assist me in creating and managing a portfolio with the balance of my funds. I understand one of you has experience in real estate business. Which one?"

"Well, that would be me." Tony tried his best to sound upbeat. "I would be happy to show you some homes. And Sam has years of experience in the investment banking field. Together we can see that you have a sound portfolio that meets all your objectives."

"That is what I wanted to hear," the prince replied. "I'm younger than my two other colleagues and single. I would like to find an attractive American girl, settle down with her, and marry."

At first both Tony and Sam were too stunned to respond.

This is absurd, Sam thought. We help them steal money and buy real estate, and now we're their American pimps?

"Sam might be able to help you there," Tony suggested. "I'm happily married."

All eyes turned to Sam.

Unamused as he was by the predicament, Sam kept things light, something he found advisable in this scenario. "So." He lifted his hands, palms up, in that gesture that says I can give you the world. "What sort of girl should I find for you?" The men, including Tony, laughed. Unlike the others' though, Tony's laughter sounded hollow, reflecting a fear, a desperation to please.

Some ten minutes passed before the next member of the triumvirate intent on scamming the government arrived, ushered into the room by one of Kidogo's male secretaries. In his mid-fifties and wearing a military uniform, Colonel Mohammed Nwapa seemed out of place.

"Gentlemen, thank you for coming to Nigeria to meet with us," Nwapa began. "Let me explain my situation." He spoke in a slow and resonant voice. "I am due to retire and unfortunately, I will have no money over and above my army pension. It is disgraceful that after all my life in the military I will have to live in harsh conditions. I have served my country well."

Sam and Tony understood that they should nod, and so they did.

"With your help gentlemen, I can now look forward to happier and more comfortable years ahead, for myself," a new sadness darkened Nwapa's features. "And I hope, for my wife and our children."

Sam watched Nwapa struggle to control his emotions, putting his head down so that no one could see the redness of his eyes. He cleared his throat a few times and raised his head again and addressed Tony and Sam.

"I want you to find me a home in California. I will need a place to live when I leave Lagos after these arrangements.

In other words, Sam thought, after you flee from the military regime you were a part of, with all the money you skimmed.

Echoing their interaction with the prince, Tony and Sam showed they would help. Nwapa began to express his appreciation to them but stopped short. Kidogo and Obete sat forward in their seats, as did the others in the now crowded office. The sound of heavy military boots climbing the staircase snagged everyone's attention. The footsteps closed in. At the door, a forceful knock. A youth in military uniform, the same one who had accompanied Nwapa, opened the door wide and saluted stiffly. Kidogo stood and beckoned everyone to do likewise.

Seconds later they heard the footsteps of someone else climbing the stairs. When the footsteps ceased, their third new friend came into view. The young soldier and Colonel Nwapa stood to attention, clicked their heels and saluted. This friend remained at the doorway while Kidogo, Ford Obete, and Prince Adedeji each offered a respectful bow. Sam and Tony involuntarily did the same.

Kidogo led Sam and Tony across the room and introduced them.

"This is His Excellency, General Sawa Tambo," Kidogo said, causing a hush of veneration to fall over the office. General Tambo was dressed in white silk ceremonial garb. In his early sixties with a large head and handsome face but hard, penetrating eyes, he struck the most powerful presence of the three—before he had uttered a word. Kidogo waited to make sure the general sat before did, the others followed Kidogo's lead.

After he looked around the room to ensure that everyone was attentive, Kidogo began.

"Excellency, these gentlemen from America, Tony Dobbs and Sam Marsh, are very important military consultants." Sam flinched. Apparently, Kidogo had not bothered to tell these friends that Sam had a shell corporation. Sam did not look at Tony but hoped his friend would say nothing.

"They are here to assist you, General," Kidogo said, "and your colleagues in transferring funds and buying homes in America. They can help you obtain green cards so you can live the rest of your lives in peace and happiness in the United States."

Now we're immigration lawyers, thought Sam. At least Tambo doesn't want American pimps.

The general raised his hand for Kidogo to stop talking, but Kidogo missed the signal. He glanced at Sam and Tony.

"They have assured me," Kidogo said.

"Shut up!" the general said. Kidogo shrank back in his chair.

The general's appraising squint made it look as though he took the entire room for some arithmetic problem he needed to solve. His gaze came to a rest on Sam.

"Mister Marsh," the general began. "I first need to tell you a few things." Sam took it as his cue to sit down next to Tambo.

General Tambo studied Sam's face for a few moments. "I have been a loyal, brave and courageous soldier in my country's army all my life, and am one of the most important men in this country. This is a big country, don't forget. General Abacha and I are very close. In fact, I am flying to Abuja, our capital, as soon as this meeting is over to see him."

Sam listened.

Tony wondered why Tambo had zeroed in on Sam. He looked every bit as trustworthy, not to mention professional. Perhaps it was an age thing, Sam was nearer to Tambo in that category.

"All my life I have been a soldier. I have been tortured during some of our military engagements. I have killed men with my own two hands. Many men." He displayed his hands inches from Sam's face, fingers outstretched.

"My country is having serious difficulties. Political difficulties. Many of my friends have accumulated vast fortunes and escaped overseas. This they have been able to do with the help of clever people like you." He still spoke, now looking also across at Tony. "Now it is my turn. I want to spend the rest of my days with my wife, in comfort and in safety. Also, my beloved wife needs urgent medical treatment that isn't possible here. Without that treatment, she will die."

Tony met the general's gaze and spoke with compassion. "General, please be assured, we understand. All of us, Sam here and myself. And our colleagues back in the states. All of us at Bedford and Clifford are at your service to assist in every way we can."

Though Sam found this speech somewhat cloying, he appreciated that Tony wasn't stupid enough to balk at Kidogo's suggestion that they were actual consultants.

After a few moments' pause, which afforded everyone an opportunity to regain their composure, the general addressed his next remarks, again, to Sam.

"First, I thought of moving not to the United States, but to Ireland. It is a religious, English-speaking, God-fearing country. The church is an important part of our lives. I believed that my wife would be thrilled in Ireland. It is green and beautiful. But it is not to be. Taxes are too high. Maybe we could find a nice Catholic community somewhere in America. I trust you. I need your help." He put his hands on top of Sam's.

Sam squeezed the man's hands gently.

"Tony and I realize what you and your associates have been through," Sam said. "We will do everything in our power to make new and successful lives for all of you."

For another half an hour, Tony held forth on houses and investment possibilities while Sam tried, without success, to relax. The general listened, nodding now and again, until he glanced at his watch and then at Kidogo. Without being asked, Kidogo called for Tambo's aide. Within seconds, the young aide's heavy boots stamped up the staircase once more. Everyone stood as the general, followed by Prince Adedeji and Colonel Nwapa, left.

The moment they were out of the room, it was as if air had been let out of a balloon. The relief seeped into Kidogo and Obete and their underlings. They exchanged congratulations for a successful meeting commingled with hellos and goodbyes.

For the first time in a long while, Kidogo assumed a polite demeanor. "It went well," he said. "You gentlemen did a good job. We are pleased."

Tony celebrated making it through the nerve-wracking meeting by chattering, while Sam remained lost in thought, not carrying to join the rounds of self-congratulations. He too had discerned the pressure and now its counterpart, relief, but their rejoicing was premature.

"Don't you think we did a good job, there?" Tony asked Sam.

Sam snapped to attention.

"Yeah," he said without enthusiasm. "Looks like everything is on track."

Both Obete and Kidogo shook their hands and told them that Joseph would drive them back to the boarding house, where they would wait with Patrick until the four o'clock meeting at the Central Bank.

As Joseph drove them back to the substandard housing that Kidogo provided, Tony continued his cheerful patter, talking of the intense moment when Tambo threatened to kill them.

Watching Joseph negotiate the terrible traffic outside, Sam slid on the back seat until he was nearer to Tony.

"Look out the window and listen," Sam whispered.

Looking off in another direction, he called out to the driver, "Hey, Joseph, we had a very successful meeting. How about turning on the radio, play some music for us?"

Joseph met Sam's eyes in the rearview mirror and smiled, he flipped on a station playing Nigerian pop. Then the driver's attention returned at once to the strenuous traffic.

"Now listen, you moron," Sam said in an intense whisper. Tony moved to pivot his head toward Sam but stopped when Sam's fingers dug in his leg.

"Don't look at me. Listen." Tony did as he was told. "There is nothing to celebrate. Kidogo didn't tell his clients we're just two guys who have experience in real estate and finance. That wasn't part of the arrangement."

Out of the side of his mouth, Tony said, "Don't louse this up with that damned temper of yours, Sam. Besides that part, it went well, didn't it?"

"Except the part where we can't believe anything Kidogo says or does? Other than that, it's great. We're handling all their affairs, getting them everything from green cards to girls, while they don't know we're not exactly with the military. Or that we're being kept like prisoners. We've got to figure out how to get out of this goddamn country."

They exchanged no more words until Joseph pulled up at the boarding house.

Joseph looked at his watch. "We will leave in one hour and a half for your meeting. I will be out here to drive you."

"Okay," said Sam. "I'll get some coffee over there." He pointed to a small stand near the house and got out of the car.

When Tony's jaw dropped, Sam felt a fresh flush of irritation that something as mundane as buying coffee, at a place in spitting distance of their lodgings, had somehow become a transgression.

"No, Mister Sam," Joseph insisted. "Patrick will make coffee inside the house for you."

"The coffee there is lousy," Sam said.

"You cannot go there," Joseph insisted.

"You can watch me," Sam replied casually, slamming the door. "I'll be right back."

"It's okay," Tony assured Joseph, who looked confused.

As Sam waited for the customer ahead of him to place an order, he watched a Nigerian man walk from a car down the street toward him. When the man took his place in line, Sam turned his attention to ordering two coffees. He still didn't think much of it when the man bumped into him, mumbling, "Sorry."

As Sam waited, however, the stranger's voice came softly. "Don't turn around. I work with Roni. There is an important envelope in your right jacket pocket. Look at it only when you have complete privacy. Do not look at me or talk to me. Nod if you understand."

Sam nodded, paid for the coffee and returned to the car where Joseph stood beside it.

Patrick greeted them when he entered the house. Tony briefed Patrick on how well the meeting had gone when Patrick noticed the coffees he held.

"Where did you get those?" he asked.

"I'm going to my room," announced Sam, "to prepare for the meeting at the Central Bank. Please don't disturb me."

He smiled as he said it, knowing under the circumstances how ridiculous it sounded. But once he was inside his room, Sam stuck a wooden chair under the doorknob in case Patrick developed boundary issues.

Satisfied with the precautions, Sam took off his jacket, kneeled on the far side of the bed so he was not seen from the doorway, and opened the envelope.

Dear Sam:

This is Roni. My operative is watching the house where you are staying. Dina believes you are in great danger, and I cannot guarantee your safety while you and your partner are here. If you want me to help you get out of Lagos, call me if you can. Here is some cash for you to bribe people you are dealing with to help you get away. I can pick you up and get you to the American Embassy. You have a supposed business deal, but you must abandon it in exchange for your safety.

Best,

Roni

By the time he had transferred the bills from the envelope to his pocket, Sam decided not to tell Tony about this. He memorized the phone number, a different one from the last. It was printed on the bottom of the page. He wrote it on the card in his wallet and then tore Roni's letter into small pieces, which he flushed down the toilet. He was reassured that Roni was there to help. He couldn't drop out of the deal, not when they'd already put themselves through so much and all the pieces were aligning. Not when they stood, if they handled this right, to walk away with millions.

CHAPTER 13

"Where is my watch?" demanded Mrs. Fusa, director of the Department for Foreign Remittances.

Her office was surprisingly modest with its functional metal desk and chairs. Mrs. Fusa herself, by contrast, would never be described as modest. A great lump of a woman whose expression fell between a grimace and sneer, she wore a bright red and black floral dress that only emphasized her bulk. She stared down Sam and Tony. They seemed to have angered her already.

In the room with them were Obete and a young man in a brown, three-piece suit wearing rimless spectacles who had introduced himself as "Doctor Johnstone," Mrs. Fusa's assistant. Neither seemed interested in helping Sam and Tony out of their new predicament.

They stood in shock. She had not invited them to sit, and they were uncertain whether they should. Finally, Dr. Johnstone told them to take their seats.

"Where's my watch?" she repeated. "You bring only men's watches? Where was my watch? I am very hurt and insulted. Also, the sunglasses do not fit."

Kidogo had not told them to bring a woman's watch.

"Madame Fusa," Sam began, determined to salvage the situation, "forgive us. When this transaction is over, we will leave for Geneva. We will buy you a watch there. I will bring it back personally to you." *At gunpoint*, he thought.

"You foreign businessmen are all the same," Madame Fusa snarled. "I see this all the time. People who cannot be relied upon to do as they say. All of you!" Like a whip cracking, her attention turned to Johnstone. "Bring me their file."

Seconds later, he reappeared with a thin manila envelope. Opening it with care, she retrieved the all-important payment release order. She then passed it across the desk to Sam for his signature.

"Passport," she demanded.

Sam produced his passport and handed it to her as he read the wording of the payment release order. Everything looked correct. He passed it to Tony.

"Where are the receipts?" Madame Fusa demanded.

"What receipts?" Sam asked, irritated. Tony looked puzzled.

"The tax receipts showing that the two and a half percent tax has been paid. I have to see the receipts before I can release the funds," she explained.

Now, Tony and Sam swiveled their heads toward Ford Obete. His mouth fell open but no words came out.

"Oh, Madame Fusa," Obete finally managed, "Dr. Kidogo has taken care of that."

"Then where are the receipts? You don't expect me to authorize the release of any funds without them, surely."

"Madame Fusa," Tony tried, "I believe that Dr. Kidogo will have the receipts. If there's any problem, the tax could either be settled by the Central Bank, deducting it from the thirty-seven million now, or alternatively, we would settle the liability immediately upon the funds reaching our account."

"That is not the way it is handled," Madame Fusa said. "You talk to Kidogo and do this thing correctly." She turned back to her desk, dismissing them without another word. The woman was every bit as inflexible as she appeared in the flesh. Nothing could be done with her though unfortunately, nothing could be done without her either.

They left her office in shock. Tony started in on Obete. "Why were we not told about this?"

Obete stammered in reply and Sam pulled Tony away, for once the calmer of the duo.

"Listen," Sam whispered to Tony as they stood among the desks in the bullpen of the Central Bank. "Obete is just an errand boy like Johnstone, or Patrick, or Joseph. It's Kidogo we're going to get mad at. And believe me, we're going to get mad."

When they entered Kidogo's office a half hour later, Obete tried explaining what had happened over Sam's frequent interruptions.

"Human error," Kidogo said, annoyed with their report. "I will sort it out. Of course, it is a setback. But don't worry, we are all professionals."

"If you are all professionals, then why didn't you tell us about this two and a half percent?" Sam demanded.

"It is not customary," Kidogo responded coolly. "It is something Madame Fusa decided must be done, since the amount of the transfer is so large. You must realize that in this country, you buy influence. You do not command it merely by being an American."

Kidogo looked at the clock. It was six. "It is too late to reach our friends now. We will meet with them here at nine o'clock tomorrow morning. Joseph will take you now and bring you back tomorrow."

"I have a suggestion," Ford Obete offered. "I am a member of the same tribe as Madame Fusa. I will invite her to a meeting here tomorrow afternoon. Maybe outside the Central Bank, she will be more relaxed and easier to deal with."

"Don't be ridiculous," Kidogo said. "She is a senior officer of the Central Bank. She cannot come to a meeting in a private office to meet with overseas businessmen. All meetings have to be at the Central Bank."

"It's worth a try, Bill," Tony gently offered.

"No, it isn't. It's a stupid suggestion. I will handle this." Kidogo's tone suggested the discussion was over. At least that discussion. He had what he deemed good news for them. "Tomorrow night, General Tambo's brother is hosting a very important party. Not only will our three friends be there but also there will be many diplomats and oil people. And some of the Arab oil people have asked me to make sure that there will be friendly and accommodating women in attendance. I think you and Sam will enjoy yourselves very much."

"Is Madame Fusa one of the *friendly* women?" Sam asked.

"She won't be there," Kidogo said, humorless. "The general's brother is one of the most important men in Nigeria. He used to be an ambassador and, like the general, is very close to the president. I will call for you at half past eight. Meanwhile," he added, "I will think about how best to handle Madame Fusa."

Joseph steered the car in a direction they had not previously traveled, through a blighted, dreary industrial area and then several miles more to an opulently landscaped suburb with manicured lawns, ornate street lighting, and smoothly paved roads.

"Joseph," Sam called. The driver met his eyes in the rearview mirror. "Why doesn't Kidogo live here? This seems like where he should live, with all the deals he makes."

There was a pause. Sam knew Joseph would never say anything against Kidogo. He expected no response.

"Doctor Beel owns a number of buildings," Joseph said. "But he lives not far from where you are staying."

"We should get a second home in this section," Tony joked.

"This is the very best area of Lagos," Joseph announced. "All the top generals and important people live here."

Underscoring his point, a guard approached as soon as he turned into a well-lit private driveway. Upon flashing the embossed invitation, Joseph was waved through. It was clear from the number of cars parked in the long driveway that the party was already well in progress. As they drew closer to the white, pillared entrance, they could hear music.

After a valet motioned for Joseph to stop, Sam and Tony stepped out into the muggy night, where, for the first time, they could take in the vastness of the house.

"This is huge, Sam. Jesus, it's bigger than the White House."

The front door was wide open, and a turbaned Somali servant stood to attention as they entered the house. Another servant approached and beckoned them in the direction of French doors that led into the garden. The party took place under an enormous silk canopy, on a tennis court covered by Persian rugs. Ornate crystal chandeliers were suspended.

The senior military officials were evident, their tunics weighed down by flamboyant medals. A score of scantily clad black women moved from a group of Arab men in flowing robes to white men in suits and ties.

"There you both are," Kidogo greeted them as he moved from the attractive black couple with whom he had been talking. "Let me see that you get a drink." Kidogo waved to a passing waiter who brought them champagne.

"It's good to get out of that damned boarding house." Sam wasn't thanking Kidogo without getting in a barb about their accommodations. He thought about broaching that nothing had come of the promise of better accommodations after their first night in all the chaos, he hadn't lost sight of this slight but Kidogo was already talking.

"Bijou, come over to meet my friends, Sam and Tony."

A tall black girl approached. She was stunning. She wore a short, backless, low-cut white dress, and her long, straightened black hair brushed lightly against her back, reaching almost all the way to her waist.

"Gentlemen," she said in a strong French accent, "good evening. It is an honor to make the acquaintance of such good-looking men."

"Are you Nigerian or from the Cote D'Ivoire?" Sam asked.

"I love your French accent." Tony drooled.

"I am Nigerian, but I lived in Paris for many years. I like to speak French. And you, where are you from?"

"We're from California," Tony said, unable to control his stare, which alternated between her large, wide-open brown eyes and her nipples, insistently pressing up against the thin fabric of her designer dress. "Do you live in Lagos?"

She smiled. "I do now. I have lived in London, Paris, New York, and now I'm here. I make a lot of money, and if one has money, one can live a good life anywhere."

"And what do you do?" Tony asked.

"Public relations."

What a damned fool, Sam thought. *He knows she's a hooker.*

Tony moved closer to Bijou, talking softly in her ear, Sam suddenly invisible to him. Sam shook his head. He thought it might be an opportune moment to remind Tony of his wife, but, thinking better of it, he drifted away from them.

"Have a grand time, Tony," Sam shouted over the noise of the party. "Don't think about anything. Just have fun."

"Let's all have fun," boomed a friendly voice.

Sam turned to look at a handsome black man in a stylish suit.

"Sam Marsh. And you are?"

"Philip Carlisle." They shook hands. "What brings you to Lagos?"

Sam took a sip of his champagne, affording himself the extra second to consider his answer. "Consultant," he said, smacking his lips. "Damn, this is great champagne. How about you? What kind of work do you do?"

"I'm here in Lagos working for Trevithick Oil. What kind of consulting?"

"I left banking a couple of years ago. I was on Wall Street with Salomon Brothers and then I bought a hotel in Palm Springs."

"And the consulting?" Carlisle seemed more than passingly interested in Sam's reply, but an observer couldn't detect that interest in his gaze. His eyes scanned the room, behind and on all sides of Sam, even as he waited in silence for the answer.

"Tony's my partner. We're looking for capital to sink into the hotel. My hotel is keeping my restaurant afloat. Barely. So, some oil money would be very welcome."

Carlisle instantly produced a card. "I think I might be able to help you." He flashed a brief but warm smile. "That's my cell, here in Lagos. Leave a voice mail message anytime. You have a card?"

Sam finished his champagne, again searching for a cover story. "I think Tony and I are changing lodging soon. But I would like to have a sit down with you about the hotel. The restaurant is five star. We just need a bit more capital to…"

Sam stopped short when he saw a loud, boorish American trying to drink, balance a plate of food, and talk to an attractive black woman all at once—and loudly failing.

"Look at this guy. Gives our country a bad name."

Carlisle took in the lout with a peripheral glance. In fishing for a business card, or something, to give the woman, he was spilling food at their feet.

"Aw, the hell with it," the man said. "Listen, I'm staying here. Guest of Minister Tambo. Just ask for Mark Woods and they'll connect you. How about your number?"

"I'm sorry. I don't have a card. Perhaps, I can write it down. Excuse me." She hurriedly escaped, and Woods, with no concern for his whereabouts, said, "Goddamn bitch. I wouldn't act so high and mighty if I charged people to screw me."

Just then, Woods caught Sam and Carlisle looking in his direction. Sam tried to look away, to avoid a confrontation. But Carlisle used the same cheerful voice that had drawn Sam's attention.

"Always nice to meet a fellow American in Lagos," Carlisle began. With introductions made, he said, "Don't feel bad about that woman. They charge too much for their services anyway."

"I don't care," Woods said bluntly. "I want some action. And besides, Tambo's paying. I think he can afford it."

"Tambo is paying?" Sam chimed in. "Maybe he'll be good enough to buy us each one."

"I don't think so, buddy. I'm his guest. Oil speculation. Working my nuts off. But you know what they say: work hard, play hard."

"We might know some of the same people," Carlisle casually suggested. "Where are you from originally?"

"Texas," Woods said absentmindedly, scanning the party guests.

"Had some dealings with Thompson Associates down there."

"Sure, I worked for Thompson back in the day." As soon as Woods said the words, his attention was gone again. "Oh my God," he said and whistled lowly. "Look at that one. I'll catch up with you guys later."

Woods moved off toward a voluptuous woman in a clingy, floor-length dress.

"What a bizarre man," Carlisle said to Sam. "If he's working for Tambo, buying oil, he must be good at his job. Why would anyone want to hire a guy like him, otherwise?"

"Good question," Sam replied. "And what about Minister Tambo?

"Our host is the godfather here in the oil business. Nothing gets bought, sold, drilled, refined, or shipped without Minister Tambo skimming something off the top. They say he's one of the richest men in the world."

"I wouldn't mind meeting him."

"You haven't yet? Come on. I'll introduce you."

As Sam followed Carlisle slowly through the crowd, he caught a glimpse of Tony and Bijou dancing cheek to cheek. At the bar, Kidogo was deep in conversation with Glanville Tambo and another man whose back was partly turned.

"I'm a guest of Bill Kidogo," Sam shouted at Carlisle. "Do you know him?"

When Carlisle looked back and nodded, there was an expression on his face Sam couldn't read.

They pushed their way to the bar.

Glanville Tambo, like his brother Sawa, was an imposing figure, statuesque and muscled. But when he turned toward them, he broke out in a smile. "Philip, who do you have here?"

The third man took the opportunity to excuse himself and move off into the crowd. Kidogo began to introduce Sam but Carlisle beat him to it.

"Sam is helping me on a project," Kidogo added. "His knowledge of banking and financial matters is most impressive."

"Thank you," Sam offered to Kidogo. "And how do you know Philip, Bill?"

Kidogo left it at, "We've known each other for years."

It was a natural juncture for Sam to ask more questions, but Carlisle jumped in. "We met in Kuwait way back, at an oil industry conference."

"It's nice to meet you, Mr. Marsh," Glanville Tambo boomed. "I hope you're having an enjoyable evening."

"I am indeed, sir. Thank you for inviting me. You have a very lovely home."

"Thank you. If there is anything you would like at the bar that we do not have, I will send men out to get it for you. Just ask."

"Thank you, Excellency. There is one question I have."

Tambo smiled and nodded, a gracious host at the ready.

"Well, I've been looking around this attractive group of guests and I haven't seen your brother, General Tambo. Will we be seeing him later?"

Glanville Tambo seemed to grow in size before Sam's very eyes, his own eyes flaring in anger. Sam could feel the tension among the three men, and Kidogo and Carlisle spoke at once, rendering both indecipherable.

When Tambo regained his composure, it was to say, "I do not know how you know my brother, and the fact is, I am not interested. I have no dealings with my brother and if you ever bring his name up in my presence again, you will regret the day you were born."

Tambo left the three men gaping.

"That was an incredibly stupid thing to do," hissed Kidogo.

"What is the problem between Tambo and his brother?" Sam asked.

"Bill," Carlisle soothed, putting a gentle hand on his shoulder. "Clearly, Sam here did not know that the minister and his brother do not get along."

"Do not get along?" Kidogo mimicked cruelly. "If Sawa wasn't in the army, he'd be in jail or executed." Turning to Sam, he growled, "Do not make my job harder than it already is."

"I didn't know, Bill," Sam shot back. "Give me a break."

Again, Carlisle stepped in. "I have an idea. How about if Sam joins me tomorrow for a nice visit to the delta? Or do you have business that cannot wait."

"Actually, Philip," Sam said, "I appreciate the offer but—"

"That is a good idea," Kidogo interrupted.

"We have business to conduct tomorrow," Sam protested.

"It can wait. I have to arrange a few things." Kidogo nodded appreciatively at Carlisle. "What time?"

"Well, we'd have to get an early start. Seven in the morning?"

To avoid Kidogo's hostile gaze, Sam turned back to Carlisle. "That would be fine. I'll be ready."

"Good," said Kidogo. "Philip, I will see that my driver brings him to your office. Now, I must apologize to his Excellency for Sam's behavior." Kidogo took his leave, throwing one more resentful look at Sam before searching among the guests for Glanville Tambo.

CHAPTER 14

The roar of the helicopter engine, the whoosh of its blades, the vibration of the craft as it rose off the ground, all locked Sam in a state of frightened fascination. He watched as the airfield below appeared, widened, and then shrank. He and Philip Carlisle sat behind a Nigerian pilot identified to them only as Alfred.

Catching Sam's enthralled expression, Carlisle told him, "Trevithick spares no expense, believe me. I come down to the Delta every week, and Alfred is my regular pilot. Nothing to worry about here."

"Thank God for that." Already at seven-thirty, Sam could see the morning rush-hour traffic rapidly building up in Lagos, just as they were leaving it.

"How much do you know about the River Delta, Sam?"

"Not a damned thing."

While Sam had said it with some levity, Carlisle's response was serious—grim, even. "It's one of the most shameful environmental issues on the planet, but if I make too much noise about it, I'll be fired. It's *that* bad."

They were above the outskirts of Lagos now, the city view now swapped for treetops.

Carlisle paused, looking agonized, and then with balled fists leaned closer to Sam. "Look, these multinational oil companies get away with murder. They grease the palms of rulers, and they can do whatever they want. What you're going to see in a short while will horrify you. Horrified me the first time."

"I'm a little confused, Philip. I mean, you're an oil guy. I know Trevithick isn't Shell or Chevron-Texaco or the other big guys, but you do make your living from oil."

"Does that mean I shouldn't care about the complete devastation of a river delta? Of Nigeria?"

Sam held his hands up in surrender. "I don't know anything about it. I admit that."

That quickly, sadness substituted Carlisle's fury. He zoned out watching a tree line below them diminish until it came closer to resembling a pencil line.

Carlisle, subdued now, proceeded to enlighten his guest on how the major oil companies had swooped in following Nigeria's independence in 1960, converting a huge wetland into four thousand plus miles of pipelines and nearly two hundred oil fields. How roads were constructed and concrete laid with total disregard for the well-being of the locals. Agriculture plummeted.

Oil, he said, should have been Nigeria's ticket to becoming one of the richest countries in the world but instead had contributed to its poverty.

The government in Lagos, he told Sam, had been kept in power for years by the multinationals involved in oil exploration. For decades, poverty and environmental damage in the Delta had gone from bad to sickening while the tribes, particularly the Ogoni and Ijaw, had suffered terribly. Anyone who tried protesting these conditions faced the tandem forces of the government and the oil companies.

When Sam wondered aloud how bad it would be, Carlisle only promised him he would see. Pollution was out of control, farming and fishing both rendered impossible in zones near the drilling and refining. Drinking water had become a commodity. As malnourishment and disease skyrocketed, so did inflation, prostitution, drugs, and violence. It was a nightmare for the locals. It was a nightmare for the bastard kids of expatriate oil works left there to fend for themselves. The *thousands* of them.

"So, there's never been any huge revolt or resistance on the part of the tribes in the Delta?"

"African journalists have been killed to prevent their stories getting out." Conveying this piece of information left Carlisle looking his most dejected. "And it's just not on the radar screen for Western journalists."

Sam retrieved a bottle of orange juice from the cooler between their seats and took a large gulp. If it were laced with vodka, a screwdriver in a plastic bottle, it might've helped wash down the information Carlisle was sharing. "Aren't any overseas governments doing anything about this, Philip?"

"The United Nations conducted investigations. Their reports condemned the oil companies, but who the hell takes any notice of the UN? You think they have more power than Big Oil? And believe me, not everything runs smoothly. Projects have been started and abandoned. Water tanks have been constructed and there aren't any pumps. Hospital clinics have no doctors. Fishponds have no fish. There's no oversight."

Philip leaned forward and tapped Alfred on the shoulder. The pilot lifted up the right side of his headphones.

"Take us down for a look at Gbaran," Carlisle shouted. Alfred nodded.

"In a minute," Carlisle explained, "we're going to be flying over the Nun River. Alfred will descend so you'll see a project operated by Shell, the Gbaran Integrated Oil and Gas Project. There'll be fifteen new oil and gas fields. More than two hundred miles of pipeline will be laid. Forests are being decimated to make room. Ninety villages will have their way of life ruined."

"Are we going to land and walk around?" Sam asked, doubtful this was something he wanted to experience up close and personal.

Carlisle shook his head. "The stench and the smoke would nauseate you—plus it's not safe. Land in an oil chopper, we'd be surrounded by thugs in five minutes. We'd never get back in the air."

"Sounds like our arrival at the airport," Sam said. "We had to pay everybody to get the hell out of there."

They flew over the Gbaran project, and shortly thereafter, Sam looked down at the slums that now appeared below the helicopter, stretching off as far as the eye could see.

"What is this place?" Sam asked.

"Port Harcourt."

The pilot flew lower so Sam could clearly view the mountains of garbage and black-smoke fires. Sam grabbed a handful of Kleenex from a box Carlisle offered him to wipe his eyes and cover his mouth. He tried to imagine the intensity of that smell at ground level; the thought made him gag.

"The oil reserves in this country are larger than the United States and Mexico combined," Carlisle said, his voice gravelly with emotion, "and just look at this shit hole. Should have been a middle-class suburb."

Carlisle reached for a can of air freshener he kept under his seat and doused the cabin. "This is the best we can do. It helps a little. We're now going to fly inland for a few miles."

Sam fought down his nausea. The manufactured lemon scent helped him recover.

"Paper bag under the seat if you need it," Carlisle said.

Sam refused. When his stomach stopped churning, he asked about the guy he'd met at the party, that odd character. Mark Woods.

"An excellent question. I asked myself, why is a rude, disgusting US oil buyer being put up by an ex-ambassador of Nigeria in his own home? And when he mentioned he worked for Thompson and Associates in Houston, I decided to call my contacts back in the States after the party." Carlisle paused for effect. "Woods had a couple of drunk and disorderly arrests in Houston but somehow, he got raises before others with seniority. Then he gets a transfer to a major consulting firm in Maryland. What do you make of that?"

"I guess he has good contacts," Sam suggested.

"I guess Woods has somebody major vouching for him. And since he got a better job in Maryland, it's very likely that person is in Washington, DC."

"I wouldn't know."

"And here's something else you don't know. You've arrived in Nigeria as someone is buying up huge amounts of Nigerian oil for stockpiling. There's also talk that they have hijacked a tanker, maybe two. That could not have happened without the cooperation of the Nigerian military. This goes beyond everyday corruption. This is the kind of stuff that starts wars."

As Carlisle's volume increased, his eyes bored into Sam.

"Here's something else you don't know, Sam. Glanville Tambo and his brother Sawa hate each other. Sawa barely earns a living wage and Glanville has never lifted a finger to help him. Glanville has thrown all kinds of corrupt, money-making deals to people, like your host Bill Kidogo, but he sees his brother as competition and doesn't care what happens to him."

"Talk about your sibling rivalry," said Sam, trying to lighten Carlisle' suddenly dark mood.

"It's not a joke!" shouted Carlisle.

Alfred looked back quickly but then swiveled his head forward again.

"What you don't know about Nigeria, Sam Marsh," Carlisle spat out, "could fill an encyclopedia. You insult one of the most powerful men in Nigeria in his home, while you're in his country working with guys trying to scam the government out of thirty-seven million dollars."

Sam felt the air rush out of his lungs. It certainly didn't feel like a joke now.

"I know exactly what you're doing here," Carlisle went on, "and unless you listen very carefully to me, odds are you're going to die here or wind up in a Nigerian jail for the rest of your life."

"Who *are* you?" Sam managed.

"Who am I?" barked Carlisle. Despite the fire in his eyes, his gaze sent a chill down Sam's spine. "Here, let me show you who I am."

Sam's eyes followed Carlisle as he bent over. Reached under his seat. A cold, loud click. Carlisle straightened himself. Thrust the .45 pistol into Sam's ribs.

Carlisle unclicked his safety belt and moved closer. The nose of his gun bore into a sensitive groove in Sam's ribs, only one of the reasons Sam suddenly found breathing almost impossible.

"Who am I?" Carlisle was now shouting. "I'm with the Central Intelligence Agency, Sam, and your idiotic Central Bank of Nigeria scam could destabilize this country, and inadvertently trigger a war in the Middle East. The only other thing you need to know is that you're going to cooperate with me. And if you don't give me the right answers to questions I ask, I have no problem throwing you out of this chopper and letting your body be torn apart by crocodiles. Do you understand?"

Carlisle grabbed him by the scuff of his neck and shoved Sam's face against the window. There was no place to look now except the river below.

Sam felt the nausea well up inside him again. But he could smell nothing. It was base, unadulterated fear that took hold of him now.

"I understand."

"Louder!"

"I understand!"

"Okay, Sam. You're going to tell me all the details of your pathetic plans with your partner. But before you do, let's be clear on a couple things. One, the likelihood is, you will never get any money out of the guys you're working with. Two, if you try and screw me, I will inform the government you are not just a white-collar criminal but a spy. You and Tony will go to prison and if they decide to execute you, I will inform the State Department here to forget about you. The US Embassy in Nigeria will not intercede on your behalf."

Carlisle's rage stunned Sam into silence. He now had two potential enemies, Kidogo and the Central Intelligence Agency. And who was he? An insolvent hotelier.

"What do you want me to do?" Sam's voice shook.

Carlisle let go of Sam and returned his .45 to its previous position under his seat. He tapped Alfred on the shoulder. Seeing the direction in which Carlisle thumb-pointed, the pilot understood it was time to go back. With a nod Alfred began a slow bank to the left.

Carlisle, to Sam's surprise, did not say anything for a long while. Sam watched him for a few moments, then, fearing his stare might set the man's temper flaring again, looked down at the murky water.

"Sam, I shouldn't even be here." Carlisle's fury had been replaced by a sense of melancholy. "I asked the agency for South America. I have friends in Buenos Aires and Sao Paulo. But no, they give me Lagos. They figured I'm black so automatically, I'll get along better with Africans. And on top of the corruption and the living conditions, I see how these people are in constant fear, under a military dictatorship, with the oil business destroying their country before their eyes."

Carlisle turned to Sam, who was astonished to see that Carlisle's eyes were red from emotion. "I can't do anything about the multinationals or the dictators, but goddamn it, Marsh, you are not going to plunge this country into worse condition than it's already in."

"I told you," Sam said cautiously, "I'll cooperate. Obviously, I have no choice. I just would like to know, how you found out about our deal and the Central Bank?"

"You don't ask questions. You answer them."

"Okay." Sam put his head in his hands, trying to process the situation he was in. He knew he had to tell Carlisle everything, but he also had to find a way to depart from this country with Tony.

"My source tells me you are posing as military subcontractors so the Ministry of Defense will pay thirty-seven million dollars for your supposed consulting. Is that correct?"

"Yes," Sam said softly. "But it's to help three men transfer their personal wealth out of the country."

"You and Tony have a shell corporation?"

"The shell is mine. Tony will confirm everything I'm telling you."

"No," Carlisle stated flatly. "Tony is not going to know you are working with me."

"But I don't understand how…"

"Listen to me!" Carlisle shouted. Sam shrank back in his seat; he had met his equal. Someone who would not be pushed around or walked over, and certainly not bamboozled. "You work for me. I will try and get both of you out of this country. But I'm telling you now, I'm working with you. Not Tony. I've seen your partner in action. I can't depend upon him."

"You're not saying we may have to sacrifice Tony to get me out?"

Carlisle looked out the window and did not answer.

"Philip?"

"If Tony doesn't do anything stupid, we'll get him out. If he threatens the plan I come up with, he's expendable."

Carlisle sighed. He reached inside his pants pocket and took out a small notebook and pen.

"Okay, let's start at the beginning. Did Tony tell you the thirty-seven million was money they felt they deserved?"

"Yes."

"Well, there's your first mistake, believing him. There's no way they could have earned thirty-seven million collectively."

Sam heard the heard the words but they sounded distant. Tony had been scamming him. The words that followed from Carlisle did not register.

"I said," shouted Carlisle, "who was your initial contact regarding this scam, here in Lagos?"

"Bill Kidogo."

"No, I don't mean who's putting you up. I mean, who is the person who contacted Tony about the scam itself."

"It's Kidogo, like I said. Tony knew him from real estate dealings and then…"

"William Kidogo is running this operation?" Carlisle looked skeptical.

"I'm telling you the truth."

"Well," said Carlisle with a groan, "then you're in even worse shape than I thought."

CHAPTER 15

Having said next to nothing to each other at breakfast, Sam and Tony kept their mouths closed as Joseph drove them to Kidogo's office. Another day following another night in their decrepit lodgings, another meeting.

Finally, a smile spread across Tony's lips. "Some party."

"I'm guessing after the main event, you and Bijou had a private party," Sam said.

"You jealous?"

"Not at all. Must have cost you quite a lot."

"Oh, believe me," Tony said lazily, "she was worth every bit of it."

"I hope you saved some of your money to bribe our way out of the airport again."

"Kidogo told me you got a helicopter tour from an oil guy from the States. How was it?"

"Not as much fun as what you were doing," Sam responded. Helicopter tours and parties be damned, he was finding it hard to care anymore whether the deal even happened or not. "I just want to go home."

Inside the office, in addition to Kidogo and Obete, Madame Fusa and Dr. Johnstone awaited them. While the latter wore the same suit he had before, which hardly stood out, Madame Fusa wore a bright green floral dress with a matching headscarf. Sam could not help noticing that she occupied the most comfortable chair in the room—Kidogo's.

The meeting began on the note of Kidogo fawning over Fusa's willingness not simply to accommodate their lack of funds but to grace his humble office with her presence. *Why don't you just get on all fours and volunteer to be her ottoman*, Sam thought. He tried to remind himself this was not his culture; if kissing Fusa's ass would help them avoid paying 2.5 percent tax on a $37 million transfer, it was a small price to pay.

When Kidogo finally ran out of compliments, he let Madame Fusa speak. She shifted her weight in the chair behind his desk, folded her hands, and surveyed the men in the room.

"I was very upset at the lack of proper gifts when you Americans arrived," she began. "Imagine, not even a watch. After all, it is because of me that you will have this large amount of money transferred. Yet, I will surprise you. I agree to the release of the thirty-seven million without the taxes being paid upfront."

Sam sat up, ignoring Tony's trusting smile. It sounded too good to be true. Did she mean the money for the taxes would be deducted later? Or perhaps she was waiving the tax altogether, which would save them a lot of trouble.

"Oh, Madame Fusa," Kidogo said, "that is most generous of you. We appreciate your kindness and your patience with us."

"I can order the release of the funds you have requested for these gentlemen." She nodded at Sam and Tony. "Provided I receive an upfront payment of three hundred thousand dollars."

Sam threw a glance back at Tony, groaning, making no attempt to conceal his exasperation. Tony's smile distorted until it was a frown.

Neither Kidogo nor Obete dared speak.

"This three hundred thousand dollars," Fusa continued, "will be shared among my colleagues, including Dr. Coke, the deputy governor of the Central Bank. It is to be wired to Vereins-und-Westbank in Hamburg for the account of Universal Holdings Limited, a company with which my husband is associated."

"Madame Fusa," Sam said, "I don't know if you have ever been to the United States?"

Her eyes flicked down then up him in a switch-like motion. "I have not."

"Well," Sam explained, "we realize that America is very different from Lagos. But I want to assure you, we are not all millionaires in America. I, for one, have absolutely no way to get you that amount of money upfront. The same goes for my partner."

If Kidogo fidgeted any harder, Sam was certain he would knock something over, perhaps himself. "Uh, Sam and Tony, we do not have to bother Madame Fusa with the details of how we will come up with the money for this considerate counteroffer she has made."

Kidogo walked over to Fusa and shook her hand, again bowing low, his behavior that of a subject honoring his queen. "Thank you so much for working with us in this way."

Madame Fusa grunted as she rose from his chair, nodding back at Kidogo, and then she and Johnstone shuffled toward the door. "I expect to hear from you tomorrow." She threw a hostile glance at Sam, the only attendant who hadn't risen for her. Then she paraded out of the office with Johnstone trailing behind.

A few moments passed before the next abrupt change in Kidogo's personality. He stormed over to the chair where Sam sat and stood over him, wagging an angry finger in his face.

"Who do you think you're talking to?" Kidogo began. "You were talking to the woman who will make you a millionaire and you question her intentions? Do you understand—"

"I don't want to hear it!" Sam not only interrupted Kidogo but topped the man's volume. "Stop waving your finger in my face, take two steps back, and you listen to me right now. Right now!"

Despite the anger steaming from his eyes, Kidogo did as asked and he stepped back.

"Now look," Sam went on, no longer interested in gauging Tony's reaction to anything he might say or do. "This deal is just about over. You want to hold us in your country, I will put in a call to some people I know in the embassy and then they can call your boss Tambo, the one with that palatial house who hates his brother, who we're helping, and tell him about this operation."

"Don't you threaten me!" Kidogo shot back. "Do you not believe I can turn this all on you? Say that you contacted me? Do you not believe I can have you thrown in jail?"

"You would go with me," Sam growled. "Do *you* think Glanville Tambo is going to think a Palm Springs hotel owner contacted you to help the brother he hates and two others smuggle millions out of Lagos?"

"Stop!" yelled Tony. In how his eyes twitched between the men, he resembled a child whose parents were fighting. And he seemed every bit as helpless to intervene.

"I have to stand up for both of us." Sam redirected all his anger from Kidogo to Tony. "You have no guts, and I'm sorry I ever got into this with you!"

The blood drained from Tony's face, leaving him ghostly. "Can we just calm down? I know we are going to find a solution."

"Kidogo," Sam said, dispensing with the overly formal *doctor* as well as the overly familiar *Bill*, "you have no control over Fusa and her demands. If you let her dictate the terms, we can't do this deal. Also, you better not think Tony and I are going to put up three hundred thousand dollars."

"Well, we certainly do not have that much money either," Kidogo insisted. "And I would remind you, *Marsh*," spat Kidogo, "that we all succeed or fail in this venture together. Don't threaten me unless you wish to make sure of your own doom."

A long silence filled the room.

Obete tried ending it softly. "Would anyone like some more coffee or cookies?"

Sam snorted.

Massaging his temples with what appeared to be painful pressure, Kidogo tried again, this time in a more moderate tone of voice. "Look you guys. We have the general coming here any moment, and complete calm is needed for this meeting. I did not expect Madame Fusa to make the deal this hard, but surely we can find a solution. We are smart men."

"Of course. We will," Tony offered. If he was charmed by the softer side of Kidogo, he was the only one. Sam looked off into space, seething, until heavy bootsteps sounded outside the door. General Sawa Tambo had arrived.

Kidogo and Obete immediately rose. Joining them, Tony shot a nasty look to Sam, who lingered in his seat before he grudgingly found his feet.

"Ah, cookies," said the general. He scooped up a handful and then sprinkled his military uniform with their crumbs. He continued nibbling the cookies after he'd taken a seat to listen to Kidogo, who sat as close as possible.

Kidogo told Tambo how delighted Tony and Sam were to assist him, which Tony confirmed with a smile and Sam allowed to pass with no comment. But when, in the same tone of voice, placid and authoritative, Kidogo conveyed Madame Fusa's new demand, Tambo stopped snacking. Slamming his hand onto the table, he turned the remaining cookies to dust.

"How can she do this? She already agreed!"

"I know," Kidogo said. "But if she was willing to change the tax from a percentage to a flat amount, we might be able to lower the figure of three hundred thousand."

"We will try to assist you," the general said. "But I do not know how to raise that kind of money. I hope our friends from America can do this.

"Listen, General," Sam said. Kidogo cocked his head as he made eye contact with Sam, warning against demands, insults, attitude. Already the general was flummoxed. Tony seconded this warning, whispering, "Easy, Sam" out the side of his mouth.

Sam took a deep breath and exhaled. "We realize you and your two partners have worked hard for your country and want to leave with the money that is yours. Tony and I want to help. But now that Madame Fusa has shown us we cannot rely upon her, there isn't much any of us can do."

"You must," insisted Tambo. "You must help me and the prince and the colonel. And think of the money you are going to make. It is worth it for you to raise this money."

"The fact is, General, Tony and I do not have that kind of money. That's why we came out here, to make money. Now perhaps," Sam ventured carefully, "Doctor Kidogo has other sources to raise the money Fusa demands. And maybe he can convince her to ask for a smaller amount of money upfront."

Kidogo did not seem to like Sam putting the responsibility back on him. "I doubt Madame Fusa will make any more concessions. You two must find those who will invest money. You will repay them and give them a substantial profit when the thirty-seven million arrives in Geneva."

"They're going to want to know what they're investing in," Sam replied. "Am I supposed to tell them they will be breaking the law? And do I give them your email as a reference?"

"You are not breaking the law," Kidogo said, an edge rising in his voice. "You are helping people transfer their own money to a foreign account."

"While posing as military consultants!" Sam shot back. "*That* is illegal."

Tony cleared his throat and actually raised his hand, like a nervous schoolboy. "May I make a suggestion, here? It seems to me, we agree to pay the three hundred k that Madame Fusa wants, but after the wire transfer goes through."

"I don't think she will agree to that," Kidogo said.

"Then the only possibility you leave us," Sam said, "is for Tony and me to fly home immediately. We will do our best to secure the money from investors. Of course, we won't be able to tell them the truth about their investment. We'll have to create a cover story."

They all sat in silence, staring at the floor, the ceiling, out of the window, anywhere but at one another.

When General Tambo beckoned him closer, Kidogo slid his chair until they were directly side by side so Tambo could whisper in Kidogo ear, something he did with much animation. Kidogo nodded his approval, and then Tambo addressed the room.

"I have another idea," the general announced. "It is not necessary for the two of you to leave. One of you should remain here. It should only be necessary for one of you two gentlemen to go on this fundraising trip."

Sam and Tony glanced at each other.

"Let me handle this," Tony whispered.

"Lots of luck," Sam whispered back.

In a louder voice, Tony asked, "Gentlemen, trying to raise three hundred thousand dollars will take both of us. We'll need to deal with clients in Switzerland, Paris, London, New York, California, Canada, Frankfurt. We both need to go."

"General Tambo," Kidogo explained, "has mentioned to me the fact if you both leave our country, we are concerned you will not come back. I think one of you staying behind is a good way to make sure you don't abandon our project."

"We're going to have to trust each other," Tony said. "It's really not helpful to prevent us from traveling. We need to contact investors."

"I do not see why you cannot contact them from here in Lagos," Tambo announced.

"General," Sam began, trying to hold his temper in check, "if you want to get out of this country, and you want us to help you, then you're going to have to let us do business the way we do business. If you keep us here against our will, we're never going to convince anyone to give us money. Your phone lines are not reliable. I do not have my contact information here. Neither does Tony. You are doing everything wrong here, gentlemen. You have Fusa changing the deal on us, you are asking us to raise money, and then you are preventing us from actually raising the money. Do you want to work with us or not? Either way, by this time tomorrow, Tony and I are on a plane out of here."

Tony looked at Sam, then down at his feet. *He* could never pull off a speech with such conviction; Sam knew he had to speak for both of them.

Sam stood. "Come on, Tony. We're going back to that shabby boarding house, the one Bill promised to get us out of after the first night, and pack our bags."

Tony unsteadily stood up. "Uh, General, Bill, why don't we all take a rest and discuss this by phone later. Would that be all right?"

Kidogo looked at Tambo, who nodded almost imperceptibly.

"Fine," Kidogo said. "Ford, have Joseph drive them back. I will call later."

"Thank you," said Tony. Sam, on the other hand, grabbed his business partner by the arm. Obete barely had a chance to open the door before they barreled through.

CHAPTER 16

The next day was one of waiting. Waiting for Kidogo, since as Patrick firmly told them again and again, the good doctor did not want to be called or visited: he would do the visiting himself. He would drop by before any international travel took place. In the meantime, Patrick pointed out to them, they were free to watch some TV. To relax. A notion that grew more farcical with each passing day in Lagos.

Sam knew how he would spend the interim hours. Lying on a lumpy mattress, far below the comfort level of the Americanized hotel he had been led to anticipate, brooding over how this deal had gone from risky to overcomplicated to a blatant trap.

If Sam could bargain the Nigerians down, in terms of the size of the bribe, and get the assistance of Pierre in Geneva, who had done little to help them thus far, it could still work. He would have to ensure they got out of here before Carlisle caught up with him again, he was sure *that* would be the end of the whole operation. Sam closed his eyes, resting, hoping to drift off for a short nap so he was rejuvenated for the next problem to land at his feet.

But he did not get the chance to rest for long; he heard the door open, followed by a familiar voice. Sam cracked Tony's door and saw his friend snoring. Even though he was still disturbed by Tony's lack of gumption, not to mention backbone, during their little Lagos getaway, he almost hated to wake him; rest was no easy commodity here. Still, Tony needed to be aware of this. "Kidogo's here."

They found Kidogo sitting in the living room, hands folded in his lap, pure serenity dressed in a suit.

"I have good news for you," Kidogo announced.

Their silence was not, apparently, enough encouragement for him to expound upon the news. Like so much else about the man, this annoyed Sam. "What? Madame Fusa doesn't need a bribe?"

"No, we will still have to pay her. But I have made a reservation for you on a flight to Paris on Air France. I have the information here." He handed Sam a slip of paper with handwritten information. "I will have Joseph take you to the airport and I will ride along. We will discuss some tactics for securing the money for Madame Fusa. All right?"

"Yes, yes, fine," Tony said, instantly awake and energized.

Sam studied Kidogo's eyes for signs of his true agenda. Weren't there always at least two with him?

"Well, go ahead," Kidogo said to Sam. "Pack. You are very anxious to leave us. So go."

There were certainly cheaper places than the Hotel De Crillon to stay in Paris, but Sam wanted nothing to do with them. He felt this former eighteenth-century palace, with its view of the Place de la Concorde and dazzlingly lit Eiffel Tower, was the proper antidote to Lagos.

The airport in Lagos had been a veritable obstacle course. They had learned upon arrival that no reservations had been made for them, as Kidogo had promised. Sam and Tony were now old hands at the Nigerian way of doing business, and after purchasing their own tickets, with an additional Lagos surcharge of two hundred dollars for the manager, they had received their boarding cards.

First things first, a few stiff drinks on the patio followed by a call to Pierre in Geneva; he needed to know the new parameters of the deal. He needed to *help* them.

After they'd elucidated the updated terms, Pierre began in his cautious, pragmatic banker's tone: "First, is it at all possible to have the funds released when the thirty-seven million has been credited to our account at UBS?"

"No," Tony said, "they wanted the three hundred k as a bribe, upfront."

"Any way this Madame Fusa might be convinced to be paid after the wire transfer? After all, you say she changed her mind about taking a percentage."

"But if anyone can convince her of that," said Sam, "it isn't me or Tony." He caught Pierre up on her hostility toward them. "And trust me, an angry Madame Fusa is not a pretty sight."

They could practically hear Pierre's gears grinding.

". . . Now that you know that the Nigerians expect you to pay a bribe to do this deal, do you still believe that the thirty-seven million is genuine? Or is this simply a way to get their hands on three hundred thousand?"

Sam and Tony looked at each other, huddled over his cell phone in Sam's room, with the gorgeous Parisian nightscape spread out before them. Were they deceiving themselves? Did they simply have so much invested at this point, bribe money, sweat, and tears, that they couldn't let themselves believe the scam was on them?

Sam, in particular, refused to believe it. He was working with Carlisle now, and he had to have faith that that meant he could salvage the deal. True, part of him had dreamed of what it would be like to leave directly from France for the US, to put Lagos behind him and never give anything in Nigeria a second thought. But that's what it was: a dream.

He certainly couldn't tell Tony or Pierre, but Sam understood that he had to go back. The only way he could now avoid prosecution back in the US was to cooperate with everything Carlisle wanted him to do. And he would. He would be as cooperative as he'd ever been in his life.

But he would also see to it that they wrung every penny possible out of this deal. It had cost them too much already. They'd put too much on the line. It *had* to work out.

"I don't like the fact that they have asked us for money upfront," Tony said, finally. "But if they were trying to rip us off, it seems like they would have tried to do so while we were in America. Now we know all the players involved in their scheme. They are vulnerable. And Sam let them know they were vulnerable."

Sam admitted he had lost his temper, threatening them. He also admitted Tony had a point. "If they wanted to just take us for a few hundred grand and there is no deal in place, why drag us all the way over there and set up meetings inside the Central Bank."

"Again, sorry to be the devil's advocate," Pierre responded, "but your dear friend Madame Fusa might be in on this scam. Perhaps Kidogo is splitting any money you put up with her and Ford Obete."

"Kidogo looked caught off-guard when she asked for it," Tony said. "The culture is based on greed and intimidation. I don't think they planned it."

"I don't either," Sam said. "But even if this isn't a scam, it's going to be hard to raise the money."

"True," Pierre said, adding, "and while I can facilitate UBS accepting a wire transfer from your Bedford and Clifford shell, there is not a lot I can do to help with the funds if they are put in this bank they want in Hamburg. I don't know that bank or anyone associated with it. It would not be as risky if it was an escrow account at UBS or at another Swiss bank that I have done business with, you know."

"I think we can convince them to use a Swiss bank and send the money to it. But do we want to take a chance on losing three hundred k?"

"Yes, it is a definite risk you would be taking," Pierre said.

Tony shot Sam a look and grabbed a pen and piece of Hotel de Crillon stationery. On it, Tony quickly wrote, *Pierre in or I am out.*

Sam nodded at Tony. "Listen, Pierre, you stand to make two and a half mil on this deal, just as Tony and I do. That means you're a full partner. If we do this, we do this equally."

During the long pause that followed, Tony added a postscript to his message. *He won't.*

"Pierre?" Sam gently said.

"Yes, I hear you, Sam. What you say is reasonable. I am thinking about my finances."

"What if we got the Nigerians to lower the figure?" Sam suggested.

"They'll never go for it," Tony said.

"I am not raising money for Nigerians" Pierre offered. "The risk is too great." Another lengthy lull in the call. "What about you?" Pierre finally asked.

"Then you are no longer our partner," announced Tony. "We'll give you ten percent of whatever we end up with when the money is transferred."

"And you, Sam, what do you say?" Pierre asked.

"I might be able to raise a hundred and fifty k. It would just about clean me out, though. No investor is going to put up money for a Nigerian deal when we can't give them the nuts and bolts. So I've got to second Tony on this, Pierre. You help raise the money or you're out."

Hearing no objection from Tony or his friend on the line in Geneva, Sam continued. "So that's the deal. Three hundred thousand total, raised by Tony and me. Pierre, you get ten percent. You're getting seven hundred and forty grand for the wire transfer."

"Assuming it is a Swiss bank," Pierre offered before, politely as ever, excusing himself. He was exhausted, he told them, and knew they must be as well. When they'd hung up, Sam and Tony drained their room-service cognacs.

On the way back to his own room, for his first comfortable sleep in what felt like ages, Tony said, "If they agree to this deal, and we successfully raise the money, I would like to go on record right now and say that I never want to go back to Lagos. Ever."

Sam smiled a tired smile and Tony left the room, quietly closing the door. The two friends may have countless points of divergence, but there were some things they would forever agree on. They would always, have Lagos.

CHAPTER 17

Sam sank deeper with every step. Now he was supposed to put up $150,000 while on the verge of insolvency. He felt he was caught in an irreversible tide, unable to stop the deal's momentum.

Yet he couldn't deny he relished the thrill of posing as a military consultant, getting tough with an armed thug at the airport. That feeling of standing up to Kidogo after he'd cut them off from outside communication and rendered them as vulnerable as possible. After months of feeling unable to control the decline of his hotel, it was intoxicating to wrench back control of this chaotic deal. In his most commanding moments, he felt like his old self, the Sam Marsh who had commanded Wall Street and swept Karin off her feet.

But now, lying in the morning sun of his room at the Hotel de Crillon, Sam thought first and foremost of being with Dina. Walking hand in hand with her, someplace quiet and secure. Sailing with her against a cerulean sky on waters as smooth as sheets on a freshly made bed. Making love to her. He barely knew the woman, he knew that, but it didn't stop him from entertaining visions of a future with her as he scrubbed his face with French milled soap.

Besides that, it was time to regain his standing in her eyes. She had witnessed him vulnerable and had even come to his aid. While it made him admire her all the more, he wanted her to see the strong side of him again. The side perfectly capable of pulling off an international deal worth millions.

Looking at his watch, he figured Tony would still be asleep in the next room and Dina would be winding down for the evening in Palm Springs, relaxing but not necessarily in bed. It would be intimate, without being too late in the evening to call, so he dialed. And when she answered, he felt his throat tighten with anticipation.

After her gasp of relief at hearing his voice came the barrage of questions. Where was he? When Roni hadn't been able to find him, had he been held captive?

How had he freed himself? Was this deal the dangerous trap it seemed from the outside?

He told her about Roni, the airport, the changed deal, and the Tambo brothers. Emphasizing how he had taken control at last. How he'd rebelled against Kidogo by threatening to expose him to Glanville Tambo, insisting on his and Tony's freedom. How, at the airport, he'd refused to be cowed by the typical Nigerian beadledom. He hoped she thought he sounded strong.

By the time Sam had finished, his tongue felt dry as paper.

"Are you still with me?" he asked.

"The busy life of the adventurer," she answered, thankfully sounding playful. "You should take off some time, now that you're coming back to Palm Springs. You should spend some time with me."

"That is exactly what I was thinking," Sam replied. "Did you have any place in mind?"

She started to answer but stopped herself. Across the vast distance, he heard the hitch in her breath. "Sam, you're not going back to Lagos, are you?"

He let his silence answer for him. He had to go back.

"Sam, listen to me. You wouldn't have called Roni unless you understood you were unsafe there. You've essentially been held hostage by the man who's supposed to be your business partner! I had no way of knowing if you were even alive."

On one hand, he was nourished by that concern in her voice. It was the sort of voice he'd dreamed of coming home to and wrapping himself in at the end of long days. On the other, he didn't want her seeing him as some rube in over his head. He wanted to prove to her, nearly as much as he wanted to prove it to himself, that he'd turned the tide in this deal, and while he'd been vulnerable at first, he could complete the job with Kidogo now playing by *his* rules.

He played down the lack of communication, allowing only that having restricted access to their cell phones had made it much more difficult. "The question now," he told her, "is whether we'll be able to raise the money. But I believe we will." *If we can't*, he added silently, *I'll have to think of some other way to save the hotel. And I have no idea what that could be.*

"Why would you go back? Roni has told me all about these Nigerian crooks, Kidogo and his henchmen. They are shady. Just forget it. You're going to get hurt."

"You really do care, don't you?" Sam enjoyed teasing her for a change.

"I'm not joking with you. You are taking a chance with your own safety and your friend Tony's as well."

"I don't mind going back without Tony," Sam said, surprised to hear himself say it aloud, but at the same time, knowing it was true. "He's a weak negotiator, Dina. When I did the talking, things got done. I'll be okay."

"Sam, do you want me to beg you?"

"No, I don't, Dina. If we can't raise the money, then believe me, the first thing I'm doing is flying back to be with you. There is nothing, nothing at all, I would rather do."

"Please think about what I've told you," said Dina and Sam heard in her voice a level of despair that made him sad and a little doubtful as well.

"Dina, I wish I was there with you." He didn't try to hide the intensity of his feelings; doing so was unnecessary. She'd been so vulnerable with him, so tender, he doubted he would have felt her presence more strongly if she were sitting beside him, stroking his stubbled chin with her strong but soft hands.

"You can be," Dina replied. "Call me soon."

"I will. I promise."

They both remained on the line, waiting to see if there was a last line, a signoff, as it were, from either one. The silence was filled with a charged passion, with words unsaid. After he'd hung up, Sam allowed his hand to linger on the receiver.

Mark Woods stared out from the Cessna window as the pilot flew low over the coast. He peered through binoculars at the tankers.

"Where are we going to land?"

"Another five miles up the coast, Mister Woods," the pilot assured him. "Mister Kidogo has arranged for a car to meet you there, to drive you to the tankers,"

"Good. This plane is goddamn uncomfortable. No legroom. Seats too narrow." Not to mention how the buckle on his seat belt dug into his protruding gut. The African pilot said nothing as Woods fiddled with the belt, trying to accommodate his own girth.

Within fifteen minutes, the plane had landed on a small coastal airstrip. Woods was driven in an SUV with tinted windows, an armed soldier in the back, to the location of the two tankers. When he got out, Woods peered around through the agitated dust: the port was crowded with armored vehicles.

He clumsily returned a sergeant's salute.

"It is Mister Woods, is it not?" the sergeant asked in heavily accented English.

"That's me."

"We have been expecting you. I will take you to the colonel."

The sergeant led the way between several portable buildings in various stages of dilapidation. *These people think these are offices?* Woods thought. Windows missing panes. Kicked-in doors. Drainpipes yanked out of sockets and rivulets of dirty water on the ground.

The sergeant knocked on a door of one of the portable buildings.

"Enter," called out a voice from within and the sergeant held it open. With an eyeroll, Woods hoisted his mass up the tottering staircase that appeared not so much attached to the building as wheeled into its vicinity.

Colonel Tazwetta had a hawk-like nose and beady eyes, but he was genial when he shook hands with Woods.

"I hope you had a nice journey, Mister Woods."

"Well, actually…" Mark Woods had never been accused of tact. "The plane was like a tin can. But anyway. Glanville Tambo asked me to come down here to check on the operation, so here I am. And I see the two tankers that you captured are still docked here."

Woods looked across a battered wooden desk at the colonel, who took a last puff of a cigarette and grinned. "The tankers are, of course, fully loaded, and we should be setting off within the next few hours for Madeira."

"Why the delay, Colonel?"

"There is no delay, Mister Woods," the colonel said, cautiously. "Please inform Minister Tambo that we have certain paperwork to complete, fresh water to take on, and we're awaiting some new crew members. You will appreciate that we cannot just sail with the old crews, given the fact that we seized their tankers."

Woods paused to light a cigarette of his own. The colonel looked out of the window while Woods broke into a loud smoker's cough and spat into a handkerchief. By the end of his fit of croup, he appeared flushed.

"Did the takeover go smoothly, Colonel?"

"Not entirely. Three men were killed. Very unfortunate."

"And what about the remaining crew members you captured?"

"You do not have to worry about that, Mister Woods." Here the colonel's amenable expression gave way to narrowed eyes. "If His Excellency wants me to report on what happened to those men, I will explain it to him. Directly."

It was no skin off Woods's nose. He moved on. "Once these tankers have left, if we need more, is that possible?"

The colonel didn't hesitate. "Of course. We just need to hear from His Excellency and we will do our best to arrange it."

"Good." Woods rose, hoping to conclude the meeting.

"Would you like to go aboard the tankers, now, Mister Woods?" Tazwetta snapped to his feet.

"Thanks, but that won't be necessary."

"But you must. Minister Tambo will want eyewitness confirmation of the condition of the tankers. I'm sure that is why you have come all this way."

Woods didn't bother agreeing verbally; he just trailed Tazwetta up long, wooden walkways onto both tankers, allowing himself to be shown around. On the second tanker, Woods stepped in a pool of blood on the main deck.

He looked down and wiped the sole of his shoe off.

"As I said," Tazwetta offered, "there was some resistance. But none of my men were hurt."

Woods darted a glance back at the SUV waiting to return him to the Cessna. "So, I can confirm to my associates in Lagos that the tankers will be leaving port within the next few hours?"

"I have been told sailing conditions will be excellent. No delays are expected. I'm hopeful that His Excellency will need more vessels. His Excellency is very generous, and I would be happy to receive my same fee for additional tankers. Please let him know that."

"Well, decision's his, but I'll tell him."

Tazwetta led Woods down the gangplank and they walked toward the SUV. The guard and driver, who sat inside the vehicle to stay out of the sun, suddenly popped up and stood to attention as the comically mismatched men approached.

Woods thought of a final question. "Listen, I need to know, Colonel. These tankers reliable? Like, in good shape? If there are any issues, I need to know now.

We can't afford to have mechanical problems. We need to get them to Madeira and hidden with no delays."

"They have been well maintained," the colonel assured him. "We will claim that pirates took control of the tankers and that we did not know who they were working for. Easy to blame on the Somalis."

Sounded like a good cover story to Woods. He shook Tazwetta's hand. "Thank you for your help."

Tazwetta headed back to the labyrinth of crude buildings that included his office. Woods tried his cell phone but it had no signal. Where in this shithole of a place did? He headed back toward the airstrip.

The pilot started up the Cessna as he saw the SUV bounce into view. Woods got out, waved to the occupants, and made his way to the open door on the right side of the aircraft. Before he got in, and against the thrumming of the plane's engine, Woods called George Laney.

It was five hours earlier in Maryland. Laney had to excuse himself from a meeting when he identified the incoming number.

"Hello," Laney said tentatively.

"George, I'm sweating my ass off in some port in Nigeria."

"Uh, I do have one of my staff in my office right now," Laney politely lied, "but if you have a brief update for me, I'd like to hear it."

"The tankers are leaving for Madeira in a just a few hours," Woods shouted into the cell phone. "I haven't even told Tambo yet."

"Well, tell him. By all means, right away. We don't want to get him mad."

"George, they had to kill three of the crew and I have a bad feeling that the remaining crew members are at the bottom of the ocean somewhere." Woods paused for Laney's reaction. It was not forthcoming; the only response was that sky-splitting sound of the Cessna getting ready to fly. "George, did you hear me about the crew?"

"Yes, I heard. I'm thinking about it. In any event, I will handle that."

"I mean, some of these guys, even in the ones in military uniforms, are nothing but thugs. It's the goddamn Wild Wild West out here."

Laney cut him off. "I know what Lagos is like, Mark. I've been there before. Let me know the reaction you get when you file your report there. Just tell Tambo what he needs to know. Do not editorialize. Do not complain. And do not show fear."

"But I got to tell you, George, I thought I was just buying oil. And now I'm dealing with guys who look like they want to kill me if I say anything wrong."

"Well, make sure you say the right things." Laney smirked. "I've got to get back to work. Remember, this is serving all of us. We're going to make a big score."

Woods wiped his greasy forehead with his shirt sleeve and shielded his eyes from the sun's late-afternoon glare. "It's just rougher than I thought it would be here. That's all."

"But you could never pull this off in the Middle East," Laney pointed out. "Just remember, Mark, be on your best behavior."

CHAPTER 18

Pierre was as immaculate as Sam had ever seen him, greeting him and Tony in a crisp white shirt and a perfectly tailored Saville Row blazer, a flower laced through a buttonhole. He brought them into a living room that featured his grandfather's mahogany bookcase with a prized collection of signed first editions and leather-bound works of Goethe, Molière, and Shakespeare.

As their hotel in the quiet, quaint French town of Annemasse was only six kilometers from Geneva, they'd decided an in-person meeting was due.

After a few minutes of pleasantries, and a discussion of mutual friends in Switzerland and France, Pierre got down to business. "Well, gentlemen, what news do you have about our mutual project?"

"We were going to ask you the same thing," Tony said. Sam shot his friend a look; the fact that Tony hadn't been keen on Pierre's involvement didn't give him the right to be rude to the man in his own home.

"When Tony and I were in Paris, we got on the phone and checked with our clients," Sam explained. "And together, we've got our three hundred grand lined up."

"Well done," said Pierre.

"Let's call Kidogo," suggested Tony, "and see what he has to say about our having the money in place."

"Certainly, Tony, but we should discuss some other things first."

"Like what?" Tony demanded.

"It would be better to put all this money in a Swiss bank. I do not know the bank your Madame Fusa named in Hamburg.

"She's not *our* Madame Fusa," Tony shot back. "You have no idea what they put us through in that country."

"We don't know that bank either," Sam said. "I don't think they're going to be flexible about the bank. We'll be lucky if we can bargain them down to two fifty, instead of three hundred."

"In a way," said Pierre, "it isn't unrealistic for them to want a fee at the Central Bank. I know the two-point-five percent was rather a lot of money. It would not be so unreasonable for them to ask for this three hundred thousand. But to reiterate, my concern is that they could be trying to steal your money. In other words, gentlemen, what if the scam is on us? What if there is no thirty-seven million?"

Tony surprised Sam by, for the first time, agreeing with their Swiss host. "I've thought of that. What if Fusa and Kidogo are duping us? Once we deposit the money, couldn't they simply claim it never got transferred?"

Feeling put on the spot, and shaken, as both men turned to gauge his reaction, Sam tried to sound coolheaded. "The three guys who want out of Nigeria would have to be phony too."

Tony just shrugged, as though the thought wasn't potentially devastating. "Maybe they are."

"We researched them, remember?"

"I don't mean they aren't the prince, the colonel, and the general. I mean maybe they don't have thirty-seven million. Or anything close to it."

Sam reached for the crystal decanter of white wine. For several beats, their surroundings were mute except for strains of a Beethoven symphony reaching them from the next room. Against such quiet, Sam's glass issued a resounding *thunk* when he set it on the coffee table.

"There is one solution then," he said. "If the Nigerians go for it, we have a safeguard. If they don't, I can't see how we can move ahead."

"This better be good." Tony responded. Sam's words may have sounded threatening but his tone was merely exhausted. He was out of ideas; Tony had to hope that Sam's idea would save them.

"An escrow account," said Sam. "I think if we set up an escrow account, deposit the money going into this Hamburg bank, we could make sure that the money remains there until the thirty-seven million hits the account. Then, they can withdraw their money."

"I'm not the banking guy here," Tony said. "You guys are. It sounds nice. What's the catch?"

"The catch," Pierre said matter-of-factly, "is whether the Nigerians will agree to it. But Sam is correct. We can monitor the account and prevent any withdrawal until the deal is done."

"Well," Tony said, "let's get it over with."

On the second attempt, they reached Kidogo's office. Knowing that Sam's aggression could alienate Kidogo, Tony had elected himself to be their spokesman. Pierre would deliver the request itself, his banking expertise, they all thought, would make him sound confident and trustworthy. Tony would soften the news.

"Bill, how are you? I'm here with Sam and Pierre, our banking partner. We're here in Switzerland and we have some news for you. We have raised a lot of money already."

He waited for a reaction, some congratulations or appreciation, but none came. Kidogo ended his lengthy pause by asking, "How long do you think it might take you to get back to Lagos?"

Sam silently pointed at Pierre.

"Doctor Kidogo, this is Pierre. We have not spoken before, but I want you to know that the three of us have worked very hard to make this transaction work. If you will accept the amount of two hundred and fifty thousand, we are willing to open an escrow account at the bank you prefer in Hamburg. I assume you have dealt with escrow accounts before?"

Another pause. Kidogo ended this one with an explosion.

"Sam and Tony know very well that the amount is three hundred thousand. I know very well what an escrow account is, and that is not the agreement. The money is to be wired to the account I gave them."

Convinced he was watching their one sure solution vanish, Tony slowly shook his head.

"We are making a counterproposal," Pierre explained. "We need to safeguard the money we send, and the best way is an escrow account."

"Why don't you ask Madame Fusa about this?" Tony asked.

He was met with a stream of invective in a native dialect that none of the three men in Geneva understood, nor cared to.

"I have changed this deal from two-point-five percent to this, and it is not going to change again. You keep complicating things, and I am doing the very best

I can with the Central Bank. I am not negotiating with you. The amount is three hundred thousand, and it will be deposited in the Hamburg account."

Pierre shrugged. Tony shook his head. These were gestures of surrender. Sam, on the other hand, had been looking forward to this. His own gesture was a raised finger that signaled his companions to *watch this*. With a wicked twinkle in his eye, he greeted Kidogo. "How are you, Bill?"

"Sam, I am not happy. You have changed the deal and…"

"The first person to change this deal was you," Sam began. "You made us come to Lagos when we wanted to conduct business from America. Then we thought we were going to stay in a decent hotel. That changed. And *then* you decided we had to put up money to get this deal done. Now, frankly, I don't care how much of this is your doing and how much of it is Madame Fusa's. We have done our best and shown good faith. We've got two hundred and fifty thousand lined up. If you or Fusa want more, you can go look elsewhere."

"You have not honored your agreement…"

"I'm still talking, Bill. Do you hear me? I'm not finished." Unlike Tony, Sam didn't worry for a moment that his natural belligerence would estrange them from Kidogo. If it did, so be it. But he knew Kidogo needed them, despite the man's games and inflexibility. They weren't the only ones who were going to compromise from now on. "You've treated us rudely and we don't trust you." Sam saw Tony flinch. He didn't care. "And the only way we are going to send that two hundred and fifty thousand to you is if it is an escrow account. We are not sending it to any regular account in Hamburg or anywhere else. You will get that money when the deal for the thirty-seven million goes through. That's it. If you don't like it, I'll hang up now, and you won't hear my voice ever again."

Sam turned to Tony and Pierre. "Am I right, gentlemen?"

Although he still looked seasick, Tony found his voice. "It's all we can do, Bill. Please try to convince Fusa."

"I think it is a fair solution," Pierre said. "And we cannot raise more money for a deal we cannot even fully describe to investors. Obviously, no investor in Europe or America wants to risk money on an illegal scheme. So you are getting a lot of money from Tony and Sam when they didn't expect to ever have to put up their own money."

Kidogo sounded very tired when he next spoke, as if his earlier outburst had used up all his energy.

"It is not my fault that a fee must be paid to Fusa and her people. You said the two-point-five percent was too much, so now this is what you get from them. If you had agreed to the two-point-five, maybe you would have the money now."

Tony leaned over and whispered in Sam's ear, "Make peace."

Sam nodded. "Bill," he started again, this time in a much more moderate tone, "we really cannot do better than this. If you can get Fusa to agree to three hundred in an escrow account, we have a deal, and as soon as you give us the account information, we can wire the money."

"I will see if Madame Fusa will agree. But I have very grave doubts about it. Talk soon."

Kidogo hung up before any of them could say goodbye.

"What is it, Mark?" Laney made no attempt to hide his anger as he headed onto the back patio of his home, his bathrobe pulled around him against the cool night air. "I told you never to phone me at home. Always leave a message for me at Annie's."

"George, strange things are happening in Lagos. We might have some trouble."

"What the hell do you mean?" By now, they had bought thousands of barrels and taken care of transportation; if they were to sell then and there, they would turn profits of over ten dollars a barrel. "You've made more commission in the last couple weeks than you've earned in years. Why are you bothering me?"

Woods's voice was, as usual, slurred with drink. "One of my best clients is an Israeli company. They're big buyers of Delta oil and they can't understand why the price is soaring. Plus, they expected a delivery last week. Then they discovered that the tanker with their oil was captured and it's gone. Oil that they had paid for. George, they're giving me a hard time over it."

"Tell them you're not responsible for any piracy."

"But, George, they're right. I bought the oil for them. They've paid for it and they were supposed to have taken delivery last week. I called to discuss it with Tambo, and he told me not to ask questions."

"Just tell them that they'll get their damned oil. It may cost them a couple of bucks more, but they'll get it."

"I'm in breach of contract with them," he said.

Laney adopted a softer tone. "For Christ's sake, Mark, it's just talk. They're not going to do anything. In another week, your ass will be back in Kuwait, where they'll never even find you."

"George, you don't understand." Woods's voice rose. "One of them threatened my life. What kind of protection do I have?"

Laney heard the panic in his cousin's voice. "Look, don't lose your cool, Mark. Stay focused. If the guy becomes too demanding, we can take care of him. Glanville can arrange for that in five minutes, okay?"

"Okay." Woods sounded unsure.

"Get some rest. Keep buying. And don't call me on this phone again."

Laney hung up abruptly. He went inside and joined his wife in bed. But he could not join her in sleep.

CHAPTER 19

Sam had tried calling Tony twice but hadn't left a message. He realized the likelihood was that Tony was out carousing, looking for women and it was likely Sam would hear nothing more from him that evening.

Checking his watch, Sam dialed Dina.

He got her voicemail as well. "I'm still in Annemasse. I wish you were here. I'm going out for a walk and I'll be back at the hotel in a couple of hours."

He was interrupted by an incoming call and he was relieved to see on the phone's screen it was Dina.

"Sam, I'm here," she said when he answered. "I was in the other room and couldn't remember where I'd left my phone. Listen, I'm in Paris." She sounded out of breath.

"What are you doing there?"

"My aunt is in the hospital. She's had a bypass operation and I flew over to see her. She's Roni's mother. Roni is flying in from Lagos tonight."

"I'm sorry to hear that." He paused. "Listen, when things are settled there, why don't you come to Geneva for a couple of days?'

"Well, I was going to suggest that you come to Paris," she said. "Give me a chance to talk you out of going back to Lagos."

Paris sounded wonderful. He did want to see her, desperately. But he had to make sure he was being clear with her. "This deal will happen. There's a delay, but we will resolve it. Anyway, I may have to fly off at any moment to Nigeria."

"Sam, listen to me." She could not conceal her anger. "That deal is not going to happen. It's a crooked deal and you're not to go back to Nigeria. I've been talking with Roni. He has excellent connections in Nigeria and he's checked out Kidogo and those other villains. You owe it to yourself to reconsider. And to me too," she added firmly.

He thought about those words carefully. "I know," he said gently. "And I don't mind telling you I miss you terribly."

"Well, you should miss me." Her tone had softened.

Sam snapped to attention on the edge of his hotel bed. "Of course I'll come. I would love to come to Paris and spend a day with you there."

"Why not come for the weekend? What's this about coming for only a day?"

"I have to stay close to the phone and Pierre too, in case anything happens."

She sighed. "You must do what you think is best. I understand."

"I'll catch the first plane I can out of Geneva and call you before I take off." As soon as they hung up, he called Air France and made a reservation. Minutes later, he heard footsteps in the hall.

Tony was trying to open his hotel room door, slightly disheveled, reeking of scotch, perfume, and sex.

"Where the hell have you been?"

"None of your business," Tony murmured.

"Out whoring around," Sam said.

"Oh, it was quite a lot better than whoring."

"I'm going to Paris tomorrow."

This jolted Tony out of his stupor. "What for?"

"I'm going to see Dina. She's there with a sick relative."

"You can't go to Paris." He gave up attempting to unlock his own door. "We're in the middle of a deal here." Stumbling over, he grabbed Sam's shirt sleeve. "You have to be ready in case we get a call from Kidogo."

"Get your hands off me!" Sam shoved Tony away. Tony's eyes grew wide with surprise and hurt. "I'm going for one goddamn day to be with her. Unlike you, I'm in love. And unlike you, I'm not married."

Sam turned back to his hotel room. "Call you from Paris," he grumbled. He slammed his door emphatically, leaving Tony alone, his head hung down.

CHAPTER 20

At a table overlooking Lake Geneva, and the paddle steamer that languidly ferried tourists across its turquoise waters, Tony convinced Pierre they needed to call Kidogo right then, rather than waiting for Sam's return from Paris. After all, he was there with a beautiful woman he professed to be in love with. Women had a way of delaying a man's travel plans.

"Suit yourself," Pierre said dryly, sipping and looking out over the lake. His gaze changed when he heard Tony shout into his cell phone, "Hello, Bill! It's Tony. Can you hear me okay?"

Tony motioned Pierre to slide closer to him at their table. After Pierre did so, Tony bellowed, "Bill, Pierre is here with me. Sam is in Paris. I am going to put you on speaker."

Tony pressed the button for the speaker function and he and Pierre huddled over the phone as they heard Kidogo's voice, mixed with static but still understandable.

"Tony, Pierre, I am sorry I did not call you first. I have some very good news."

Pierre smiled at Tony, who still looked skeptical.

"I have had a serious talk with Madame Fusa and she has agreed to your request of an escrow account being set up for the three hundred thousand your investors have contributed. All we ask is that the account be set up in Lagos."

"We just wish to be clear," Pierre said, leaning down toward the phone Tony held. "Can you confirm that Tony and Sam would be the only ones able to access the money until the thirty-seven million is transferred?"

"Yes," said Kidogo. "And *we* wish to be clear that the three hundred thousand is real before we go ahead with the rest of the plan."

"It's real," Tony assured him. "We've got it in a bank here in Switzerland, and our investors want to know when they can expect their return."

Kidogo assured him it would be soon, very soon. He asked Tony to simply let him know when Sam had agreed to the plan.

"Right away," said Tony enthusiastically. "Bill, good work. We'll be in touch soon."

The Ritz was one of Sam's favorite Paris hotels, and he was surprised that he still recognized the concierge and doorman from his last visit, three years earlier. Walking through the lobby, he passed the impressive arcade of jewelry showcases leading to the Rue Cambon entrance. Instantly he flashed back to the days when, on a whim, he could buy an expensive gift for Karin just to let her know he was thinking of her.

Knowing he'd arrived early, Sam wandered outside, where the splendid Place Vendome buzzed with the usual excitement of Paris. His concentration on the Column was interrupted when a taxi came to a screeching halt just a few feet away from him. The doorman rushed to open the car door.

There was Dina, wearing a tight sweater, dark skirt, and seamed stockings.

"Sam, you're here already. Am I late?" Dina asked.

He hugged her tightly. The driver leaned forward and looked through the open window at him and smiled at Sam before whisking the cab away. "You look very Parisienne, Dina."

"Thank you, darling. You look tired."

"I am but never mind. How is your aunt doing?"

"The doctors say she will recover, thank God. She's tough. Roni is very relieved. I was over at her apartment on Avenue Foch, assuring friends she is doing okay."

Already wishing he could stay longer, and wishing he'd planned the single day he had to spend with her, Sam asked, "What should we do?"

"Well, first I want to go upstairs and change," she said. "Wait here. I'll be down in five minutes."

Watching her stride toward the elevator with the step of someone ten years her junior, Sam couldn't help feeling disappointed he hadn't been invited up. Their last conversation had felt as intimate as a call could be between long-time lovers. He wanted her, needed her, with a passion he hadn't felt since the days when he and Karin were still in love.

True to her word, Dina was soon back downstairs, dressed in her familiar white jeans and a light blue designer T-shirt. She flashed a smile at the doorman as they ran from the hotel.

Before they departed, she said, "I'm sorry if I'm pushing you too hard on this deal." Then she smiled. "I just want you to be safe."

"And I love you for that," said Sam, and unable to hold back, he gently placed his hands on her strong shoulders, drew her to him, and kissed her. When they pulled apart, their expressions matched: lust, relief, and tenderness all at once. The feeling of being in their own world faded when Dina spotted a taxi.

"Sacre-Coeur, *s'il vous plaît*," she said to the driver.

Silent but brimming with words, they held hands while the car climbed the hills toward Montmartre.

"Take off your tie." She giggled. "You look far too formal."

He happily complied. The taxi dropped them off at La Butte, and they looked over the entire city that lay before them.

They walked toward the Place du Terte, busy with artists selling their paintings. Some offered, aggressively, to draw portraits of the passing tourists. A black musician blew a piercing off-key riff on his saxophone that was intended to sound like the opening chords of "Around Midnight." A longhaired unshaven youth with rimless spectacles, whose red eyes suggested he regularly replaced sleep with drugs, strummed a guitar, a Gauloise dangled from his lips.

Dina, hand in hand with Sam, swung her arm in a forward, pointing toward a sidewalk bistro.

"This is where we are having lunch," she exclaimed.

Sam pointed in the direction of La Mère Catherine, one of the oldest Parisian restaurants.

"I know this place," he said, pleased. "They are famous for their onion soup."

"If you decide to stay longer," Dina said as she sat at the table, "I'd love for you to meet some of my friends and family here in Paris."

"I wish I could," he whispered.

After a long and relaxed lunch they walked around the back of the Basilica, where the crowds of tourists thinned and disappeared. A gateway led into a small garden square. They stopped to admire the alcoves covered in vines, the waterfall fountain, the flowerbeds with abundant clumps of lavender. They sat on a bench under a tree and basked in the seclusion.

Sam gently put a finger under Dina's chin and turned her face toward his. She smiled back.

"Look around us," Dina said. "This is probably one of the most romantic places in the world. It's wonderful to be here with you, but let's keep our feet on the ground. Get that Nigerian deal out of your system, and when you get back to California, we'll have more time together. Okay?" Her eyes were large with worry.

He found it hard to restrain himself from wrapping his arms around her and kissing her. Instead, they rose from the bench to spend an hour sauntering, hand in hand, around the narrow streets of Montmartre.

"Sam, it's four," she noted. "It's rush hour. If you need to be at the airport for a flight at seven, you'd better start looking for a cab. That is, unless I can persuade you to change your mind about staying."

"You could persuade me to do anything, I think. I'm only going back to Lagos to complete the deal and save my hotel. Then I'm coming back to spend all the time I can with you. I swear it."

"I know. So what do you say?"

"I say, the hell with it. I'll take the nine o'clock flight. I can call Geneva and tell them to expect me later."

She smiled. "Well, in that case, come back to the hotel," she said softly.

Feeling as though he'd awakened in a sumptuous dream, he followed Dina to her room at the Ritz. Inside she pulled him to her tightly; he could feel her breasts, full and warm, against his chest.

"Sam, I want you to know I admire you for sticking with what you started in Lagos."

"You do?" he asked, a little surprised. "I'm glad to hear it. Because before…"

She put a glossy red fingernail gently up to his lips. Then she moved her finger into his mouth. He sucked on it and the rest was a whirl of kissing and touching, of sighs and caresses, of clothes being unzipped and unbuttoned and hitting the floor.

They never made it to the bedroom. He eased her onto the sofa and knelt before her, moving his mouth, his tongue, between her parted silky legs. After she gasped and thrashed from the pleasure, he got on top of her.

"Sam," she whispered, concern still in her eyes. "I don't want anything bad to happen to you."

"Don't worry," he assured her. "Something wonderful is about to happen to us both." And with that, their bodies and lips drew together in dizzying symmetry.

CHAPTER 21

Roni leaned back in the armchair. Philip's apartment was a typical American expatriate bachelor pad, comfortable without being luxurious, on the outskirts of the area where the Nigerian elite had their mansions. It was the closest thing in Lagos to a middle-class neighborhood.

Roni sipped Russian vodka from Philip's private reserve and nibbled on canapés. "I hope I can assume you're not taping our conversation," he said. "That would be bad. For both of us."

"Roni," Philip said with false shock, "we may work for different countries, but we are partners in this endeavor."

"That's why I intend to help you," Roni agreed. "And I must ask you, as my partner, to make sure Sam Marsh never learns of my involvement or who I work for."

"You have my word, Roni. I'd like to return the favor of you telling me about him. The name of the man I believe to be buying up oil for Glanville Tambo is Mark Woods. I met him at a party at Tambo's, where he is a guest."

"And who is this guy?"

"He worked for a company in Houston, that I know. They tell me he got transferred to a company near DC after screwing up. He has some connection in Washington. And that connection sent him to Tambo."

"So, who do you think Woods is working for?"

"I don't know. But it would help both of our countries if we found out as soon as possible."

"You realize," Roni said carefully, "that this could embarrass your government, if Woods's identity is revealed. An American cooperating with a military dictatorship to destabilize the oil market."

"That's true," admitted Carlisle. "So what we need to do is put pressure on Glanville so he stops using Woods, stops the oil stockpiling."

"Is it possible that Woods is working for the Agency?"

Carlisle chortled. "This guy is too loud and obnoxious to work as a spook. What about Marsh? How do I know he isn't Mossad?"

"He's an American citizen. Owns a hotel in Palm Springs."

"What, an American citizen can't secretly be working for you?" smiled Carlisle.

Roni set down his drink and rubbed his temples, thinking.

"Come on, Roni. Full disclosure."

"Without naming names."

"Yes. Full disclosure without names."

Roni gritted his teeth. "Sam Marsh is a friend of a good friend. This good friend is former Mossad. I said I would try to keep Marsh out of jail, despite this stupid scam he's trying to pull off."

"I need another vodka." Carlisle sighed. He poured Roni another as well without asking. Both drank quietly for a few moments, both lost in thought, schemes shooting through their minds.

"You know as well as I do," Roni said, "that Kidogo is working both sides. He's Glanville's man but he might also be helping steal from the Central Bank."

"Right. We'll never be able to turn Kidogo against Glanville. He can't know anything about what we're doing."

Roni reached for another canapé. "These are really good. Who knew you had such taste in food and vodka?"

Carlisle only grunted in reply. "We've got to get to Woods. But as a guest of Tambo's, I can guarantee you he has a bodyguard if he goes anywhere."

"What about intercepting some of Glanville's emails and humiliating him into stopping?" Roni mused aloud.

"I would have trouble getting authorization for that," Carlisle contended. "We still want to buy Delta oil from these guys."

"Well, you can understand that after our oil shipment disappeared, my government is willing to take some serious action."

"How serious?" asked Carlisle.

"We have to do something with Woods," Roni suggested. "But I realize that if you kidnap him and force him into a confession, that could be a death warrant for him and any agents from your country or mine who are discovered. Then you have an international incident and we still don't stop Tambo's oil plotting."

Carlisle paced his living room. Physical movement always helped get his mind moving as well.

Roni reached into his jacket. "You're making me nervous with your pacing. Do you mind if I smoke?"

"Do you think better if you smoke?"

"As a matter of fact, I do."

"Then go ahead," Carlisle said. "I think better when I pace."

Roni inhaled deeply a few times and Carlisle, head down, walked back and forth on the Berber carpeting covering most of his living room floor.

"Can't use Kidogo, can't use Glanville," Roni summarized. "And you've got Sam Marsh to contend with."

Carlisle stopped walking.

"What have you got?" Roni asked dourly.

A small but hopeful smile turned up one corner of Carlisle's mouth. His pacing this time was short-lived. At the window, looking out on the working class neighborhood, he turned and faced Roni.

"Let me try this out on you, Roni. Woods met Sam Marsh at this bash at Glanville's little palace. What if we used Sam to get Woods away from the residence and away from his bodyguard."

"How in hell are you going to do that?"

"I don't know. But Woods is a loudmouth and a slob. And we might just find a way to leak information about what he is doing."

"That could work," said Roni. "But if you use Marsh, we're back to your promising me he won't get hurt or caught."

"If I get approval, I will do my best to keep Sam Marsh safe. But we'd be using him as bait. There are risks."

The flight to Lagos was on time. Sam insisted on a first-class ticket, assuming it would be the last real comfort he would have for some time. But his concerns about returning to Nigeria came in flight.

Engaging his Nigerian seating companion in small talk, Sam learned she had been visiting her four children in Paris; she was headed home to reunite with her husband. She was pleasant company, but he noticed her fidgeting with her handbag and necklace on their descent.

"You seem upset about something," Sam commented. "Are you okay?"

"I am always nervous when I go home," she answered. "If it were not for my husband, I would not go back at all until the present regime is ousted."

"What makes you so nervous?"

"There are dangerous and terrible people at the airport. I am not happy until I am back in my own house."

Sam nodded. "We had to keep bribing people to get out of there. I assumed that Nigerians have no problem at the airport. I thought it was only the foreigners, like me, who were exposed to danger there."

"In some ways it's even worse for us," she told him. "The workers at the airport are badly paid, and many envy Nigerians like me who can afford to travel. They know we have some money, although not very much."

Studying the fear in her eyes, Sam gently took his hand in hers. "I'm sorry it's like that for you."

"You are a gentleman," the Nigerian woman said. "If you already know how Lagos is, why would you go back?"

"Good question," Sam chuckled softy. He looked out his window to see the airport looming through the hazy overcast of Lagos.

When they landed, Sam walked off the plane through the familiar muggy terminal to begin the mandatory obstacle course for all arriving passengers. His travel companion walked on ahead, deliberately distancing herself from him. It was ten o'clock at night. Sam was exhausted.

After running the gauntlet with minimal delays and bribes, Sam recognized one of Kidogo's henchmen carrying a hand-scrawled card with "MARSH" on it. He led him to Joseph, who was sitting in the Volvo in the nearby parking lot.

On their way to Chateau Kidogo, they soon hit roadblocks. A tall, muscular soldier waved a flashlight and beckoned them to stop. Sam turned around and saw two parked military trucks and several armed soldiers holding up traffic, seemingly at random.

"What's all this about, Joseph?" Sam asked.

"Don't worry, sir. It's the army."

One of the soldiers approached and asked Joseph to step out of the car. Sam was ordered to remain in the backseat. Sam closed his eyes and said a small prayer, resigned for whatever was to happen next.

A few minutes later, Joseph returned with the soldier, who ordered Sam to lower the window. He asked to see Sam's passport, which Sam handed over. The soldier took it to show to his superior officer.

Moments later, the officer ordered Sam out of the car, demanded to inspect his belongings. That was no disaster, after a swift inspection, Sam was commanded to return to the car. He would have been terrified as this was his first trip to Lagos. It was miraculous, how immune he'd become to these indignities.

They arrived half an hour later at Chateau Kidogo. Joseph led the way through the darkened house up the staircase to the living room. It reminded Sam of a scene from a Hitchcock movie. Kidogo was seated in the room, lit by just two flickering candles.

Kidogo rose from the armchair and went to a card table in the corner of the room. "Here are the passports of the men at the Central Bank. Write down their names, addresses, and passport numbers. When the power returns, fax your colleague in Geneva so he can arrange the visas for them to travel to Switzerland."

Sam bristled, as usual, at Kidogo's domineering attitude.

Kidogo continued casually, discussing the escrow account and that Tony had already arrived the night before. Sam's mind was foggy from travel and lack of sleep. That, coupled with the lack of light due to the outage made it even harder to concentrate.

Sam finally spoke up. "Bill, it's late and I haven't slept in a while. I've had one hell of a day. You agreed to put me up in a hotel. Where am I staying?"

"At the Gestec." And then Kidogo promised, "You will be comfortable there."

Perhaps he had just grown accustomed to most statements uttered in Nigeria being lies, but Sam somehow doubted it.

CHAPTER 22

After half an hour of driving, Joseph turned off the main road onto an unlit highway. In the car's headlamps, Sam could see ramshackle homes whose lawns were piled with trash bags and old tires, smoke battling the faint illumination along the roadside. It was surreal but true: he was back in Lagos. They approached a four-way stop sign, with one more military roadblock.

"Pull in here!" shouted a soldier, who directed them with his flashlight. Joseph followed directions, glancing in the rearview mirror to see how hostile Sam's reaction might be.

But Sam was resigned. He had traveled thousands of miles for the privilege of being driven in near darkness in a city he secretly feared.

"Show me your passport," the soldier demanded. Sam handed it to yet another uniformed man, who snapped it out of Sam's hand and inspected it with a flashlight. Sam remained in the car while Joseph negotiated their "free" passage, at a cost of an additional two hundred dollars, to the Gestec Hotel, less than a mile away.

When Joseph drove off, Sam mumbled, "Twice in one night. I don't even want to think what else can go wrong."

"I'm sorry." Joseph mumbled as well, but loud enough for Sam to hear. "I know it is very different from what you are used to in America."

"It's all right, Joseph. I'm just tired. But tell me, how long is this power outage likely to last?"

"Maybe just a few hours more. It was caused by someone who was angry."

"What do you mean?"

"When you were away," Joseph hesitated as though someone from the military regime might hear him speak, "there was a public demonstration against the government. One of the protestors set off a bomb."

Driving up to the Gestec they saw a security guard with his back turned. As they got closer, Sam leaned forward to see a group of woman shouting and waving their arms at the guard.

What the hell was it this time? Some of the women yelled, some grinned. Others looked bored as they smoked cigarettes. Some were toothless and drunk. All were scantily clad. Sam didn't have to speak the language to grasp their profession.

When they noticed Joseph's car with a white man in the front seat, a few of the prostitutes rushed toward the car. Some raised their skirts, revealing all; others unbuttoned their blouses.

"Can we avoid these women?" Sam asked.

Joseph nodded and quickly drove around the women. A few of them got close enough to smack the car with their open palms but Joseph pushed down on the accelerator and left them behind.

Sam entered the hotel through a service entrance, feeling like a fugitive. On learning that Tony's room was next to the one Kidogo had arranged for him, Sam knocked, even though he felt utterly depleted.

"Who's that?" came Tony's sleepy voice.

"It's Sam." He heard nothing from inside and so Sam opened the door to his own room. Finally, Tony appeared, sticking his head out to confirm it was Sam, then unlocked his door and closed it behind him.

"So you decided to come back," Tony joked.

"Can you come in for a minute? I won't keep you long."

Tony followed Sam into his room; while the bed was made and the scarce amenities were in order, there was an unidentifiable scent Sam disliked.

"It appears our proposal about the escrow account has worked," Tony observed. "Well done."

"Well, we'll see tomorrow," Sam said, throwing his bag in a corner and himself on the bed. The springs complained. "Every day here is a new challenge."

They both fell silent. The wall that separated Sam's room from the next suite was paper thin. The groans, shrieks, panting, and screaming suggested some unambitious orgy next door.

"See the hookers out front?" Sam asked.

Tony nodded. "This Kidogo spares no expense. Next time, we book our own rooms."

"There's not going to be a next time."

"I'm worn out," Tony said. "Wake me up or I'll wake you up in the morning and we will make this deal finally happen." He stretched, yawned, headed for the door. "Sorry we had words about Dina. You have every right to do whatever you want in your personal life."

"I know I got in your face too. I don't approve of you going outside your marriage, but you don't have to worry about me. I won't say anything."

"This trip, this deal . . ." Tony struggled for the words. "It's been more than I was prepared to deal with. Think I just wanted to forget where I was for a while."

"It's the sort of place where beliefs go out of the window," Sam said. "I get it."

"Maybe you can plug your ears with some toilet paper." Tony smiled. "Block out the orgy next door."

Sam waited until the door closed and he heard Tony open and then close his own door. After washing, Sam looked at his face in a mirror that was chipped along the bottom edge. It was drained of blood and dripping wet.

"You're *going* to do this," he said to himself. "You're going to get through it. And the only person you'll ever tell is Dina. Only Dina will know the truth."

While the feral sounds of sex drifting over didn't excite him, they did allow his mind a segue to his time spent at the Ritz with Dina. It had been perfect, he thought, like a dream. The memory of her insistent body, her firm mouth, drowned out the chaotic noise.

As the broadcast from next door grew louder, he retreated into his thoughts, his fantasy of seeing her again.

They were lying poolside. It was warm but not hot with a slight breeze. It was not his hotel. It was somewhere else in Palm Springs. Dina wore a blue velour bikini, edged in lacy white material, and dark sunglasses. He leaned over to her and removed them.

Her cobalt-blue eyes captured him, invited him. He took the cocoa sun block and with index and middle finger, scooped some out and smoothed it over her shoulders and her arms. Then gently coated her chest.

Dina took his hand in both of hers and moved his hand.

"Lower," she said.

Sam complied with a smile. His lubricated fingers dipped under the fabric of her top. He squeezed next to her on the chaise lounge, dosing himself with the sweet and salty scent of sunblock. She wrapped her legs around his. She sucked his lower lip.

"Lower," she purred.

A phone rang, and the fantasy dissolved.

Sam grabbed the phone. He knew his raspy voice sounded unwelcoming.

It was the front desk clerk. "Mister Marsh, you asked us to call you."

"Yes, I have a number I want you to call. It's a cell phone, here in Lagos. Please charge it to my room."

The clerk dialed the number. Sam heard it ring.

"You can hang up now," Sam said. He heard a click. Two more rings, and then, "Hello."

"Carlisle, it's Sam Marsh."

"Where are you staying?"

"The Gestec. You know it?"

"I can be there in twenty minutes. We all set?"

"I called him from the airport and he agreed to meet me at this place called the Club Bobo. Is that a real place?"

Carlisle snorted. "Too real. Kind of a low-end singles bar. A real meat market."

"Well, he agreed to meet at ten. Meet me at the left side entrance of the hotel," Sam said. "It's less conspicuous."

"You're getting the hang of this," Carlisle joked and hung up.

After getting ready, Sam eased his door open, mindful not to wake Tony. He hoped that by not looking at anyone, during the elevator ride and then on his way to the side door, he would discourage anyone from looking at him.

Outside a car with blackened windows idled. Sam wasn't sure it was Carlisle until the driver's door opened and the man motioned, aggressively, for Sam to get in.

"I didn't know if it was you," Sam said. "All that tinted glass."

"Nice, isn't it?" Carlisle replied, putting the car in gear. "Cuts down on UV rays. And it's bulletproof." Carlisle pulled away and drove swiftly down the same highway that had led Joseph and Sam to the Gestec.

"Listen carefully," started Carlisle. "I have a lot of questions, and you don't have much time to answer."

"Got it."

"Did the hundred and fifty K we sent hit your escrow account?"

"Yes."

"Have you seen Tony since you arrived?"

"Yes."

"Did you tell him anything about where you're going tonight?"

"He went to bed before I left."

"Good. What did you tell Woods you wanted to talk about?"

"As you instructed, I was vague. I mentioned an oil buying deal. I told him I wanted to talk in person."

"Good. Keep him drinking and feel free to talk about women and sex. If he wants specifics about the oil buying deal, tell him you want to get to know him better. You can say it's oil from a Middle East country but go no farther than that. We've got to make this happen tonight. You'll never see him again. Did Woods say anything about bringing his bodyguard with him?"

"No."

They rode in silence for a while. Carlisle scratched his chin, deep in thought.

"What if his bodyguard shows up?" asked Sam.

"It can still work," Carlisle replied. "You'll just have to think on your feet."

"You think it'll be that easy? You got much experience with bodyguards around here?"

"Oh, I've got one of my own," Carlisle said. He reached behind him and, from the small of his back, brandished a .38.

Carlisle saw the blood drain from Sam's face and put the gun back, chuckling. "Aw, come on, Sam. It's going to be fine. There's not going to be any gun fire."

Sam nervously stared outside. They were approaching another area where soldiers randomly stopped cars.

"I hope you have some bribe money ready," said Sam, mustering some false sense of calm.

Carlisle, not fooled, smiled at him. "Sam, you need to relax. We're just going out for a night with a fellow American."

Carlisle rolled the sedan up to a soldier who waved them to a stop with his flashlight. Carlisle produced his passport and rolled down the window, opening it smartly with thumb and forefinger and shoving it at the soldier, who studied it. He compared it to Carlisle's face, returned it. A flicking flashlight beam indicated they could proceed. Sam had never gone so quickly through a Nigerian checkpoint.

"How the hell did you do that?" Sam asked. "You have CIA stamped in your passport?"

"Only residents and tourists have to bribe these people. They don't want to scare off foreign businessmen working inside their country." Carlisle turned onto a better-lit highway and headed for the downtown section of Lagos, close to Kidogo's office.

"Sam, you've been very cooperative. I appreciate it."

"What choice do I have?"

"You don't, really. But I wanted to thank you for doing what is best for your country. I know you wanted those millions."

"Sure," Sam said glumly.

"And because you're cooperating," Carlisle went on, "and because I personally like you, I have to say something I wish I didn't have to say."

"Don't tell me I have to carry a gun during this thing," Sam said, immediately tense again.

"No, no, nothing like that. I just have to remind you."

The car came to a stop at the side of the highway. Carlisle's voice took on the edge Sam remembered very well from their helicopter flight.

"Sam, this night's going to be simple. You'll be fine. But if you try to screw us, if you reveal anything, even by accident, that fucks up this operation, I will make sure you are arrested and thrown in jail here. And believe me, if I tell the Embassy to ignore you, you'll forget what daylight ever looked like."

Weeks, even days, before, a speech like this would have sent Sam's pulse into overdrive; now he'd grown accustomed to threats from high-level officials. It was just part of the backdrop of Lagos. "What if something goes wrong even though I don't say anything and I still get arrested? You better be there for me. I'm putting my ass on the line."

"Yeah, just like you put your ass on the line when you decided to try and rip off the Nigerian military for thirty-seven million dollars."

"So if Kidogo thinks I've sold him out..."

"Of course we'll protect you, Sam. If for some reason you're arrested, you say nothing to them. You tell them you're innocent and that you demand to talk to the American ambassador. But you'll probably be okay."

Probably. With that, Sam geared up for yet another Nigerian sting, this one in the service of the US government, at the end of which he would *probably* be okay.

CHAPTER 23

Carlisle dropped Sam off at Club Bobo, where expatriates with expense accounts and wealthy locals drank the night away, shoulder to shoulder, and wished him good luck. When he'd made it past the bouncer with thigh-sized arms, Sam's eyes instantly teared from the ozone of cigarette smoke.

Taking a table near the fluorescent bar, Sam ordered a scotch. Ten thirty. He looked around. No Mark Woods.

He spent the next half hour slowly sipping his drink, wondering what would happen it Woods didn't show. As he contemplated life in a Nigerian jail cell, again, a flock of hookers swept by, evaluating him and apparently finding him too miserable to pay for pleasure that night. The distorted tunes thumping from the jukebox made it hard for Sam to think. Not that thinking had done him any good so far.

A sultry waitress asked him if he wanted another drink.

"After my friend arrives."

A few minutes later, Sam recognized Mark Woods at the bar. He didn't recognize the tall Nigerian with ropes of muscle beside Woods, but it was easy enough to figure out who he was.

"Of course. A bodyguard. Why should this be easy?" Sam murmured to himself. He waved across at Woods, who looked around, not seeing him.

Sam stood up, took a few steps forward, and cupped his hands around his mouth. "Mark, over here!"

Woods squinted. He nodded and padded over with his bodyguard behind him.

Sam shook hands with Woods, warily eyeing his bodyguard.

Woods noticed. "Oh, don't mind Jethro."

"Jethro?" Sam couldn't keep the amusement from his voice.

"No, that's just what I call him. He reminds me of a good old boy back in the States who was built like him. Like a brick shithouse."

Woods sat and Jethro joined him. It was Sam's cue to fork over a hundred-dollar bill to the bodyguard.

"Would you mind getting me another scotch and whatever you and Mark want to drink? I have some business I have to discuss with Mark."

Jethro looked at Sam intently, saying nothing.

Please don't punch me, thought Sam.

Woods made the standoff mercifully short. "I'll have the best scotch this dump has, Jethro. Get yourself what you like."

"That's what I will do." Jethro's deep, basso profundo made Sam even more nervous. Sam's previous waitress eyed Jethro, she was annoyed at losing a tip, but made no complaint.

"To what do I owe the pleasure of a free drink?" Woods asked.

"I like to get to know everyone who is doing business here," Sam said, "especially if they're American and in the oil business. I believe you let on as much at Tambo's party."

"We didn't talk much," Woods said.

"I was with Philip Carlisle, another oil guy here."

"And what are you doing?" Woods asked abruptly.

"I'm actually a military subcontractor. We advise governments about the purchase of weapons systems." Sam paused dramatically. "And oil purchasing too."

"Really." It didn't have the impact Sam would've hoped; he had maybe half his companion's attention. The prostitutes who'd earlier brushed by Sam had at least the other half.

In Woods's obsession with sex for sale, Sam saw an opportunity. "You like some of the women in here?"

Woods swiveled his head back to Sam. "I wouldn't mind trying that one over there on for size."

"Tell you what. If you'll let me buy the scotch and, afterward, buy you some female company, I'd like to talk to you about what I do, and what you do. Maybe bring you some more business. We'd need to talk one on one."

"One on one," Woods repeated. "You mean somewhere else?"

"No, right here," Sam corrected. "I'm happy to buy you and Jethro all the scotch you can drink. But if you don't mind, I need the conversation to be between you and me only. Can he be your bodyguard from the bar?"

With perfect timing, Jethro walked up, balancing all three drinks in his large hands.

"Jethro, Mister Marsh here and I have some business to talk. Can you wait over by the bar?"

"But feel free to order whatever you like," Sam quickly added. He clinked glasses with Woods and Jethro before a reply came. "In fact, bring us over a bottle, would you?"

Jethro eyed Sam cautiously, nodded, and while grasping the bills left from Sam's hundred-dollar bill, drained his glass of scotch. He returned to the bar, which seemed to be getting more crowded by the minute.

"He's a good guy," said Woods. "He can tear your head off with one arm but basically, if you don't piss him off, he's a frigging teddy bear."

"Right."

"Who'd you say you work for?"

"Bedford and Clifford. Sorry if I didn't have time to mention it at Tambo's. Oh, man, look at that woman over there."

This time Woods didn't take the bait. His hard stare made Sam feel a rush of blood. "Why haven't I heard of you? How long have you been in business?"

"Twelve years," Sam shot back, letting himself sound angrier than the situation called for. "We're on the web."

Woods pulled out his expensive smartphone just as Jethro arrived with a bottle of scotch. He set it down on the table so hard some would have it called it slamming.

"It's still loading," said Woods.

Jethro leaned down until he was inches away from Sam's face.

"Okay if I have a drink at the bar?"

"Go right ahead," Sam said, eagerly. "You order what you like. When you use that hundred up, come on back and I'll have another one for you."

"Thank you." Jethro lumbered away.

Woods stared at the cell phone screen. Sam poured him more scotch. The website he and Tony had made did not give away their names but suggested they were contractors for the military and industrial development of other countries.

"Hm. Not much on here," Woods observed.

"We don't like our web designer. We're getting another. But speaking of getting some," Sam said, wincing inside for the ridiculous segue, "did you catch up with that amazing-looking woman at Tambo's? Bijou, wasn't it?"

That did it. Woods was content to polish off the majority of scotch, while Sam took sips now and again. Woods delivered a discourse on the exotic locales he'd visited around the world, the equally exotic prostitutes he'd taken to bed. Sam was adept at feigning lurid interest.

"So, anyways," Woods slurred, having just finished his third prostitute story and fifth scotch, "what was the deal you were offering me?" He relied on his plump forearms for balance.

"I want to eventually propose giving you major finder's fees for each private meeting you set up with me with major investors in Kuwait. But before we get into all the details, I just wanted to have a night out, relax, talk a little, you know?"

"Absolutely." Woods rose unsteadily. "I've got to drain the weasel," he announced loudly.

"I'll join you," Sam said, rising with him.

Woods looked over at the bar and Sam followed his eyes.

Jethro seemed a consummate professional, even with a drink fit for Vikings in front of him. He watched them the whole time. His eyes as sharp as the weapon Sam imagined he carried, always ready to defend the precious cargo that was Mark Woods.

"Bathroom," called out Woods.

Jethro got up from his bar stool and moved toward them.

"Is there room for three of us in there?" joked Sam.

Woods looked at him, confused for a moment and then, thinking about it, and seeing Sam smile, Woods guffawed loudly, stupidly. Jethro was at his side, one large hand placed on Woods's shoulder in case he needed assistance walking.

"I got it," Woods assured his guard. "We're hitting the bathroom. Watch our table, will you, buddy?"

Jethro humorlessly nodded and sat in one of their chairs as Sam and Woods wended their way to the small bathrooms in the back of the club. Sam sighed in relief seeing no one else hovered at the urinals. And no legs visible under stall doors.

"Ahhh," Woods sang as he relieved himself.

This is the moment, Sam thought. *Right now. Don't wait. You do it now or you don't get another chance.*

"Ahhh," Sam said loudly in reply. He smacked Woods hard on the back with his left hand while simultaneously dipping his right hand into the right-hand side pocket of Woods's jacket.

"Hey," shouted Woods turning his head partially but unable to look directly at Sam, who slipped the cell phone he had just taken into his own right-hand pocket.

"I got to take a dump," Sam said, loudly, crassly, trying to sound as drunk as Woods. "I'll catch up with you."

Woods finished shaking himself as Sam disappeared into the stall and locked the door. There Sam sat on the toilet, listening for Woods's departure. Sam prayed he was too drunk to check his pocket.

"Well, I better get out of here before you stink up the place," Woods volunteered. Then the door slammed. All was quiet. He wondered how long to wait. It should be long enough that Woods was out of sight and back at his table. But it couldn't be too long, since he might discover his phone was missing.

Sam waited ten more seconds to slip out of the door. He headed past a kitchen through a narrow cement walkway that required him to duck, then through a screen door into the Lagos air and to the back of the club, where the garbage bins were kept.

He froze as a rat scuffled across the toe of his right shoe. Then Sam hustled to the back of the club, where he pulled his own phone.

"Carlisle. It's Sam. I've got it. I'm walking behind the club."

"Nice job," said Carlisle. "Keep walking down the alley and then turn right, then left. Keep walking toward the Sheraton and stay by the curb. I'll swing by and pick it up and you take a cab back to the Gestec. I'll call."

Sam maintained a rapid clip as he followed his directions, not looking back for fear it would bring bad luck. He breathed easier once he spotted Carlisle's car pull up to an open spot. The passenger door flew open.

"I'm impressed." Carlisle smiled, admiring the phone now in his possession as though it were a rare jewel. Then his expression grew serious. "Say goodbye to Woods and get a cab back to the Gestec."

"What if Woods accuses me?"

"Well, let him search you," chuckled Carlisle, who waved Woods's cell phone in the air.

"Call you after I download this stuff?"

Carlisle pulled away while Sam was still closing the door. He darted off into traffic and was gone quickly. Sam trudged back to Club Bobo. Stepping lighter now. He was nearly done with all of it.

But to his consternation, both Woods and Bobo were outside the club looking for him. Sam slowed and Woods walked right up to him, still drunk but now red-faced with anger. Jethro moved in too.

"Where the hell did you go?" demanded Woods.

"I needed to get some air," said Sam. "Don't know about you, but I am *drunk*."

"My cell phone," Woods shouted. "Where's my cell phone?"

"How do I know?"

"Because you took it."

"I did not."

"It's missing."

"It's probably on the floor of the club."

"We checked. It isn't. I'm going to search you."

Sam had had enough. He was done with being manipulated and lied to and living in the worst place imaginable. He was done with Woods and his giant henchman.

"I don't have it," barked Sam. "And I don't appreciate your tone. I think I'll head back to the hotel."

"You're not going anywhere." Woods lurched to stuff both hands in Sam's jacket pockets.

"Get off me, you fat scumbag," Sam yelled and pushed Woods backward.

Woods, already so drunk that walking was a challenge, went down easily.

But Sam never got to see Woods land because Jethro launched a large right fist into Sam's cheek and darkness was upon him.

CHAPTER 24

Dina was making a list of groceries to purchase for her aunt's Paris apartment, grouping them according to where she would purchase them. She marked down the open-air market nearby for fruits and vegetables, a favorite patisserie for deserts and breads. She put down shop addresses for the butcher and the fish market and prepared for a walk in the cloudy, cool air of the neighborhood.

The phone rang, she set down the pencil and cheerily answered.

"Hello, Dina. It's Roni, in Lagos."

"Roni, how are you? Is there news about Sam?" Her words came out in a rush.

He sighed. "Dina, sit down if you're not. There is news and it's bad."

Dina didn't sit, but she did, without realizing it, let the list flutter from her fingertips. She leaned forward on the counter, feeling her hand sweat around the receiver.

"Oh, God, tell me he's not hurt, Roni."

"He's alive but he's in jail, Dina."

"Damn it, Roni! You promised me you'd protect him." She slammed her fist onto the glossy wooden surface. The candelabra and some dishes jumped from the force. "What happened?"

"According to Carlisle, Sam was in an altercation with this American I told you about, who is buying oil for Tambo, this Mark Woods character. Woods's bodyguard knocked him out, and now he's in jail. I don't even know what they're charging him with."

"A fight? I don't believe this. You need to get a hold of this CIA guy and tell him—"

"Dina, Dina, calm down."

"Don't tell me to calm down! I asked you to watch him and you let me down!"

"Watch him? Your idiot boyfriend tried to scam a bunch of scammers. The only way I could *protect him* was to tell Carlisle about him. Did you think Mossad was going to have his back?"

"If you don't intercede on his behalf, I will fly down there myself and do the job you were supposed to."

"Wait a minute!" When Roni's temper kicked in, he matched his cousin's volume. "First, you don't work for us anymore. Second, you knew about the deal and you also knew there was a chance it could go wrong."

"He's in jail in Lagos, Roni. He doesn't have anyone to rely on. Including you."

"Carlisle will get him out. All Sam has to do is keep his mouth shut and Carlisle will work with the US Embassy to secure his release."

"What if they torture him? What if they force him to confess to whatever they want him to confess to?"

"I'll call you after I get more information. And remember, it was up to you to talk Sam out of going back to Lagos. So just keep that in perspective."

"So now this is all my fault?"

"Call you later!" Roni promised, just before the line went dead.

Sam woke to a metallic taste in his mouth and an ache on the right side of his head. One dingy window filtered light into the concrete room. He marveled that he'd been able to sleep on the thin stained mattress.

Sam had no idea how much time had passed since Jethro had sent him into unconsciousness. He touched the side of his face and winced. There was no mirror. Just as well, he thought.

A toilet bowl, sink and metal bed represented the room's furnishings. He checked his pockets: watch, wallet, passport, cell phone—gone. He threw some water on his face, but there was no towel. He sprinkled water on his wrists and the back of his neck.

The hunger pangs in his stomach and the coolness of the water beads on his head helped him focus. He must have been arrested for fighting with Mark Woods. Woods had accused him of stealing his cell phone but he had no proof. He couldn't have seen Sam hand the phone over to Carlisle.

But who could he call? Carlisle had told him to keep his mouth shut, as long as he did so, no matter what went wrong, he would be bailed out, eventually. That's what Carlisle said.

But was it true? Or was it what he'd been told so he would cooperate? Perhaps it would make more sense to call Roni. But no, he needed the help of his own government. He had to trust that Carlisle would honor his pledge. But when and how would Sam be able to contact him?

There was no one he could hear and the door to his cell was solid, without a window. Would they even hear him if he yelled? As though to test it out, he shouted, "Hey! I need some help!" He repeated the loud plea until his throat grew sore.

"Wait until my lawyer in Los Angeles hears about this," Sam murmured to himself before lying down again on the thin mattress.

It was only then that he noticed his shoes were still on. Unlike their counterparts in the United States, authorities here did not confiscate shoelaces. His belt, too, was still on. *They don't care if I commit suicide. Maybe they see it as an easy way out of dealing with me.*

Accepting that Carlisle really was with the CIA, as he claimed, was Sam's only hope. If he kept his mouth closed and refused to talk to anyone in the Nigerian government, Carlisle would back him up Sam had to believe it was true. But what about Kidogo?

Nigeria was utterly corrupt, but someone inside the military or the bank or the government would have to be working with Sam for the scam to work. How could Kidogo pass the blame?

Unless it was all a scam on the part of Kidogo to start with, as Sam and Tony and Pierre, too had pondered in Switzerland. If they never had intentions of releasing $37 million, if it was all a setup to see how much money they could get out of Sam and Tony's investors, they could easily claim the scam started with Sam and his partners. And it was doubtful Kidogo would ever be punished for trying to work a scam on some gullible Americans.

After what felt like hours of fruitlessly contemplating his dilemma, he heard voices outside his cell. A key was inserted into the lock of the door and turned.

Sam was instantly on his feet, waiting. The door creaked open. A Nigerian guard with a club entered, followed by a second carrying a tray. Before even looking at the food, Sam demanded, "I want to make a phone call right now. I want you—"

But the words died in his throat. As the guard with the tray set it down, Sam saw Tony, his hands behind his back, pushed forward into the cell by a third guard. Tony fell on the floor. Sam moved forward to help but one guard pushed his club up against Sam's chest, pinning him up against the bed frame.

Tony's handcuffs were removed. The three guards withdrew. Sam again demanded the right to make a phone call. In answer, the cell door was slammed, and locked.

Sam helped Tony up and then laid him on the lower bunk. Except for Tony's ripped shirt and his wrists reddened from handcuffs, Sam saw no marks on his friend.

"Can you talk, Tony?" Sam asked, holding back a score of questions.

Tony opened his mouth, but no sound emerged.

"What?"

Sam made out the shape of the word *water* on his friend's lips.

Seeing that the tray contained two bowls of gray-brown indeterminate soup but no cups, Sam put Tony's arm around his shoulders and walked him to the sink, where Sam held him up while Tony cupped water into his mouth from the running tap. Then Sam helped lower him back to the bunk.

"Tony, I've got so many things to ask you," Sam said, "and to tell you."

"Why weren't you there? At the meeting with Kidogo?"

"First did they beat you?"

"They knocked me around a bit. Said you were a spy and I was too."

Sam winced. He sat on the edge of the lower bunk, wondering how much to tell Tony. Under the circumstances, it seemed better to rely on Carlisle than share too much information with Tony. Only one of them could help them get out, and that person wasn't in the cell.

"All right, Tony, tell me about the morning meeting."

"Kidogo was furious. He had a laptop and demanded I log into our escrow account. I did, and when I got there, the three hundred thousand was gone."

Sam felt his blood pound in his ears. "Gone?"

"Yes, the account was zeroed out. We were cleaned out and Kidogo accused me, us, of trying to scam them."

Sam paced the small cell, his mind whirring. Tony had to hold onto a metal bedpost to remain upright on the little mattress.

"Sam, you don't think Pierre screwed us, do you?"

Sam stopped pacing; despite Tony's battered state, he couldn't keep his anger from rising. "Tony, don't you get it? This whole thing has been a scam on the part of Kidogo. There isn't any thirty-seven million. They just wanted to get our money and now they have it."

Tony shook his head. "It—it doesn't make sense, does it, Sam? We set up an escrow account that only we can access, and then you're arrested and the money is gone."

"What are you suggesting?"

"I didn't take that money." With this indirect accusation, Tony's voice gained strength.

"Well, I didn't take it either, pal," Sam shot back.

"Then, it's your friend Pierre."

"Pierre did not rip us off!"

"The three of us were the only ones who had access to the account."

"There's no way it was him. He would never do that." Sam paced again, keeping his laps tight in this constricted space.

"And what's all this about you being a spy?" Tony now sat on the edge of the bed, eyes burning. "Kidogo said you stole the cell phone of some oil guy, Mark Woods."

"I went out drinking with Woods and the next thing I know," Sam insisted, "he's accusing me of stealing his damn phone. He searches me, I push him away, his bodyguard knocks me out. End of story."

"Then why is Kidogo saying you were spying for the CIA?"

"I didn't steal his phone." Sam flung his arms around like a fire-and-brimstone preacher at the pulpit. "And how do you get that I'm a spy? It's Kidogo, you idiot. How can you possibly believe the crap he tells you? I'm a spy—ripping off a cell phone from some oil-buying jerk from the States? Does that make sense to you?"

Tony hung his head. Joining his friend on the bed, Sam placed a gentle arm around his shoulder, but Tony shrugged it off.

"Are you hungry?" Sam asked. "I think they left us some stuff that looks a lot like dog food." Sam smiled but Tony's bitter expression did not change.

It was Tony's turn to pace. "At the very least," he said, "even if they don't prove charges of spying, they've got us supposedly trying to scam the government. Think they're going to believe anything we say if Kidogo's telling them otherwise?"

Sam practiced his tone in his head—he needed to sound calm, confident, convincing. "Kidogo is playing both sides, Tony. He scams people for a living. He has no credibility."

"No credibility! Are you mad! Can you possibly be so stupid?" Tony's eyes bulged. "If you're a spy, and you haven't told me, you're the stupidest spy on record."

Sam now stood up and went face to face with Tony. "You seem awfully willing to believe anything the Nigerians tell you. To you, Pierre and I are just out for ourselves. But anything your good friend Kidogo tells you—"

"My *good friend Kidogo* had his thugs rough me up," Tony yelled. "Then he tells me that this Woods bastard had information on his cell phone that implicates him in an oil stockpiling scheme. If you handed that phone to someone, then you've just been involved in spying against the Nigerian government. That's an offense they execute people for, here, Sam. Tambo has been embarrassed. Woods is the focal point of an international scandal. Kidogo said that our State Department and the CIA have both demanded an explanation about oil stockpiling and oil tanker piracy. And the Israelis are furious too! They claim their oil was stolen by this scam. And no matter what you have actually done, you and I are going to be blamed for it! Do you get the full picture now, mate? We're doomed. We're the scapegoats."

CHAPTER 25

There were no signs of life in Woods's room, and the houseboy hadn't been yet. The main thing that greeted Kidogo was an overpowering stench of tobacco. The once elegant room was now buried under unemptied ashtrays, unrinsed whisky goblets, and unwashed clothes. Wandering into the bathroom, Kidogo discovered puddles of gray dirty water.

He walked through an open doorway to the room that Woods used as his office. More of the same: papers everywhere, wastebasket overflowing. But added to this mayhem was Woods himself, sitting there in his standard uniform of T-shirt and boxer shorts, drinking from a nearly empty bottle of Chivas Regal as he listened to country music and stared at pictures of Texas on his computer screen.

Woods turned slowly to see Kidogo, who was approaching.

"Bill, I guess you heard about what happened."

"Yes. I am sorry about it, Mark."

"You going over to talk to Tambo?"

"I have a meeting with him in a few minutes."

Woods lowered the volume on the drawling, sad-sounding song emanating from the computer's speakers. "Bill, do me a favor. I can tell he's really mad at me. But I had no idea who that Sam guy was or what he wanted. He stole my goddamn phone out of my jacket while I was taking a piss. I didn't drop it. He stole it."

"I believe you, Mark. You did good work for us. I will remind Ambassador Tambo of that fact when I talk with him."

"I sure would appreciate that," said Woods, pathetically.

Kidogo looked around the office.

"Why hasn't the staff cleaned up here?" asked Kidogo.

"I sent them away. They tried three times, but I was too depressed to have anybody here," Woods explained.

Happy to be out of the disheveled office, Kidogo returned to the main residence. A bodyguard met him on the second floor and led him wordlessly to Tambo's palatial bedroom, the size of a ballroom in a small hotel.

A first-time visitor might have chuckled at Tambo's green silk pajamas with his initials sewn into the lapels, but Kidogo stood at attention in the doorway, waiting to be noticed. Between his computer and cell phone, Tambo's attention was consumed.

Finally, after a few minutes, Tambo looked up, Kidogo motioned him to come closer. He clicked off his cell phone and cursed loudly, throwing it down on the bed, which was as big as two king-sized beds pushed together. He turned his iciest stare on Kidogo.

"Do you have the slightest idea how humiliating this all is for me?" he began. "My position in the government is jeopardized because you allowed some greedy American . . ." Tambo suddenly was at a loss for words. "What is he? Is he a military subcontractor? A spy? Is he a criminal?"

"Ambassador." Kidogo bowed his head and prepared the same low, shame-filled voice he always used when something went sideways. "This Sam Marsh, along with his partner, Tony Dobbs, approached me as military subcontractors, who wanted to launder money through our Central Bank. I agreed to help them, with the intention of turning the money over to you."

"What does this have to do with Woods?" Tambo's fury was softened only by his confusion. "Did this Marsh man take Woods's cell phone and release information to embarrass me?"

"It's a very complex situation."

"I don't care!" thundered Tambo. "I am a complex man! I can understand anything you can tell me."

"Of course, sir. I only meant we don't have all the facts yet. We think Marsh may be a spy for the US, trying to humiliate us and stop the oil purchases. He most likely offered that money to be laundered so that he could get close to me and—"

"And you invited him to my home, to my recent party, didn't you?"

"Yes, Ambassador. But as I say, he had already sent money to an account for laundering, and I thought that was all it was. I apologize humbly, sir."

Tambo slammed his hand into the carved mahogany side table, making Kidogo leap back.

"Damn it, Kidogo. You have never made an error like this. And now look at the Internet." Tambo turned the screen of his laptop so that Kidogo could view it as well. The website for the *Washington Post*. "Look! Page five. 'US Oil Man Accused of Oil Fixing in Nigeria.' Regardless of how Marsh got that phone away from that idiot Woods, he turned it over to someone working for the CIA, the Energy Department, someone in Washington. And this is their way of threatening me. They're saying, "stop or we'll print more.""

"I know," Kidogo said simply. "It is terrible. I humbly apologize. There is only one bit of good to come of all this treachery from America."

"Something happened that is good?" Tambo appeared puzzled.

"Yes, Ambassador." Kidogo took the opportunity to sit down on the bed so he was level with Tambo. "You recall that Marsh claimed he wanted to launder money. I recommended a bank that we do business with, Union Bank of Switzerland. When I learned of his deceit, I immediately contacted one of our people, who hacked into UBS's computer network. He withdrew the money, and I have transferred it over to your regular account."

With his eyes growing wide, Tambo typed furiously on his laptop. He seemed to be waiting for something. He looked at Kidogo again.

"You are saying you took all of Marsh's money and sent it to me?"

"Of course, Ambassador. We have had cases like this before. I automatically send it to you."

Tambo typed in a password, keeping his eyes on Kidogo as he did. Kidogo averted his own eyes; he seemed to find something on the far side of the room fascinating.

"Two hundred thousand dollars!" said Tambo loudly. "Ha! That ought to teach him to mess with us."

"Yes, Ambassador."

Tambo turned his attention back to the screen with the *Washington Post* story, "You did well about the money but this, this must go away. Normally, I would reward you for the money. But this remains a terrible matter. One you must straighten out."

"Of course. I must mention one more thing. Sam Marsh was attempting to not only launder money but help three of our officials steal money from the Central Bank and leave our country permanently."

Tambo looked gravely at his aide. "That is not acceptable. They must be punished. Who are these men? Do you know?"

"Yes, Ambassador. They will lie and protest their innocence, and claim I was working with them. But it is not true."

"Of course not. Tell me who they are, and I will have the military arrest them."
Kidogo sighed.

"Why do you hesitate?" Tambo demanded.

"It will cause you pain to hear their identities."

"Tell me at once!"

"Prince Adedeji, Colonel Nwapa."

"Yes? And?"

"Your brother, Sawa."

A feral, ugly scream of anger forced Kidogo to jump back in his chair. Tambo leaped from the bed and stormed about the room in bare feet, shouting, cursing the day his brother had been born. He griped the walls, only letting go to throw a punch. His fist hitting the wall with a loud thump.

Kidogo sat, letting Tambo spend his rage. He flopped onto the bed and hung his head in his hands. When he finally raised his head again, there was a redness in his eyes that had not been there before.

"Do you understand how painful my life is, Kidogo? For every victory, there is a horrible defeat. I make millions of dollars trading oil but now, I must put my own brother in prison for life. It's unfair."

"Yes, Ambassador, it is unfair."

Tambo picked up his phone. "Kidogo, I will take care of the traitors. Your job is to get a confession out of Marsh, proving to the world he is a spy."

Tony and Sam were eating bowls of unidentifiable stew with their rusty spoons when the key sounded in the lock. As they attempted to wolf down what was left, a guard yanked Tony aside.

"Where's he going?" yelled Sam.

The guards ignored him.

When the cell door had slammed shut, Sam stood at it shouting, "We're US citizens. Don't forget it!"

Kidogo didn't even look at Sam after the two guards deposited him in the same chair Tony had previously occupied. Whatever thuggish violence they'd held back with Tony, they unleashed full force on Sam. They threw him into the chair so hard he tumbled out, putting his hands out so he wouldn't fall on his face. Before he had recovered from the fall the guards were kicking him in the ribs and back, knocking the air from his lungs. With both arms held behind his back, the guards lifted him into the chair. They hit their target.

On the other side of the table, Kidogo looked into Sam's bloated, reddened face. Blood trickled from his left nostril.

"Wipe your face. It's bleeding."

"Where?" asked Sam.

"Your nose."

"What? I didn't hear you."

Annoyed, Kidogo leaned in closer to yell in his face. "Your nose!"

As soon as Kidogo got close, Sam spit with all the air he had left in his lungs, spraying blood-stained saliva into the man's face. The two guards lunged toward Sam but Kidogo held up his hand. Deliberately he took a handkerchief out of his breast pocket, carefully wiped his face, folded the handkerchief; put it away, before rearing back and slapping Sam's face with all his might.

The blow threw back Sam's head. Still, when he had recovered, he fixed Kidogo with a winning smile.

"What are you smiling at? You're a spy and we will either execute you or merely keep you in jail for the rest of your life, where we will dole out this kind of treatment every day."

"Oh, really?" Sam said in the most offhand way he could manage, considering the pain coursing through his body.

"Your money is gone. Your friend is ready to admit that you are a spy, in order to get himself free. If you tell us yourself, we will go easier on you. Do you understand?"

Sam continued to stare at him, neither dropping his smile nor wiping away the blood that dripped down his lips and onto his chin.

"We are giving you the opportunity to confess and we will ask the court to show mercy. Who was your contact regarding getting Mark Woods's phone away from him?"

Sam looked around the room. "I don't see any tape recorders. How are you going to take down my confession?"

"It will be a written confession."

"And if I confess, you'll let Tony go."

"Yes, Sam."

"And you will give me a lesser sentence. You promise."

"You have my word," said Kidogo, his voice instantly comforting.

"All right," Sam said, the smile leaving his face. "Leave your guards outside. There's something I have to tell you, one on one." Sam continued in an attempt to soothe Kidogo's hesitation. "It's embarrassing. Have one of them get the paper and pen and the other wait outside. Please."

It seemed to Kidogo that Sam's will was broken. He gave the orders, and the door clanked shut behind his guards. Sam put his head down, breathed deeply a few times, and looked at Kidogo with unmistakable hatred in his eyes.

"Kidogo, listen to me very carefully. I am an American citizen. Not a Nigerian, who you bribe or beat or have one of your soldiers threaten with a rifle in the chest, I'm a US citizen. My government stands up for me. I'm sure you don't understand what that's like. And more than that, I have information about your attempts to steal money from the Central Bank and help the brother of Glanville Tambo escape this hell-hole of a country. You know what else I've got? I've got someone to work for our side in your country. I don't know who it is, and you don't know who it is. But whoever it is, Kidogo, they've already ended your pathetic oil-buying scheme and ruined the names of Mark Woods and Glanville Tambo. I'm not sure who Mark Woods is working for in the US, but I'm guessing they're going to be on the phone to Tambo pretty goddamn soon. As soon as they've read the papers."

"I have told Glanville of your attempts to launder money."

"Oh, you mean the three hundred thousand you stole from us?" interrupted Sam. "The three hundred thousand you forced us to come up with? You want to see the email on that? I mean, this gets better and better, Kidogo. You beat up and falsely imprison a US citizen helping you rip off your own country. And you're so goddamn greedy that you try to help Sawa Tambo. What do you think Glanville will think of that? And Woods is obviously working with someone as well as Glanville. Do you think my government wants me on trial here, talking about Woods's involvement with this oil scheme?"

"What do you know about Woods and your country?" Kidogo asked but Sam was going full throttle.

"Listen, Kidogo. Don't talk. Just listen. Because you're not as intelligent as you think you are, and you've got a lot of catching up to do. My government wants this whole oil buying scheme to go away, and I've got a feeling you don't want me giving details to the rest of your government of your attempts to screw them over."

"You're guilty of money laundering *and*..."

"I'm not guilty of shit. You touch another hair on my head, and the phone calls I audiotaped of our plans to free the prince, the colonel, and the hated brother of your boss will be sent to everyone above Tambo in this pathetic country. And we'll see which cell *you're* in."

The door opened, and both guards entered, one with paper and pen in hand.

With his clenched jaw, Kidogo couldn't have spoken if he'd wanted to.

Finally Sam wiped the blood from his face. "Would you like me to write all that down for you?"

CHAPTER 26

In their booth at the small restaurant in Lagos, Philip Carlisle and Roni Kahan compared newspapers. All of them contained news of Sam and Tony's arrest.

"Why are they in jail? And why are they accusing them of spying?" Roni's forehead was wrinkled with worry.

"It's a case of bad timing," Carlisle mumbled. "If Marsh had said goodnight to Woods and left the bar, before Woods discovered his phone was missing, we might have got away with it. The whole idea was to get Woods drunk and make him believe he lost the phone himself."

"You got Marsh to steal his phone." Roni's eyes bored into him.

Carlisle poured cream into his coffee and stirred it, taking a gulp and not answering.

"I told you, I wanted him safe," Roni growled. "Now you've got him and his partner in jail, on spying charges."

"Comes with the territory" Carlisle responded "as you and I both know."

"Think this is a joke? To put a guy's life at stake for some bizarre operation? You promised me you would not put him in jeopardy. And now—"

Carlisle grabbed the edge of the small wooden table. Then, with a jolt, he shoved the table into Roni's midsection. "I got authorization for this, and it *should* have worked. It was the plan with the least risk to Marsh. I at least got the phone, but now the world knows some of what's going on here. Your government included."

"Don't pretend you were doing this for my country," Roni said.

"No, it benefits you and me and a lot of other countries not to have Tambo screwing with the oil market."

"And now you'll sacrifice Marsh and his friend?"

"Sacrifice them? Listen, Roni, do I need to remind you these stupid bastards came here to help others rip off the Central Bank? And I didn't see you trying to help. Tambo rips off your oil tanker and you get the agency to do your dirty work. And then you complain because Americans got caught."

"Screw you," Roni hissed. The table screeched as he returned the earlier assault. The sound, moreover the threat of it drawing attention caused both men to snap out of it. To breathe and calm down.

"As far as volunteers, I didn't see you or anyone on your side put themselves at risk, either." After he finished the roll on his plate, Roni plucked crumbs from his dish with one moistened finger.

"You're right," Carlisle agreed. "I still have to work here. And so do you. The idea is to not risk blowing one's cover if one can avoid it."

"And now what happens to them? Sam Marsh has your name and mine. You think he will remain silent in some prison here?"

Carlisle mopped sweat from his cheeks and temples with a paper napkin. "No we'll get him out."

"Oh? You have a plan for that?"

"Roni, you were a lot more fun at our previous meetings. Obviously I have a plan. It involves both of us, both of our employers, and both of our countries."

"What is it?"

"Look at the paper. Who do they mention in the story?"

"Sam Marsh. Tony Dobbs. Mark Woods."

"Right. Two guys accused of spying, one for having stolen the cell phone of an American oil buyer working for Tambo. The way to get our guys out is to concentrate on Woods, make him even more of an embarrassment to both Tambo and to whoever he works with in the US."

"We've already stopped Woods and Tambo's oil buying."

"Now both of us need to put more pressure on Tambo. What can you do?"

Roni contemplated for a few moments. "Okay, I can get Jerusalem to condemn the Lagos government and accuse them of stealing our oil. Even if we don't get the oil back, we can demand that Woods gets deported and your guys get released."

"Or else?"

"Or else we cut back our oil buying and freeze all new construction contracts."

"And I'll get the agency to use the State Department to lean on Lagos. They can threaten to get other countries to cut back on Nigerian oil buying, unless Woods is deported and Sam and Tony released."

Roni reached across the table and shook Carlisle's hand.

Sawa Tambo's prison location was significantly bigger and more secure than the jail that held Sam and Tony. For security reasons, Sawa has been given his own cell, where he now sat alone. The prison wanted to ensure nothing happened to the man before his brother saw him.

The jailer assigned to walk back and check on Sawa Tambo periodically snuck in his cell ensuring no one was looking. He smuggled packs of cigarettes and some chocolate, for which Sawa thanked him.

During another pass by Sawa's cell, the guard stopped outside it and looked around. Though the other prisoners could surely see him, the jailer spoke out of the side of his mouth toward Sawa.

"I'm sorry about all this," the jailer said. "If I was Glanville's brother, I would have expected more from him. It's wrong for a brother to ever turn against brother."

"Thank you," Sawa said humbly. "I served the country well, but I let greed get the better of me."

"I overheard that Glanville is coming to visit you soon, I just wanted you to know."

Sawa kicked the iron bars in front of him, making them clang. "Unbelievable. He has me arrested and then comes to the prison to laugh at me."

"Sawa, many of us here are with you. But we are helpless to do anything against the government."

"Yes. But thank you anyway."

True to the guard's warning, in less than an hour a retinue of security personnel and other officials surrounded Glanville Tambo as he strode toward the cell that housed his brother.

Seeing him approach, Sawa wandered off to the deepest corner of his cell. He sat on the floor and hugged his legs, curling up into a tight ball in a dark corner. Thinking Sawa was sleeping; a guard bashed the cell bars with a thick baton to rouse him.

"Stand up! Ambassador Tambo is here to see you!" the guard shouted, as his colleague opened the cell with his keys and swung the door open for Glanville, who waved them off and took three strides into the cell.

The door was locked behind Glanville, but one guard remained, standing a few feet away to give some privacy. The others retreated to their posts.

"Why don't you greet me, brother?" Glanville asked.

Sawa turned from the corner and looked upon Glanville's face, devoid of emotion.

"Are you my brother?" asked Sawa, disgusted. "Are you the boy I grew up with, who came from the same mother? You've turned your back on me your whole life and now, when I try to do what you have done, you have me thrown in jail."

Glanville Tambo looked around the cell for a place to sit but, seeing no furnishings that met his approval, walked a few feet closer to the curled-up figure in the corner. He propped himself against the wall.

"You're confused, brother. I've improved the quality of life for my country by selling our oil for a good market price. You are a mere functionary in the military. And now, you've been caught as a thief, trying to steal from our Central Bank."

Sawa jumped to his feet coming face to face with his brother.

"You don't care about what happens to me so I won't beg you for help. But I also won't stand here in this prison and listen to your lies and agree with you. You've spent a whole career, Glanville, enriching yourself, and a few of your friends with money you steal from the deals you make. Don't pretend you don't."

"Stand back," Glanville ordered. "You're filthy and you reek."

"It disturbs you, doesn't it, to think of what you've done to your own family? Why did you even come to see me? To wipe away your guilt?"

"Guilt?" Glanville laughed. He continued chuckling as he settled for the edge of the uncomfortable bed. "You are the one who's guilty. Tell me, how does it feel to not only betray your country but to use Americans to help you do so?"

"Do you know why I tried?" asked Sawa. "Do you have any idea?"

Glanville studied his brother for a few moments. "I suppose you'll tell me."

"You already know, don't you?"

"Already know that you don't have the makings of a man?"

"I'm as much a man as you, Glanville. Your position brings you power and money. Most of the people live horrible lives, and what benefit do we see from the sales of Delta oil? Virtually none, the corporations and people like you are the ones who benefit. I served the military for decades. I lived on little money. You never offered to help me. I asked you once for a loan and you turned me down. That is the person you are."

Sawa sat back on the cold floor, his knees pulled up to his chin to support his weary head.

"I made something of myself," Glanville insisted. "You, you were always weak. You wanted me to help you get a job, get you tickets to football matches, get you girls. You're incapable of doing anything on your own. I'm not responsible for you, Sawa. When you tried to steal money from the Central Bank, you did it because you are weak."

"I did it because I am poor!" shouted Sawa. His outburst brought over the guard, whom Glanville waved away.

"Millions are poor," said Glanville. "They don't resort to the behavior you have."

"We're not beggars in the street," Sawa shot back. "The prince runs the airport authority."

"*Ran* the airport authority."

"And Nwapa. Like me, he served the military honorably. And what do we get for our troubles? We have delays in getting our pay. And we cannot afford to live on our pensions. You steal millions of dollars and live in luxury and we have to have our children work to help support us. How can you defend that? How can you possibly believe that's right?"

"It's neither right nor wrong, little brother," Glanville said. "It is the way of the world. You made a bad decision and now you have to pay for it. I cannot change that. If you will sign a document, though, telling us that the Americans you worked with are spies, I can make sure they shorten your sentence. Somewhat."

Glanville took his brother's silence as deliberation over what to do.

"Consider it. It might be your one escape from dying in here."

"Spies," Sawa repeated. "Are the Americans spies? Let me ask you something. Isn't Kidogo a spy? Everyone knows he's always looking to make his cut, whether or not it is legal. When he was trying to get the money out of the Central Bank, wasn't he a spy? Wasn't he as guilty as I am? Are you going to put him in jail, too?"

"I was waiting for you to condemn Kidogo." Glanville sighed. He stood at the bars, scanning the other cells within his sight. He cut the image of a well-to-do tourist gawking at the exotic architecture of another land. "Kidogo has served me very well over the years. If he takes money for himself, it's because he deserves it."

Sawa stood behind his brother, now whispering hoarsely into his ear. "Tell the truth, brother. You never wanted me to succeed. You wanted to have much more money, more power, and higher status. And you did. You could have let me leave Nigeria. You could have let me find a new life in America and bring my wife and son. But it was not enough that you win. I had to lose."

Inches from his brother's face now, Glanville shook his head, and a sad gaze replaced the coldness.

"It doesn't bring me any pleasure to tell you this, Sawa," Glanville stated. "But Kidogo was working for me the whole time. The transfer of the money never would have taken place."

"Yes, it would have. And I would have been out of your life, forever. You won't admit that Kidogo will work for anyone who can make him money. He's loyal to you out of fear, but greed will always attract him to others. And you cannot admit, brother, that you want to punish yourself not me for what you have done to our country."

At the bars again, Glanville shouted, "Guard! Guard!" One quickly appeared, letting him out. "You will be here a long time," Glanville Tambo said, leaving the confines of the cell, stepping outside, hearing the clanging of the cell door but not looking at his brother.

"And you'll spend the rest of your life trying to forget what you've done to me and to our country" Sawa Tambo replied.

CHAPTER 27

Glanville Tambo felt dark and surly after visiting his brother in prison. His assistant's wide-eyed, stuttering report of the negative stories being circulated about his brother did not improve his mood.

"There are many requests for comments from newspapers, TV, and radio from all over, Ambassador. The president also requests another meeting with you tomorrow." The assistant, only twenty-five, timidly produced a slip of paper with typed words. "This is a list of everyone requesting interviews."

Tambo ripped the list from his assistant's hands. "I am not talking with anyone. There is enough trouble without trying to explain all this to any of them."

"And what shall I tell the president, sir?"

Tambo puffed himself up.

"I will call the president's office myself to make an appointment to see him, but first, I want that bastard Woods in my office. Right now."

"Uh, yes, Ambassador. I will get him. It might take a few minutes."

"I don't have a few minutes. I want him in my office right away. While he's here, pack his bags. When he leaves here, his next stop is Kuwait."

"I will wake him up, sir."

Tambo checked his watch. "He's sleeping? It's the middle of the afternoon! That's it!"

Tambo stormed out, shouting back at his assistant to follow. The assistant had to double-time his movements to keep up. Tambo stormed across the patio, along the way kicking a flamingo that dared cross his path; the animal stumbled forward but quickly righted itself, then hopped from Tambo's presence. His assistant wished he could do likewise.

"Sleeping in the middle of the day after creating this disaster!" Tambo grumbled as he stormed down the hallway of the guest residence toward Woods's room.

"I believe he has been drinking a lot, Ambassador, he's depressed."

"I'll give him a reason to be depressed." Finding the door locked, Tambo pounded on it loud enough to wake the dead, or the drunk and lazy.

"Open this door! Woods!"

After a few moments, Tambo heard signs of life from the other side. And a faint reply that did not sound as intimidated as it should have. "I'm coming, I'm coming."

The door opened and Woods stared at Tambo. His T-shirt and boxer shorts were unwashed and wrinkled.

Tambo shoved past him, followed by the assistant. A scent lingered in the room of cigarettes and sweat-stained clothing. Tambo turned to his assistant.

"Start packing all his belongings."

"Do you want me to launder his clothes or…"

"Pack!"

As the assistant hopped to his orders, Woods, more alert now but otherwise expressionless, studied Tambo's furious face.

"I'm sorry about what happened, Glanville, but I'm telling you, that son-of-a-bitch has got to be CIA. If I were you…"

"If I were you," thundered Tambo, "I would keep my mouth shut before I wound up in prison. You are a drunken idiot. I would never have used you to buy oil but Laney insisted on it. And now, I never want to see you again. You are going back to Kuwait on the first available flight."

"Listen, I understand you're mad. But I did not lose that phone. It was stolen from me. It could have happened to anyone."

"You Americans." Disgust surpassed Tambo's anger. He watched his assistant scurry around, jamming clothes, rumpled and worn, into the two suitcases Woods had brought. "I could have done this better without Laney, and certainly without you."

"Listen, Glanville, give me another chance. I'll stop drinking."

"I don't want to see you ever again, Woods. You are pathetic."

"Glanville, the thing is, I'm not certain what'll happen with Laney and the papers and all this. And if I go back to Kuwait, well, they have an extradition treaty with the US. I think I would be safer staying here for a while."

"Nothing would make me happier than to read that both you and Laney are in jail in your own country." Tambo turned to his assistant. "Arrange for him to be taken to the airport and put on the first flight to Kuwait. Do not leave his side until he is gone."

"Now wait a minute. I made a bunch of money for you, didn't I? Come on."

Back in his office, Tambo placed a call. He had to leave a voicemail message: "George, it's Glanville. I must talk with you immediately. Call me back."

He hung up and checked his watch and paced and paced until he could no longer stomach the waiting. He redialed the number.

"Laney," said the voice on the other end.

"George, it's Glanville. I need to talk to"

"Glanville, listen, I saw you just called but I have another problem to attend to. I'm going to have to call you…"

"No," Tambo interrupted. "There is nothing you have to do more important than listen. I am sending Mark Woods back to Kuwait and I am trying to convince the president not to fire me."

"What are you talking about?" Laney's volume now matched Tambo's—no small feat. "You're sending Woods back? Are you insane? If he's extradited, if he talks, it's the end of me, and the end of you. Get him back. Did he leave yet?"

Tambo sat at his desk, put his feet up, and leaned back in his chair. "You don't order me around anymore, George. Your CIA has ruined this operation, and now we are both in jeopardy."

"I read in the papers about the two Americans who were trying to scam your government. They weren't CIA."

"You think we are idiots? Woods has his cell phone stolen and someone talks about his contacts to the worldwide media. Who else would be behind it?"

"This is as bad for me as it is for you," Laney insisted. "No one has contacted me yet but, goddamn it, Glanville, my number is in his phone, and yours."

"That's what I expected." Tambo hauled himself to his feet. His fists weighed on his wrists like balls of iron; they ached to punch holes in the wall. "It's okay for your country to ruin my reputation as long as you don't get mentioned. I warn you, Laney, you had better protect me or you will need protection yourself."

"Protect you?" Laney sounded flustered by the very idea of it.

For the first time, Glanville Tambo hung up on George Laney.

Tony and Sam sat in the interrogation room in Lagos where each was individually questioned. Sam still stung from his run-in with Kidogo. Still, he was glad he'd stood up to the man, answering his threat with one of his own.

Sam had told Tony of his response to Kidogo's intimidation. He wanted Tony to know he had not turned over any information. Not to mention that a part of him enjoyed showing Tony he could withstand the pressure in a way Tony could not or at least did not. Though a guard waited outside the closed door, they were alone for the moment.

Sam broke a long silence. "It'll be all right."

"How do you know? You can't guarantee what will happen next."

Despite his general exhaustion and the veil of grime on him, Sam placed his hands behind his head as he leaned back in his uncomfortable metal chair, making a comical picture of a relaxed prisoner.

"For all you know," said Tony hesitantly, "they'll transfer us to a larger prison, which I for one do not want."

"I don't think so." Sam sounded almost cheerful.

"What aren't you telling me?"

"I told you, you just don't get the bigger picture. We're an embarrassment to this government. They can't afford to keep us around here. If I'm right, the next person through that door is here to help us."

"I think you're hiding something." His accusation wiped the confidence off Sam's face. The peaceful prisoner vanished.

"Need I remind you this whole Lagos deal resulted from you hounding me for help? If we lose the money…"

"It's already lost."

"If we've lost that money, screwed up our credit, are questioned by the IRS, or go to jail back in the US, understand it all started with you. So don't question my loyalty."

"You did this with me, Sam. You will not make me the scapegoat."

The room, now claustrophobic with tension, fell silent again. It was a few minutes more before the door opened and a white man with graying hair and an attaché case made his way into the room, studying papers.

He took his time meeting Sam's and Tony's eyes.

"Gentlemen, my name is Arthur Rebenack and I'm the American vice consul here in Lagos. I'm happy to report that after you sign a few papers, I'll be able to take you out of here."

Sam shot Tony an I-told-you-so look as he shook Rebenack's hand. "Thank you very much, sir. Sam Marsh."

"Tony Dobbs." But the handshake Tony offered lacked enthusiasm.

Rebenack pulled out papers and an expensive-looking pen for signing them.

"Yes, right there, please. And there. Read it if you wish, but the long and short of it is you are being released without charges against you and, in exchange, you promise to press no charges through the American Consulate against anyone here, and you further agree you are leaving the country within the next twenty-four hours."

"Trust me," said Sam, "we're happy to leave and never come back."

"I can't wait to get back to California," agreed Tony.

"We'll give you a ride to the airport," Rebenack offered.

Although he'd believed they would be rescued, Sam was flooded with an overwhelming sense of relief. It surpassed what he had experienced, a lifetime before, when he'd asked Karin to marry him and she had said yes.

For Tony's part, the news was incomprehensible. He could respond to it, with the words of a composed man, but he couldn't process it. Five minutes ago, his vision of the future had extended no further than those cell walls. To now be going home, it was a dream. Better yet, it was waking up from the nightmare of Lagos.

Still, all Tony said was, "Well, I'm glad we're done with all this. Air France, here we come."

"Yeah, we've got a business partner in Geneva we need to visit," Sam said.

They handed the papers to Rebenack, who checked the signatures, nodded, and for the first time, really looked at Sam and Tony, sizing them up.

"I have more good news," Rebenack said. "The US government will pick up the cost of your flights."

"Really?" asked Tony.

"We're as anxious as you are to have you leave the country."

Sam chuckled.

"We've got your belongings," Rebenack assured them, "and they'll give you back your passports after I turn in these papers. So, if you'll follow me?"

Were there scorpions in their seats, Sam and Tony would not have stood quicker.

"So, Mr. Rebenack, what did you have to go through to get us out of here?" Tony asked.

"It's a long story so let's hold that thought until we're in the car heading to the airport."

There were few words of any sort until they were in the back of a town car with bulletproof glass and tinted windows; such a contrast to their lives over the past two days, the ride felt like an unparalleled luxury.

Rebenack had the car wait for him as he accompanied them toward the Air France area at Lagos International Airport, showing the manager at the counter copies of the papers that were signed and the confirmations from the government. He then escorted them through security checkpoints all the way to the gate. There Tony, looking significantly more relaxed, shook Rebenack's hand with much more vigor than before.

"Thank you very much," he said, earnestly. "We could have used your help at the airport earlier."

"It's nice to go through customs without having to pay a bribe," Sam agreed.

"Good luck to you both," Rebenack said, nodding briskly before disappearing into the seething mass of humanity in the waiting area.

Tony turned to Sam. "I'm going to get rid of the rest of my Nigerian money and buy some drinks and snacks. You want anything?"

"Bottled water would be nice."

Tony nodded, slung his carry-on bag over his shoulder, and headed for the cafeteria they had passed on their way to the gate.

When Tony was out of sight, Sam's cell phone rang. It startled him as he had not used it in days. The number on the screen didn't bring to mind a face or a name.

"Sam Marsh."

"It's Carlisle."

Sam's throat tightened.

"Sam, just listen. I just saw Tony walk away from you. I'd like one more brief chat with you, face to face, without his knowledge. Look to your left. See the bathrooms there?"

"I see them."

"This will just take a minute. Take your bag and walk into the men's room, while Tony is away."

Sam stood. "I'm headed there now."

When he entered, he saw a few men but no Carlisle. He was using the urinal when he heard the familiar voice.

"I thought we'd have a last meeting in here, since you do your best work in bathrooms."

Zipping himself up, Sam saw Carlisle casually washing his hands at a sink. Sam did the same.

"You got us out, didn't you?" Sam asked.

"Oh, ye of little faith," Carlisle smiled as he energetically lathered his hands with soap. "I told you I would. And you did a good job. Sorry I had to strong arm you at times."

Sam realized that the water was still running in his sink. He turned it off. They dried their hands in silence as another man finished his ablutions and then left the restroom.

"Carlisle." Sam moved closer. "When I go back to the US…"

"Your hands are clean," interrupted Carlisle. "You and Tony have no problems with the US government."

Sam nodded.

"Anything else?" Carlisle asked.

"Just between us. Will anything happen to Kidogo and Glanville Tambo?"

"Most likely no. But if I were you, I'd read the newspapers back home. Look for the name George Laney, head of the Energy Department."

"Laney. He was in on this?"

"We didn't have this conversation, Sam. But this deal was a lot bigger than you realized."

Sam began asking another question.

"Don't forget your bag, Sam." Carlisle pointed to it lying on the floor under the sink.

Picking it up, Sam turned toward his companion.

"I just wanted to…" Sam trailed off realizing Carlisle had already left.

An African man who had entered the bathroom looked at Sam curiously.

As Sam rejoined the throng of travelers in the terminal, he dialed Dina in Paris.

The sound of her voice, even if it was her voicemail telling him she was unavailable and to leave a message, opened his floodgates. "Dina, it's Sam. Tony and I are about to get on a plane for Geneva. We're free. Is there any way you can meet me in Geneva? Please. I can't wait to see you. I love you, Dina. You were right. I'm done with all this crazy stuff. Call me soon."

He clicked off his cell phone and put it back inside the breast pocket of his jacket. His mind now free of the worries that had plagued it, free to entertain visions of being reunited with the woman he loved.

When he got back to the waiting area, Tony had still not returned with the snacks. Sam walked to where Tony had gone to make his purchases. However when he could not find Tony, the relief, even the happiness experienced only a moment before, vanished.

CHAPTER 28

Two men gripped Tony's arms, forcing him to walk through a doorway at the end of the long row of check-in counters and then into a corridor that ran parallel behind all these counters. He passed various small offices, each one belonging to an airline.

"What is this about?" he protested. "The American Vice Consul arranged all this. We are supposed to be on that plane to Paris to connect to Geneva. We've been ordered out of the country!"

The two burly men answered by tightening their hold. After what seemed like ages, the three of them reached an office with an unlabeled door, its window opaque frosted glass.

"My friend is on the plane. I need to talk to him."

One of his escorts opened the door, the other shoved him. Between the force and the weight of his bag, Tony was propelled face-first on the floor. He looked up into the emotionless eyes of Doctor William Kidogo.

At his nod, Kidogo's accomplices closed the door behind themselves.

"Bill?" Tony gasped. "Sam and I are legally obliged to leave the country. We've got to catch that plane to Paris."

"Get up," said Kidogo. "You look ridiculous. Sit in that chair."

Tony complied, leaving his bag where it sat, crumpled. He finger-combed his hair in an effort to regain some sense of dignity, hands clasping his knees and sweat pooling under his arms. He waited for Kidogo to dispel the mystery.

"I brought you here to give you one more chance."

"To do what?"

"To tell me the truth about what Sam Marsh was doing when he met with Mark Woods."

Desperation crept into Tony's voice. "Bill, I told you before, and it's still true. If Sam had any plans for dealing with Woods, I was left in the dark."

"If you admit he was spying, we will not press charges against you."

"Bill, I swear, there's nothing I can tell you. Look, the American Embassy told us that your government agreed to the release. We're trying to do what *your* government ordered."

Kidogo stood so abruptly that the metal chair he was sitting on shot out from under him. His patented equanimity now replaced with red, inflamed eyes.

"You are not going anywhere!" Kidogo shouted. "Right now, I am the government."

Sam checked his watch again. There was one seat open on the Air France flight about to leave for Paris where he will make his connection for Geneva. The aisle seat next to him. He had boarded under the assumption that Tony had already done so. When he tried to call Tony on his cell, there had been no answer.

Sam hoped Tony would greet him soon with an explanation for whatever mishap had delayed him. Maybe he'd lost something he was tracking down. Or he had suffered some stomach ailment and was now in the bathroom where Sam had his last meeting with Philip Carlisle.

But with less than seven minutes before the scheduled departure, a departure Sam looked forward to more than any other in his life, Tony was not to be found.

Sam had asked a flight attendant to let him off to search for Tony, but their regulations prevented it. If he left the plane, that was that. And Sam wasn't condemning himself to Lagos any longer. He didn't think there was another Air France flight out of Nigeria that day. Rebenack had told them they had to be out of the country within twenty-four hours. What might happen if, for whatever reason, they didn't comply?

Sam stood from his seat. Immediately a flight attendant with her blonde hair clinched in a severe bun, her name tag reading *Dominique* instructed him to sit.

"Please, my friend is in the airport and something is wrong. We're about to leave. Why can't you ask the captain to page him or something?"

"I told you," Dominique insisted, "we cannot do that. Please sit down."

"I want to talk to the captain," Sam said. "I believe my friend is being detained in this airport and I want help."

"There is nothing we can do about that."

"I'm not leaving this country without him, so you better put on your thinking cap!" Sam's burst of anger quieted the entire cabin.

Dominique didn't need to raise her voice to sound threatening. "If you do not cooperate, we will have to ask you to leave the plane, and we will not allow you back on board."

"Just get me the captain or someone official who can help me then." Sam lowered his voice, realizing that she was within her authority to have him thrown off the plane. The thought of never leaving this doomed country struck him in the chest.

Dominique headed toward the front of the plane. He saw her unlock the door to the cockpit and walk inside, closing the door. He glanced at his watch again. Four minutes to takeoff, and he hadn't a clue what to do. Should he leave and come to his friend's aid? What if the authorities detained him? He could be accused of violating the agreement and jailed, once again, in Lagos. Rebenack would never get him out a second time. And he was certain neither would Carlisle.

There was an announcement that the plane would soon push back from the gate. The cockpit door opened and Dominique emerged with the copilot, a man whose expression would make fidgeting school children sit stock-still.

Sam began before either could speak. "My name is Sam Marsh. I'm an American citizen who was illegally detained here for two days with my partner, Tony Dobbs, in a Lagos jail. The American Embassy got us out, and we have to leave today. Tony is in this airport. He came with me. I believe the authorities have detained him again. Can't you get someone from security to accompany me as I look for him?"

"Mister Marsh," said the copilot, his jaw set, eyes unblinking, "I'm sorry about your predicament. But international aviation law says once you are on this plane and leave, you cannot be readmitted."

"A man's life and freedom are as stake here. Doesn't that matter?"

"You're making the other passengers nervous, sir."

"Listen, you know what it's like here in Lagos, don't you? He and I had to bribe our way through the airport. Can't you at least call airport security from the cockpit and ask them to page Tony Dobbs? Please."

"We can wait an additional four or five minutes before leaving the gate and hope your friend makes it. This is out of the ordinary for us, so I hope you will acknowledge we're trying to help you."

Sam prepared to return to his seat when, from the jet-way, he heard a shout.

"Wait! Wait! Don't leave!"

Rushing to the door, Sam peered into the jet-way: it was Tony, scurrying as fast as he could, bag over shoulder, bouncing around, a man who worked for Air France jogging alongside him.

"Where the hell have you been?" yelled Sam.

Dominique gently but urgently guided Sam toward his seat, the copilot headed back to the cockpit, and Dominique checked Tony's boarding pass and then pointed him toward the empty seat next to Sam's.

Sam opened the overhead compartment, but it was full.

"Under the seat," said Dominique. "And put your seat belts on right now."

When Tony was buckled in next to Sam, they exhaled in unison. The engines revved. The plane began to taxi.

"Do you have any goddamn idea…"

Tony held a hand up, silencing his friend. "Two big guys dragged me into a room. I was interrogated again. By Kidogo."

"Kidogo?" Sam was astonished. "He came here, after the deal, and interrogated you?"

"I guess they figured they'd get nowhere with you. So Kidogo threatened to keep me here, forcing me to miss my plane and go back to jail."

"That bastard, unbelievable. What did he say?"

"Funny you should ask." Tony spoke with as much nonchalance as he could muster given that he was still panting. "He seemed convinced you were spying for the CIA and wanted me to confirm it."

"That's insane. What did you tell him?"

"I told him I knew nothing. I told him there was no way you were a spy and that if he forced me to miss my plane, he would be in trouble with others over him in his government."

"You said that?" Sam sounded skeptical. He had experienced first-hand what his friend was and was not likely to do when cornered.

The engines roared as the plane sped along.

Tony leaned back and closed his eyes. "You're not the only one around here who can act tough."

Sam turned to stare out of his window, worn out and confused, but relieved.

Le Bouveret, the Geneva district with a colorful marina where Pierre kept his boat, was the perfect location for Sam's reunion with Dina. Pierre offered to let

Sam, Dina, and Tony take out his boat, *Dolphin*, for a relaxing cruise on Lake Geneva to help make up for everything that had happened in Lagos.

All throughout lunch, as a counterpoint to Tony's sullen silence, Sam and Dina sat hand in hand, cooing at each other. But for Tony's presence, they would have rushed through lunch to make love on board the *Dolphin*.

Over coffee and dessert, Dina said, "I hope you gentlemen are done with deals in Nigeria. You need to find a more legitimate way of making a living."

"I believed it was for real," said Tony.

"We'll never be certain if the thirty-seven million was for real or not," said Sam. "All I can tell you is, there has to be an easier way to make two and a half million apiece." Even Tony had to laugh.

Sam excused himself to go to the men's room. On his way, he observed an African man dressed in a windbreaker looking around nervously. Sam thought back to his recent trip and to Joseph, the driver who seemed so drained of life, so defeated, expecting so little of his future.

When Sam came out of the bathroom, Tony was signing the credit card receipt.

"I planned to get this," protested Sam.

"Oh, no," Tony teased. "You left to go to the bathroom, that's the universal signal of not wanting to pay."

"I thought it meant I drank too much."

They left the restaurant and made their way down the walkway, up another passage, past a few boats. Sam took out the keys Pierre had loaned him and set down his bag. Tony ambled along a few yards behind them, seeming to inspect the scenery.

Dina paused as Sam unzipped the bag. She bent down and whispered in his ear, "I don't want you to react, but we're being watched."

"Who? Where?"

"When you stand up, glance to your right. There's a black man on a boat with binoculars. He's looked over at us a few times. I'll put on some makeup; don't make it obvious you've seen him."

Dina opened her purse and stood in front of Sam, who straightened up and looked at her. She took out some lip gloss.

"See him?" she asked.

Sam glanced subtly over her shoulder and glimpsed a man with binoculars. The man lowered them and began puttering about on his boat's deck.

"Son of a bitch," Sam murmured. "I saw that guy outside looking around when I went to the bathroom."

"What should we do?" she asked. "Are we safe on the boat?"

"Yeah," Sam said. "Pierre has a rifle on board. He's a member of a shooting club here in Geneva."

They may have discussed it further, but Tony, holding his clammy-looking forehead in his hands, approached. "Sam, Dina, I hate to disappoint you, but I've got this awful migraine. I need to skip sailing. Really, sorry about that, mate."

Dina's expression was one of intense concern and doubt.

"A migraine," Sam echoed. "I've never known you to have one." Not that he wanted Tony on board. At the moment, Sam would've loved nothing more than a lake cruise for two. But he was positive that Tony wasn't bowing out to give the reunited lovers their privacy.

"Well, I'm telling you—"

"I'm telling *you* I don't believe you." Sam grabbed Tony's shirt. Tony's eyes widened, and he tried to wrest Sam's hands from the fabric. "Actually, I'm sure you don't have a migraine. And maybe you have something to do with that African guy on the boat down there who's been watching us, same guy who was outside the restaurant."

"What are you talking about? Get your hands off me."

"Not till you've heard me, Tony. I don't trust you. What, you struck some kind of deal with Kidogo?"

Tony wrangled himself free and looked, still wild-eyed, between Sam and Dina. "Are you mad? If anyone struck a deal, it's you."

"I'm the one who stood up to Kidogo. You're the one who whimpered like a puppy every time he pulled his crap. What did you do, Tony? Get a cut of the money?"

"Go to hell!" Tony shouted. "If anyone is not trustworthy, it's you." He turned again to Dina. "You know what your heroic boyfriend here did? He did a deal with the CIA, ripping off a cell phone from a corrupt American oil buyer." Pivoting back toward Sam, he shouted, "Were you working for the CIA from the start? Or was that an idea that came up later?"

The accusation worked. Dina looked as alarmed as Tony had hoped. Sam visibly swallowed.

"All right, Tony. I'll tell you, which is more than you'll do for me. A CIA agent told me that either I helped him or we would rot in jail in Lagos. Do you get it? I didn't have a choice. I saved your ass and mine. While you were off at Tambo's palace, getting laid, a CIA agent used me to discredit Woods."

"You didn't tell me."

"I didn't tell you because I couldn't count on you!" When Sam took one step toward Tony, Tony took several back. "You're weak, you're lazy, and you're unreliable. You got us into a mess and you weren't about to get us out of it. Thank God, I did something, or we'd still be there!"

"You're a liar, Sam," Tony said with a note of finality, moving away from them. "You lied to me in Lagos and you're lying to me now." He turned on his heel.

"*I'm* a liar?" shouted Sam. "What kind of migraine medication are you taking, Tony? What's the name of it?"

There was no reply. Sam looked over at the boat where the suspicious man had been but he was no longer in sight. He stepped onto the deck of Pierre's boat and held his hand out to Dina. "Come on," he insisted. "Let's try to have a relaxing time."

CHAPTER 29

George Laney paced outside the Oval Office. The president's cantankerous assistant didn't look up as she said, "I'm sure he'll be with you shortly."

"You never mentioned the exact nature of the meeting," Laney said.

"The president didn't give me any other information."

A buzz on her desk drew her attention. She picked up the phone. "Yes, sir? Right away, sir." Hanging up, she told Laney, "Go right in. I hope you have a pleasant meeting."

Laney cleared his throat and straightened his tie, grabbing his briefcase. "Sure you do," he muttered. He put on a warm smile for the president.

"Good evening, Mister President."

"George." With folded hands, the president invited the new arrival to sit.

But Laney sat stiffly as he noticed Zeke Reilly in the corner.

"George," the president began, "because of the responsibilities we have in running the most powerful country on earth, and our need to preserve our integrity as a political party, as well as our long friendship, it pains me to tell you that I need your resignation immediately as head of the Energy Department."

Laney froze, unable to move or speak.

The president sighed. "There's a reason Reilly is at this meeting, George, and it isn't so I can get a status report from you on Nigerian oil stockpiling. We've solved that problem."

"Mister President, I understand it's an embarrassment to learn that an American was working with Glanville Tambo in the oil stockpiling scheme. I'm sure though, that after Woods is brought back and prosecuted; the public will see him for what he is, a fraudulent lone wolf trying to make a fortune for himself."

"Woods worked with the direct help of the head of the Energy Department of the United States of America." Whatever tones of camaraderie initially warmed the president's voice had dissipated. "We know. We have all the evidence, George. Show us the courtesy of not treating us like idiots."

Laney gripped the arms of the chair. His voice climbed. "Is this because I helped Woods get jobs in the past? He's a relative, for Christ's sake. He can't take care of himself. Listen, I'm not sure what he told you, but he was working on his own on this. I had no knowledge of what he was doing. I've tried to help him in the past but he keeps getting into—"

"George, stop it!" Reilly stood over Laney. "You want me to spell it out for you? Tambo had to send Woods back to Kuwait. We contacted our people there, he's now in a cell in Qatar, at a military prison. We have his phone, George. That means we have the texts you have sent him, the call log. He's not very brave. Our people tell us he talked for three hours straight. We also have paid a visit to the office of Annie Curtis."

Laney shrank before their eyes; the fight in him was ebbing away.

"We've got her in jail too," Reilly announced. "There is enough evidence to put you away for the rest of your life, George. Espionage, international monetary fraud, and that's before we mention the IRS charges. Not to mention that you tried to exploit a tense geopolitical standoff between Iran and Iraq for your own monetary gain. And, threatened to create more civil strife in Nigeria. That is the last thing that nation needs. You should be executed, in my opinion"

Laney's laugh was involuntary, and it had nothing to do with amusement. "Executed?"

"George," the president offered, coming around his desk and sitting on the edge, looking down at Laney in an admonishment that seemed almost fatherly. "We've known each other so long. How could you have done this? Reilly sees the betrayal of our country. I see it as a betrayal of me."

"What will happen?"

The president opened a drawer, took out an envelope. From it he extracted the single sheet of paper he handed to Laney.

"Sign it."

The succinct document took only moments to read, and less time to sign.

"What does this mean?" Laney asked.

"It's hard for me to say, at this point. I'll direct my press secretary to explain that your resignation has to do with personal problems. You will not talk to anyone in the press. In fact, George, we will relocate you for now. When you leave here, Secret Service will accompany you to your home, where you may take some personal items and then we will take you to an undisclosed location. If Woods and Annie Curtis cooperate and do not talk, we will give them reduced sentences."

"But if anyone talks about this," Reilly said, his bitterness now welling over, "if any of you do anything or say anything about this oil stockpiling, you're all going away for the rest of your lives. It will be considered espionage. Do you understand?"

Laney looked down. His energy had dipped too low for even a nod.

"Say it!" barked Reilly.

Laney raised his head with labor. "I understand."

The president sank back in his chair. "That's all, gentlemen. I'm tired and I still have a lot more to do this evening."

Reilly stood, waiting for Laney to rise.

"Good night, Mister President," Reilly said.

"Good night, Zeke. Thank you."

"Mister President?" Laney's voice was that of a child caught lying to his father, hoping for but not expecting mercy. "I'm sorry, I mean it sincerely."

"You'll never be able to apologize enough."

Two Secret Service men waited for them when they left the Oval Office.

"Goodnight, gentlemen," the president's executive assistant offered.

Reilly nodded but Laney walked in a trance. Reilly walked him out of the West Wing, followed not far behind by the Secret Service escorts.

"So I guess I'm in the Witness Protection Program." It was more in response to the surreal twist of events than anything else that Laney smirked.

Reilly grabbed Laney's elbow at the joint and squeezed until his eyes popped open in pain.

"You think this is a joke?" Reilly hissed in his ear. "He didn't have the heart to tell you. Even though you've threatened the stability of this government, he still had too much class to say it. So, I'll say it for him—you corrupt, stupid thug. There is no way you're not going to prison. You are not walking away from this."

Laney yanked his elbow out of Reilly's grip. They had reached elevators and Laney pushed a button to take him down and away from the director of Central Intelligence.

"You're going down, in more ways than one," Reilly said. "Your career is over. With Woods and your assistant, I don't see how we can keep your name out of this. To minimize damage, we'll wait until the next election finishes. Then we're not going to just throw the book at you, we're going to beat you to death with it. It might take a year or two, Laney, but you'll go to trial. You're going to prison. It's *over*."

Reilly watched the blood drain from Laney's face.

A light *bing* sounded and as the elevator car arrived. Reilly and Laney looked up. Reilly held the door for Laney who stepped inside.

"Oh, one other thing. The boys at FBI have frozen your financial accounts, pending a full investigation. I hope your wife has her own money."

Laney's mouth opened but Reilly extended his arm, indicating the Secret Service should join Laney. A grim smile flitted across Reilly's face as the elevator door closed.

Outside, Laney had an escort, one car in front of his and one car behind him. His entourage headed toward his home in Georgetown.

Out of the muddle of confused half thoughts, only one clear one arose. *Where can I go?*

He reached inside his pocket for his cell phone and pressed a speed dial number. He listened. After the fourth ring, his wife answered. She said "hello" twice. His words caught in his throat. He hung up, unable to say goodbye to his wife.

George Laney slammed his foot on the accelerator. He struck the lead Secret Service car. With a sickly smile, he imagined the expression on the agent's face.

"Oh, sorry," Laney said as he bashed the car again. In his headlights, the bridge ahead closed in. He swerved out of his lane, smacked into the SUV alongside him and stopped short so that the Secret Service car behind him rear-ended him. He turned on the radio, found a rock station, and turned it up all the way.

Laney let out a scream at the top of his lungs, aimed his car at the first set of oncoming headlights, gripped the wheel, closed his eyes, and waited for the impact.

Pierre had spent a fortune equipping the boat he called *Dolphin* with the latest electronic wireless system, autopilot, searchlights, radar, and alarm.

After sorting out their bags and putting away the food they had brought, Dina and Sam explored. "Very impressive, this should be fun. By the way," she said mischievously, looking around, "are you sure you can drive this thing?"

"We'll soon find out." They both laughed. "It's a heavy old tank compared with mine."

They anchored in the middle of the lake, far from other vessels. Both changed below deck; Dina reappeared in a stunning white bikini that set off her tanned and toned body.

"Very nice," he said with a grin.

"I'm glad you think so."

"If we get too distracted and run out of fuel," he said smoothly, "then we can summon the Swiss Guard to help us home."

"I hope they won't come too quickly." After a few torrid moments of kissing, his hands began to wander, and she pulled away. "I wonder what's in here. It's locked." She was trying the handle of what looked like a broom closet.

Opening the closet, with the keys Pierre had given him, Sam saw bottles of whiskey, gin, and brandy on the top shelf and, beneath, a rifle. On the back of the door, Pierre had taped a note that read, "The bar is loaded and so is the AR-15. Be careful."

Sam shut the door. "And I thought the Swiss were such a peaceful people."

They stood on the deck and marveled at the sunset. He went into the cabin to grab his camera to take a picture of the glorious pinkish-white clouds that interspersed with the blue sky over Lac Leman.

"Are you enjoying yourself, darling?" Sam asked her.

"It's wonderful, Sam," she said. "It's good to be here. I constantly worried about you when you were in Lagos."

"You don't have to worry anymore." When he wrapped an arm around her waist, she rested her head on him.

At first it was nothing more than a blip on their radar: another powerboat on the lake. There was nothing unusual about it; it wasn't enough to divert Sam's eyes from the beautiful body leaning against him.

It was an annoyance, though, that the boat pressed in their direction, not giving them a wider berth.

"What's the matter," Sam mused aloud, "not enough room on the lake for you and me?"

Dina's chuckle was aborted by the sight of the other boat coming closer, almost dangerously so now. Both could make out the outlines of two heavyset black men, one commanding the boat, the other pointing a rifle directly at them.

"Get down!" shouted Dina as she shoved Sam to the deck.

Two shots rang out and clipped part of Pierre's hull, sending fragments into the air.

"Jesus!" Sam shook off the impact of the fall. "It must be that guy I saw outside at the marina and a friend. It's Tony. He's working for them. That's why he got that supposed migraine."

"Sam, listen." Dina may have convinced Sam to keep quiet, but his heartbeat was cannon fire. The only other sound was the boat closing in.

"Get this thing started. I'll get the rifle."

"Can you work it?"

"I was in the army, remember. Go."

Sam crawled on the deck as two more shots zipped overhead. When Dina reached the closet she had noticed earlier, she snuck a look around. The other powerboat was now within a few hundred yards. The next bullet, meant for her head, pierced the closet door. She ducked, flipped open the door, and hoisted her rifle.

Sam started up the engine and saw one man aim his rifle in his direction. He flattened himself on the deck just as another bullet splintered the hull. Splinters cut into his arms and chest. There was no time for taking stock of wounds.

Dina, already resting the barrel of the AR-15 on the edge of the deck, took careful aim. She squeezed off two shots at the boat torpedoing toward them.

While she hit neither shooter nor pilot, both ducked, shocked at a counterattack. The pilot swerved, barely dodging the *Dolphin*. The boat's sweeping turn made clear they were not deterred.

"Get after them! Full throttle!"

Despite his fear, Sam found this so strange he smiled and shouted, "Yes, ma'am!" He hit the throttle.

Dina, a ferocious militant in a bikini, came up alongside Sam, resting the AR-15 and trying to steady it again.

"Stay on their tail," she shouted. "Right behind them, don't let them turn toward you!"

"Got it!" Sam gave the *Dolphin* a workout like it had never known.

The Nigerians' boat was faster, but Dina's quick thinking ensured it couldn't face the *Dolphin* again.

The Nigerian shooter's next attempt didn't hit their boat.

"It's too choppy!" Dina shouted. "Stay out of their wake! Go alongside!"

"Are you sure?"

"Stay low. I'll take out the pilot, not the shooter."

Following his orders, Sam stayed slightly behind and to the side of the powerboat. The shooter could not get a steady position and kneeled out of sight, but the pilot had nowhere to hide.

"Okay, Sam, get ready to throttle back. Ready? Now!"

Sam cut the speed on the *Dolphin*, slowing it, steadying it.

Dina squeezed off three quick shots, and the pilot went down. The shooter crawled for the controls; he pushed the pilot aside and jammed the throttle.

"They're running!" Sam said.

"Go after them."

He did. The *Dolphin* sped up but couldn't close the distance.

"He's too fast!" yelled Sam.

"Where's the fuel tank on their boat?" The calm in her voice astounded him. It's true that more pressing matters commanded his attention just now, but in pockets of clear thought, he could swear he was falling deeper in love with her.

"It's under the cockpit. Their hull is fiberglass. If you can penetrate the side with a round or two, you might hit the fuel line."

She checked the AR-15. No time to reload.

"Get me as close as you can!" Dina shouted.

Sam pursued and the shooter, now manning the controls, looked back at them, worried. The man Dina had already shot wasn't moving.

As the attacking boat got closer to the marina, it was closing in on other boats moving lazily about, clearly on a collision course with another boat. The shooter shifted his angle which gave Sam a chance to gain on his starboard side.

The shooter reached for his rifle again.

Sam throttled back. "Now, Dina!"

She emptied the AR-15 into the hull. Instinctively Sam and Dina brought their hands up, attempting to protect their faces from the explosion.

CHAPTER 30

From a hotel at the marina, Tony Dobbs heard the explosion. Fidgeting and looking around wildly from his doorframe, he saw Swiss police steering Sam and Dina into an awaiting police car, the light on top pulsing as it roared away.

When the siren had reduced to a whisper, Tony made his way into the lobby where, unknown to Sam and Dina, he'd reserved a room prior to their lunch date in Le Bouveret. He sat on a chair, his head in his hands, thinking.

A few minutes later, a tall Nigerian man carrying a briefcase sat next to Tony, whose head snapped to attention.

"Mister Dobbs," said the Nigerian man.

"What happened?" whispered Tony. "I saw them alive, taken away by the police."

"They just killed my men," the Nigerian said.

Though Tony kept his tone low, there was an edge to it as he asked, "What about the money?"

After a surreptitious scan of the lobby, the Nigerian cracked open the briefcase and turned it towards Tony, who glanced inside. The Nigerian nodded as Tony assessed stacks of hundred-dollar bills.

"Half the money," said the Nigerian. "You get the other half when they're released by the police and we can exterminate them. This is in addition to the 150 thousand we gave you for the escrow account."

Tony reached for the case and its contents, but the Nigerian popped it closed. "Not here," he said. "Count it alone in your room."

"Right."

Tony headed to the elevator, and the Nigerian followed. They rode up and walked down the hallway to Tony's room in silence. Inside, the Nigerian unlocked the briefcase again, more casually now.

"Please, count it and confirm that half of the agreed amount is there," asked the Nigerian.

Tony began to pull out banded stacks of notes and counted them. It was the click that stopped him. Tony turned to see the Nigerian aiming a pistol, a silencer on the end of its barrel.

"What are you doing?" Tony demanded. "Kidogo agreed to this. Your boss agreed to this."

The Nigerian smiled. "You are not very smart, Mister Dobbs," he said. "Did you think the fact that you weren't loyal to Sam Marsh meant we would be loyal to you?"

There was no time, not even for the scream to leave his open mouth. The Nigerian peppered Tony's heart with three shots, the force of which threw his body against the sofa. He was still clutching one stack of bills. The Nigerian grabbed the money out of Tony's fist and put it back in the briefcase with the other banknotes. He left the room as quietly as he had entered.

Sam floored the accelerator, for once the traffic lights in Palm Springs were with him.

"Aren't you driving a bit fast?" asked Dina, watching the colorful businesses outside blur as they whizzed by.

"I want to get this day done with as fast as possible." They were headed to his hotel.

Dina rested a hand on his knee. "We'll get through it together."

He nodded, thinking despite how happy he was to be with Dina, he also felt suddenly old, as if some infirmity had invaded him overnight, making him slower and less sure of himself. Even with all he'd been through, he'd incurred no serious injury; still, he understood this day marked an irreversible change in the way he would live his life.

Sam turned onto the palm-lined side street to his hotel and restaurant and then drove at the sluggish pace of a tourist seeing these sights for the first time, astounded by them.

As he reached his office, he asked her, "Would you like to relax by the pool while I take care of what I need to?"

"Sam," she said, "I came here to make sure you get your business done, not to work on my tan."

Sam wrapped his arms around her and kissed her. "You are too good to be true."

Her features darkened. "Don't say that."

"You know what I mean."

"How about you just sign the papers, like you said you would?"

He glanced through a few phone messages and bills. Most were from credit card companies requesting calls back regarding a "personal banking matter."

Dina gave him some space and wandered into the bar, asking Rod for a Perrier.

"How's he doing?" asked Rod.

"This will be very difficult for him, at first. But I'm sure he'll adapt. He's very sweet, but he's no wimp. And that's why I love him."

"Well, he's lucky to have you, Dina."

"He'll need a lot of understanding these next few weeks. We need to transition as easy as we can."

Rod gave her a resolute half nod. "You can count on me."

Dina smiled warmly and raised a silent toast to the bartender. She made her way back to Sam's office, where she noticed him rummaging through envelopes.

"How's it going?" she asked gently.

Sam rubbed his temples. "I haven't signed it yet!" Refusing to be alienated by his harsh tone, Dina positioned herself behind Sam, where she began massaging his shoulders.

"God, that feels good," he murmured.

"I'll bet," she said.

"This would be so much easier if I could blame it all on someone else."

Dina chuckled. "Sam," she said, "I don't think any less of you for having to do this."

When he tapped her hands, she pulled away, allowing him to open his right-hand desk drawer and pull out the envelope that had been gathering dust there for days. One last time, he reread the document's words.

"She'll take good care of the place," Dina said.

"Better than I did I'm sure."

"And you'll get a payment every month."

"It's not the same as running it myself."

Dina tried lightening the mood: "Karin told me we can eat here for free anytime."

Sam flipped to the last page, signed, and then, drained, dropped the pen on the desk. "I think we'll find other places to dine."

"It will all be over soon," Dina assured. "And don't forget, we have to leave in about twenty minutes."

A lump began to grow in his throat.

"I didn't want to go at first," he told her in a voice raspy with emotion. "I didn't believe in it myself. Why did I let him convince me to go to Nigeria?"

It was an unanswerable question. With his arm linked through Dina's, he headed for the car.

Forest Lawn Cemetery in Cathedral City hosted the unknown and the famous alike. Sam and Dina listened to the preacher extol Tony's adventurous spirit, how he could not be held to earthly bonds because of his need to experience life to its fullest.

Sam obsessed about that phrase, even as others came to the front of the chapel and spoke. A few times, he noticed Tony's widow, Shauna, staring at him.

When the service was all over, Shauna, red-eyed, sniffling, pale, hugged many people and handed them directions to the gathering that awaited them at her house. Sam hung back with Dina.

"We will talk to her, right?" Dina asked.

"Just waiting for the right moment."

When Sam and Dina approached, Shauna excused herself from the four people surrounding her.

"You're coming over to the house?" she asked, lifeless.

"Shauna, I'd like to take you out to lunch when you're available."

Shauna Dobbs looked at him urgently, moving him away from the others who had gathered nearby.

"Sam, when you got back from Lagos you told me nothing of what you and Tony went through. You were in jail together. But the embassy told me you weren't with him when . . ."

Her voice trailed off and her eyes filled with tears.

"We were separated when the attacks happened in Geneva. I don't know the full story, but the Nigerians went after us."

"But I don't understand. If they stole the money you invested, why would they be mad enough to come after you?"

"I'm not sure," Sam said. "I hope by the next time we're together, I can give you more information that will put your mind at ease."

Her eyes bore into him. "I don't believe you. You're not telling me everything." She turned on her heels to rejoin the other mourners.

At Dina's house, now their house, Sam changed out of his dark suit into a short-sleeved shirt, shorts, and sandals. Dina's walk-in closet was capacious but filled with her own clothes; when Sam had moved in, she'd given him a closet in a spare room.

He found her on the back patio, lying on a chaise lounge near the swimming pool. Sinking down next to her, he took her hand and kissed her palm.

"Thank you," he said.

"For what?"

"For everything. For letting me move in here, supporting me about signing over the hotel and restaurant, and contacting Roni to help me in Lagos."

Dina turned away. "You don't have to thank me. I love you."

"I love you too. Dina?"

He took her face in his hands and turned her head gently, forcing her to look into his eyes.

"Dina, what's wrong? Whatever it is, you can tell me."

"It's Roni. I called him to help you."

"I know."

"But what you don't know" he had never seen her look so vulnerable, "is that Roni is Mossad."

At first he didn't comprehend. She continued in a nervous rush.

"Please understand, Sam. I didn't know about the oil stockpiling, when I told Roni about you and Tony. I just wanted you protected; I couldn't reveal his identity to you. Roni would watch out for you. I just didn't know that you would be there during an international crisis. And I didn't know . . . "

Sam's body was now stiff. "Didn't know what? Say it, Dina."

"That Roni would talk about you with a CIA agent. He and Carlisle used you to solve the problem with Tambo."

His chest was like a balloon that had been stabbed with a needle, the air leaking out. He was deflating. He was falling from the sky. "You and your cousin used me!"

On his feet, Sam hurled his cushion from the chaise lounge into the pool, where it landed with a soft, unsatisfying thwack. He stormed the patio, unable to speak. When he circled back to Dina, all he could do was stare, angry, embarrassed, and hardly able to think.

"Sam, please sit down."

He shook his head, but he sat.

"Roni must have told you he planned to involve Carlisle," Sam said.

"Yes, he told me. There was nothing else I could do but tell him to protect you."

She put her arms around him and buried her face in his neck. After a few moments, he sighed. Returning her embrace, he thought for a moment of the conflation of factors that would have had to go differently for this tortured Nigerian scam to work, how if they had, he wouldn't have had to relinquish custody of his hotel to his ex-wife; he would be in charge, and he would still have the life he'd worked so hard for. He wouldn't be sitting here now beside Dina, watching the cushion float on the aimless currents of her swimming pool.

ABOUT THE AUTHOR

Photo Credit: Nathan Sternfeld ©

Stephen Maitland-Lewis, a dual citizen of England and the United States, is an award-winning author and a former international investment banker. He has lived and worked in London, Kuwait, Paris, and Munich prior to moving to the United States.

Stephen owned a luxury hotel, an award-winning restaurant, and was the director of marketing at a Los Angeles daily newspaper before becoming a full-time writer.

Maitland-Lewis is a jazz aficionado and a Board Trustee of the Louis Armstrong House Museum in New York. A member of PEN, the Palm Springs Writer's Guild and the Author's Guild, Maitland-Lewis is also on the executive Committee of the International Mystery Writers Festival.

Thank you so much for reading one of our **Crime Fiction** novels.
If you enjoyed the experience, please check out our recommended
title for your next great read!

The Ice Maiden by B.D. Smith

"*The Ice Maiden* deserves a spot at or
near the top of your reading list."
–BEST THRILLERS

View other Black Rose Writing titles at
www.blackrosewriting.com/books and use promo code
PRINT to receive a **20% discount** when purchasing.

CPSIA information can be obtained
at www.ICGtesting.com
Printed in the USA
BVHW030407021120
592184BV00001B/1